Strike a Pose

A Celebrity Friends to Lovers Romance

Blame It on Fame
Book 1

Lilah Morris

Striped Cat Publishing LLC

For Lee, the Willow to my Heena

Access Book Playlists Here!

Contents

POP CULTURE PULSE PODCAST	1
1. Willow	3
2. Riley	8
3. Willow	11
4. Riley	19
5. Willow	25
POP CULTURE PULSE PODCAST	33
6. Riley	35
7. Willow	40
8. Riley	46
9. Willow	52
10. Riley	58
POP CULTURE PULSE PODCAST	63
11. Willow	65
12. Willow	71
13. Willow	79
14. Willow	84
15. Riley	93
POP CULTURE PULSE PODCAST	101
16. Willow	103
17. Willow	107
18. Willow	112
19. Riley	117
POP CULTURE PULSE PODCAST	123
20. Willow	126
21. Willow	130
22. Riley	134
23. Willow	138
24. Willow	146
25. Riley	151
26. Willow	156

27. Willow	164
POP CULTURE PULSE PODCAST	173
28. Willow	174
29. Riley	180
30. Willow	186
31. Riley	194
32. Willow	201
33. Willow	208
POP CULTURE PULSE PODCAST	215
34. Willow	217
35. Riley	225
36. Willow	231
37. Willow	239
38. Riley	247
39. Willow	253
POP CULTURE PULSE PODCAST	261
40. Willow	265
41. Willow	272
POP CULTURE PULSE PODCAST	277
42. Willow	278
43. Willow	284
44. Riley	289
Epilogue	294
Author's Note	301
Acknowledgments	303

POP CULTURE PULSE PODCAST

Caroline: Hey guys, welcome back to another episode of Pop Culture Pulse. I'm your host Caroline—

Jenna:—and I'm your host Jenna! What do you have for me first?

Caroline: A video is going around of Willow Jordan rolling her eyes at a teenage fan after posing for a photo with her. Have you seen this?

Jenna: No, I haven't. Can we pull it up?

Producer: Sure.

A video plays of a teenage fan running up to Willow excitedly, asking for a photo. Willow is wearing a black silk robe while getting her hair and makeup done. She smiles gracefully and consents to a photo, posing with the young fan as her hair and makeup artists pause their work. The beaming teen fan thanks Willow and leaves. Once the teen has turned to leave, Willow's smile instantly falls, and she rolls her eyes. Video ends.

Jenna: Wow, that's *really* bad. I mean, I know Willow's spoiled, but that's just ridiculous. She seriously can't take five seconds out of her day to pose with a fan? Why does she have to be so *ungrateful?* Her fans are the reason she has modeling work in the first place.

Caroline: If you can even call that work. I mean, she has people doing her hair and makeup, choosing her outfits, telling her where and how to pose...she literally doesn't have to do anything. She just sits there looking pretty. I don't know if I'd classify that as work.

Jenna: I agree. She doesn't know how lucky she is. It's pretty fucked up that she was blessed with those looks. I mean, she's a nepo baby already, and a bitchy one at that. Why couldn't the universe have given her beauty to someone more deserving?

Caroline: Totally agree. Someone like us.

Jenna: Exactly! Ugh, I don't even want to talk about her anymore. She's making my blood boil.

Caroline: Let's move on, then. What's up first from you?

Jenna: Have you seen this new shirtless post from actor Grey Aldridge on the set of the second James Bond movie? He looks *incredible*.

Chapter 1

Willow

"*Frigid Nepo Princess*. Seriously? That's the best headline they could come up with?"

I set my phone on the marble countertop of my family's New York penthouse. I had just returned from a whirlwind trip to Paris to shoot the cover of *Elle*, dragging my best friend and fellow model, Heena Badahl, with me.

"Hey, at least they're calling you a princess." My sister Aspen shrugs before wrapping me in a hug. "Nice to have you home, Will. And you too, Heena."

She gives Heena a tight hug, too. Heena doesn't have a great relationship with her family, so she's an honorary member of ours.

"*Scorned by the Starlet: Frigid Nepo Princess Willow Jordan Rolls Eyes at Young Fan*," my other sister Maple reads the full headline as my parents engulf me in hugs of their own. "Yikes, Willow. What did you do?"

People like to poke fun at the fact that my parents named us Willow, Aspen, and Maple. But really, as far as Hollywood names go, my parents kept things pretty tame. Our names never bothered me—although as the first-born, I was given the most normal one. Maple might feel differently.

"I didn't do anything," I defend. "The fan in question was some *Elle* employee's daughter who shouldn't have even been allowed into the models' dressing room to begin with. I mean, she interrupted my entire glam team—they all had to stop their work and back up—so that she could get a photo with me. Not to mention the security and privacy concerns. I wasn't rolling my eyes at the fan. I was rolling my eyes at whoever let her into the dressing rooms in the first place. Those are, understandably, high-security areas."

"I agree wholeheartedly." My mom nods. "But, unfortunately, being captured on your worst days and having moments taken out of context are just a part of living in the limelight. I remember all the accusations they used to hurl at me. Uninventive stuff really, like 'trailer park trash,' 'white trash,' or 'gold digger.' Once they find someone new to bully, they'll leave you alone."

"But it's been six years since I first started modeling, and they haven't gotten tired of hating on me yet. And really, I've been in the spotlight since the day I was born," I add, motioning to my famous parents.

My father, Robert Jordan, was born famous. Both his mother and grandmother were well-known actresses, and his dad was the heir to a large real estate fortune. My mother, on the other hand, Isabelle Michalski—AKA Izzy Michaels—Jordan, was born to a single mother in Indiana before being scouted at sixteen while working at a fast food restaurant. She quickly rose to fame as a model before meeting my father, who had already made a name for himself as a talented young director. He inspired her to switch paths and become an actress, which in turn classed up her image.

"I just don't understand why they keep dragging me

through the mud, persisting with this mean girl reputation they've given me. I'm not mean, am I?" I continue, asking my family earnestly.

I know I shouldn't believe what the media says about me, but it's hard to ignore insult after insult. At some point, they start to stick.

"Don't even ask that. You're not mean, sweetie. Far from it," my mom assures me, moving behind me to gently rub my shoulders. "Don't listen to a word they say. They're just trying to make a headline."

"Anyone who knows you will know that what they're reporting is the furthest thing from the truth, Willy," my dad adds. "You're one of the nicest girls on Earth."

"Why does Aspen get the good girl reputation?" I turn my head to look at my sister. "How did you do that?"

Aspen shrugs. "Honestly, I think it's because I play an innocent, good-girl type on *Fairview Ridge*. People think I *am* my character."

Around the same time that I started modeling, Aspen began acting. She's almost as well-known as I am, having played the lead role in the most popular teen drama of the decade for the past six years. The show is gearing up to start filming its final season, which has given Aspen a mid-life crisis at twenty.

Since we stepped out from behind our parents' shadows and into the limelight, Aspen and I have become known as a sort of dynamic duo, especially since we attended most events together for the first few years of our careers. Even now, it's incredibly common to hear our names in the same sentence. It doesn't hurt that we look similar enough to be twins (both the spitting image of our mother) despite Aspen being two years younger.

"Maybe prancing around in lingerie while scowling makes people think you're a bitch, Willow," Maple offers.

"Maple!" my dad gasps, shocked, as always, by his youngest daughter's frankness.

Maple is sixteen, and my parents often call her 'the greatest surprise of their lives.' But age isn't the only thing that differentiates Maple from Aspen and me—she's decided to stay out of the spotlight, and instead tries to live as normal of a life as possible.

"It's the truth." She shrugs. "I'm just trying to find a constructive answer."

"Well, if that's the case, why don't other models have that reputation, too?" I challenge.

"Most of them do, to be fair," Heena says. "Me, Polina, Lottie, Anja, Seraphine, Vivi–"

"I think we get it," Aspen interrupts her, trying to spare my feelings.

"But none of them have it as bad as I do. You have to admit, it seems like I'm being dragged through the mud *every day* for something," I complain. "And you guys get to be mean girls in the cool way, while I'm a mean girl in the rude bitch way."

"You're the most famous model in the world. Naturally, you would get the brunt of the hate," Heena offers.

"Maybe that explains it. But it sucks either way."

"It does," my mom sympathizes. "I know you're tired, honey. It's been such a long day for you. What time did you leave Paris? Five?"

"Four."

"You should get some sleep," she prescribes. "I guarantee by the time you wake up, the tabloids will have found someone else to torment."

I sigh. "I hope so."

"And besides that, you need your energy for New Year's Eve tomorrow," my dad points out.

The Jordan Family has cemented itself as a staple of Time Square's New Year's Eve celebration. For the past twenty-five years, my parents have introduced an act together, and six years ago, Aspen and I began introducing an act together, too. Maple wants no part of any of it, but she still comes along and sits in our VIP tent every year.

Making it back to New York in time for New Year's Eve was the main reason why my Paris trip was condensed into only two days. I'm so messed up from all the traveling I've been doing lately, between modeling and the holidays, that I don't even know what time zone I'm operating in anymore. I just hope whichever time zone it is, it allows me to stay energized all night tomorrow.

Chapter 2

Riley

"Are you nervous?" my manager, Tracy, asks. I'm minutes away from walking onstage in Times Square. This is *by far* the biggest show I've ever played, with over a million people watching in person and millions more tuning in on TV.

"More excited than nervous." I smile. "It's crazy how far I've come in the past year."

"It is. Just think, last year, you only had an EP. Today, you've had a Billboard Number One song and a Top Ten album."

"It's surreal." I nod. This is only my second time in New York City, and I'm performing in Times Square on New Year's Eve. It's enough to make me pinch myself to prove I'm not dreaming.

I never would have even dreamed that this would be my career. When I was a boy, I dreamt of being a mechanic, like my old man. Growing up in rural North Carolina, most men went into trades of some kind. But, despite money being tight, my parents prioritized my and my sister's education, scrimping and saving enough money to put us through college. Then, my dream shifted toward business in 'the big city'—Charlotte. All of a sudden, one of my songs went viral on the internet, and I had a record deal with one of the most prestigious labels in the industry.

"Well, it's a good thing you enjoy playing live. You're going to be doing a lot of it next year," Tracy says, referencing my eighty-one-night North American tour beginning in a couple of weeks.

"Oh, I love it. It's exhilarating. And the fact that so many people want to come see me play is just...amazing."

"I've missed working with new stars." Tracy sighs. "You're so awestruck by everything."

"Riley?" a stage manager calls. "You're up."

"That's my cue." I grin at Tracy as I walk onstage.

The crowd somehow gets even *louder* as the lights find me.

"Hey, everyone." I beam out at the sea of people flooding Times Square. "Thank y'all for coming out tonight. I still can't believe I'm here." I chuckle into the mic and am met with encouraging whoops from the crowd. I hear the drums start up behind me, and I begin strumming along on my guitar. "This is for my parents back home," I squeeze in before jumping into the first verse.

To my surprise, it sounds like every last audience member is singing along with me. The cameras are circling, and I throw them a wink, earning me a collective squeal from the crowd. This stage is *exhilarating*, and I easily get lost in the music. The song goes by in what seems like mere seconds, and before I know it, I'm singing the closing lines.

"RILEY! RILEY! RILEY!" the crowd chants for me. There's truly no better feeling than hearing a crowd cheering your name, *especially* a crowd this size. I don't think I've ever smiled as wide as I'm smiling now, looking out over the sea of people cheering for me.

"Thank you all, and Happy New Year!" I yell into the mic as I watch the aerial camera hanging in front of me zip backward along its line.

"That was Riley Coleman, performing his number one song, 'Moonlight and You.'" I hear a host saying as I'm ushered off the stage so they can reset it for the next performer.

Chapter 3

Willow

After the ball drops, Aspen, Heena, and I head to the unofficial (but pretty official) afterparty. The party is thrown by one of the wealthiest socialites in the city, incontestably known for hosting the best events in the city. Tickets to his parties are invite-only and rarely cost less than $5,000 each. Tonight, he's rented out the top of the Empire State Building for a whopping $20,000 per head.

On the ride here, we all quickly change out of our warm Times Square clothes and into much skimpier outfits. Heena's gorgeous dark green dress is covered in finely bedazzled snakes with dramatic shoulder pads. Aspen is wearing a simple blue slip dress. I'm in a sheer glittered dress with a plunging neckline and slits along either side. I'm only wearing a nude thong underneath, leaving my bare chest visible through the transparent fabric.

"How do I look?" Aspen asks before we exit the car.

"Gorgeous. What about me?" Heena asks as she tightlines her eyes with black eyeliner.

"Perfect. And me?" I ask.

"Naked." Heena grins.

"You can thank my stylist for that," I parry.

"As if you didn't ask for something sheer."

"Well, if my dad asks, it was all my stylist." I wink.

When we walk into the party, all eyes immediately turn in our direction. Thankfully, most turn back around disinterestedly—that's what I like about these parties. They're so exclusive that nobody here is gawking at me or begging for an autograph...because I could be doing the same thing to them. I recognize almost everyone here, either from the tabloids or the internet. I heard that every celebrity from the New Year's show was invited and, judging by the assembled group, I'd say most of them came. I mean, even the hosts of the New Year's show are here.

The three of us head toward the bar, where the crowd parts to let us through. Even in a room full of famous people, the three of us have sway. We order our drinks, and the bartender gets to work on them immediately.

"You're Willow Jordan, aren't you?" I hear someone ask Aspen.

"No, I'm Aspen Jordan."

"Oh my gosh, I'm so sorry," the girl says.

"Don't worry, it happens all the time. I'm Willow." I smile good-naturedly, peeking my head out from behind Heena.

And it's not just a polite white lie; Aspen and I truly are always getting confused for each other. We both look just like our mother, sharing her sky-blue eyes, golden hair, and sun-kissed skin. The biggest difference between us is our height—and with me standing at 5'10 and Aspen at 5'8, that's not saying much.

"Oh my God, you're both here," she squeals.

"And Heena Badahl is here too," Heena adds, not one to get lost in the crowd.

"Wow, I–I'm," the girl stutters, opening and closing her

mouth several times without saying anything. Now that I'm looking closer, she looks around Maple's age. "I'm a little starstruck," she finally gets out. "Don't worry, I don't want a photo or anything. I just wanted to tell you how much of a fan I am."

"Thank you so much," I answer. "Who are you? I mean, how did you get an invite?" I ask out of curiosity. As I mentioned before, not many people gawk at these parties.

"My dad's company owns the building," she admits.

"Wow, good for you." Aspen laughs. "Other than us, of course, have you met anyone else interesting tonight?"

"Oh, *tons*," the girl says. "Sam Carter, Isolde Vega, Henry James–"

"Where is he?" Heena interrupts. Heena has had a massive crush on Henry James since he picked up a clutch she'd dropped on the red carpet a few months ago. She's been looking for him ever since, claiming it was her 'Cinderella moment.'

"Who, Henry James?" the girl asks.

"Yeah," Heena replies.

"I saw him about fifteen minutes ago, near the back."

"Well, it was so nice to meet you," Heena responds, already leading the way toward the back. Aspen and I shoot the girl apologetic smiles as we follow Heena.

"It was nice to meet you guys, too!" the girl earnestly calls out after us.

"I don't see him," Heena says, craning her neck. She's the tallest of us all, and with tonight's four-inch heels, she's taller than most of the men here.

She goes off in search of him, and Aspen finds one of her friends, leaving me alone in the sea of people. As I scan the crowd for someone worth talking to, a man sidles up beside me.

"Willow Jordan, right? God, you're even hotter in person," he says. He looks vaguely familiar. I think he's internet famous or something like that. Nothing notable.

"Yeah, thanks. I'm actually here with friends, so I'm not looking for any—" I start as his hand wraps around my waist. "I'm serious. Back off." I shove the man.

"Come on, don't play coy with me." He smirks, tightening his grip.

"Fuck *off*," I say, pushing him with all my strength as he stumbles backward.

He sneers. "Wow, I guess what they say is right. You really are a bitch."

"Oh really, just because I don't want to fuck you, I'm a bitch?" I ask. I know I'm making a scene and should just walk away, but I'm fuming.

"Well, when you show up wearing that, yeah," he says, staring at my chest. "I mean, you have your full tits out."

"Yeah, dumbass, I'm a supermodel. I get paid thousands to wear shit like this."

"Yeah, well, maybe you should have some more self-respect and not whore yourself out like that."

I scoff, finding the sense to walk away before I start swinging. Needing to cool off, I head out to the secret 103rd-floor balcony, snagging a bottle of champagne on the way out.

It's freezing outside, but the champagne warms me up quickly. After a few minutes, I get tired of looking out at Manhattan and decide to sit down, leaning against the lookout's half-wall.

I hear the door open behind me and turn my head sluggishly to see who it is. The champagne has done its job and I feel pleasantly fuzzy.

"Shit, what are you doing out here?" a man asks.

I don't recognize him. He's wearing a grey hoodie underneath a brown Sherpa-lined jacket, jeans, and cowboy boots. He looks to be around my age, with a five o'clock shadow and wavy dark blond hair peeking out from under his hood. He's tall and broad enough to be a professional athlete, but something tells me he's not.

"Having a drink, if you don't mind," I slur.

"You must be freezing! How long have you been out here?" he asks, taking off his jacket and walking towards me. He has a charming southern twang.

"What do you care? Shouldn't you want me half-naked anyway?" I bristle.

"No," he says, looking slightly offended. "Put this on. Do you have any friends here? What's your name?"

That last question stops me in my tracks. I seriously don't think I've been asked that question in months.

"You don't know my name?" I ask cautiously.

"Should I?" he asks, shaking his jacket in front of me, trying to get me to take it. I obligingly shrug it on.

"No...I'm Willow. Who are you? I haven't seen you before."

"I'm Riley."

"What brought you to this party?"

"Um...an Uber?"

"No." I laugh. "Wait, you take Ubers?"

"You don't?"

"Only a few times." I don't want to mention that I can only use screened drivers for security reasons.

Most of the guests here wouldn't use Uber either. I take another swig of champagne.

"Hey," Riley says slowly, like he's approaching a spooked horse. He sits down next to me and gently takes the champagne bottle from my hand. "I think you've had enough for tonight, Willow."

"Seriously, what brought you here, cowboy?" I slur, looking at his boots stretched out in front of us.

"I'm a singer."

I knew he wasn't an athlete.

"What do you sing?"

"I only have one song you might know. But my first album just came out, and I'm going to be going on tour soon. So, maybe you'll be hearing more of me soon."

He's just starting out. That makes sense...the boots, the accent, the kindness. Fame tends to chip away at those things after a while.

"What's the song?" I ask.

"'Moonlight and You.' Have you heard it?"

"I don't think so." I shake my head. Everything blurs even more than it already was. "I'll listen to it later."

"You don't have to."

"No, but I want to."

"Well, thank you." He smiles. "Do you mind if I smoke out here? It's kind of why I came out," he adds after a brief silence.

"Sure," I say.

I'm expecting a blunt, but instead, he pulls out a cigarette. I accidentally laugh out loud. He's just so...different from everyone else at that party. It's like a breath of fresh air—metaphorically speaking, of course.

"What?" he asks out of the corner of his mouth as he lights up.

"I thought you meant weed."

"Do you smoke weed?"

"Sometimes."

"Then I'm sorry to disappoint," he says.

"You didn't disappoint."

He gives me a friendly smile out the side of his mouth *not* pursed around the cigarette. "So, what do you do, Willow?"

"I'm a model."

He raises an eyebrow. "Ah, like high fashion and all that?"

"And all that," I confirm.

"So you do the runways and stuff?"

"I do," I answer, keeping it vague. It's so refreshing to have someone treat me normally, and I don't want it to end.

"And ads?"

"Yep. All of the above."

"Wow, that must be so cool." He takes a deep inhale of the cigarette.

"It is pretty cool. But it can be exhausting."

"What do you mean?"

"The constant traveling, the toxic diet culture, the creepy directors, the eyes on you at all times, the shit-talk you hear about yourself online, the perverts thinking they're entitled to your time, or worse, your body..." I trail off.

"Oh. I guess I didn't think about that."

"Don't worry, Riley. I think your karma is too good for any of that to happen to you. And surely you're too nice for anyone to shit on you." I grin at him sincerely, patting his shoulder like I would a dog.

"Thank you?" He laughs. "You seem pretty friendly too."

I reach for the champagne again. Riley gets there first, moving it to the other side of him, out of my reach.

"Give me that," I pout.

"No. You're already drunk. You don't need any more."

"You know, most men would want me drunk."

"So you keep saying. Lucky for you, I like my women conscious, consenting, and ideally not hypothermic." He takes another puff.

"You know those things are really bad for you," I respond.

"So is getting drunk on the balcony of the Empire State Building in January." He laughs, a sound I've decided I enjoy.

"It's hardly January," I answer.

"Would December be any better?"

"Touché."

"Speaking of which, I think it's time we get you inside before you actually get hypothermia." He stubs out his cigarette.

"Ugh," I whine. "I feel fine."

"You're three sheets to the wind. I bet you can't feel a thing right now."

"Where are you from?" I ask. His accent is alluring.

"I'll tell you if you get up." He stands, offering me his hand. I take it, and he pulls me up. "North Carolina. What gave it away, the clothes or the accent?" He grins bashfully. "And where are you from?"

"New York City."

"Ah, so you're home," he says, holding the door open and guiding me back inside. Maybe I *was* cold...the blast of warm air feels so good.

"Willow!" Aspen calls. "I've been looking all over for you. It's late. We should get going."

"Where's Heena?" I ask.

"She's off looking for you too. I'll text her to meet us by the car," she says, grabbing my hand.

Riley clears his throat.

"Yes?" Aspen asks him pointedly.

"Um, she has my coat," he says, nodding toward me.

"Oh, sorry." I shrug the coat off and hand it back. "It was really nice to meet you, Riley." I smile as Aspen drags me to the elevator.

"You too," he calls as the doors shut.

Chapter 4

Riley

"I can't believe this is finally happening," I say, unable to hold back my grin as the tour bus pulls onto the highway.

It's now mid-January, and the tour has just officially begun. I couldn't be more excited since I've never been on tour before, not even as an opener.

I first picked up a guitar as a kid and spent hours teaching myself how to play by watching videos I found online. But I always thought of it as more of a hobby, something that would give my life meaning while a real job would pay the bills. And now, after the release of my debut album, I'm sitting on my tour bus with my three closest friends, pursuing my passion and making more money in the past month than I thought I'd see in my entire life.

"I can believe this is all happening. You have raw talent, Riley," my best friend, Nash, says, smiling from behind his dark curls.

He and I have been inseparable since kindergarten, and he was the one who convinced me to record my first song. He's a bona fide genius, and—even though his specialty is in math and computers—when I asked him if he'd be my bassist, he learned to play the bass guitar in a single week. Not only did he learn to play, but he did it well enough to have fooled my record label into believing he's been playing for years.

"Alright, alright, let's not give Riley *too* much of an ego," Ethan chimes in.

He and I met in college and hit it off due to our mutual interest in music. He was my right-hand man while recording and producing my first few songs before my label picked me up.

"I don't think Riley could get an ego if he tried. When we were little, I accidentally knocked over a cake that took my mom hours to make. She started yelling at me, but then Riley came in and took the blame. He's not exactly known for his ego," Waylon, my cousin, adds. He's practically a guitar prodigy, blowing my skills out of the water. But I have the voice.

When my label came to me about assembling a backup band for me—even though I'm technically a solo act—I knew I needed my friends and family surrounding me, not strangers. The label was surprisingly receptive to this idea and asked the guys to come in and audition. After hearing them play, they were completely sold.

And now, we're all four heading out on tour: Nash as my bassist, Ethan as my drummer, Waylon as my lead guitarist, and me playing rhythm guitar alongside my vocals. It's a dream come true. I've gone from recording songs in my dorm room with Ethan to signing with a record label last January, to having all four of my singles on the Billboard charts (one of them reaching number one), to having an album released last month (still holding steady on the Billboard Top Ten albums). My head spins just thinking about it.

"Yeah, how could Riley have an ego? It's not like his face is plastered on the side of a bus or anything." Nash smirks, referencing the ten-foot-tall photo of me on the side of our bus.

"I'm really glad y'all are coming with me." I change the subject as we settle on the couch at the back of the bus to play video games. From what I've heard, they keep the boredom at bay while touring.

"Yeah, yeah. As if we'd let you tour the country without us," Waylon jokes, grabbing a controller.

"Have any of you been to Utah before?" I ask, referencing our first stop: Salt Lake City.

We're set to arrive there in two days, leaving now from my labels' stronghold in Nashville. We're kicking off the tour with two sold-out nights at the Delta Center, which seats 20,000 people. I literally cannot comprehend how so many people want to see me, especially in a state I've never even stepped foot in.

"Nope," Ethan says. A beam of sunlight moves directly onto him as the bus takes a curve, illuminating his auburn hair and blue eyes.

Waylon shakes his head.

"Me neither. I'm ready to scratch it off," Nash answers.

"What?" I ask.

"My sister gave me one of those scratch-off maps of the country. I only have five states scratched off so far."

"I should get one of those for all the women I sleep with," Ethan says. "I want one from every state."

Nash, Waylon, and I groan in unison. Ethan has always been a playboy, taking advantage of his incredibly good looks. I gave up keeping track of the women he slept with in college. It seems every woman on campus knew him by name.

I chuckle. "That's disgusting."

"No, it's not. Don't worry, dad, I always wear a condom," he teases.

"I like Nash's map better," I say.

"So do I," Nash states. "And don't get any ideas about my sister." He glares at Ethan.

"Speaking of her, how is Nellie?" Ethan smirks.

Nash pales. "You haven't."

"I haven't," Ethan confirms. "Friends' sisters are off-limits."

"At least you have *some* decency. Keep away from Olivia, too," I add, referencing my older sister.

"Come on, guys, don't you have any faith in me?" Ethan asks.

"No, we don't," Nash answers.

"I have *some* boundaries. And anyway, it's not like I don't respect women. I respect them a lot. I just also want to sleep with as many of them as possible." Ethan grins roguishly.

"Shut up, Ethan," I joke.

"Yeah, man, quit while you're ahead," Waylon says, clapping Ethan on the shoulder affectionately.

"So who's going to cover me when I head into this cave?" I ask, drawing our attention back to the game.

After a few hours of gaming, we pull over at a rest stop so our driver can fill up on gas and stretch his legs. We head inside, craving some beers and snacks.

As we're in line for the checkout, junk food in hand, Ethan points to a magazine. "If anyone could get me to give up my bachelor ways, it's her."

I turn around to look, shocked to see Willow, the girl I met on New Year's. She's sitting in a glamorous midnight blue ball gown, angled slightly away from the camera, looking over her shoulder directly into the lens. She has her elbows propped up on her knees, her face in her hands as she stares out at me. She looks...colder than she looked on New Year's, no pun intended.

"She's so hot," Ethan repeats, practically drooling.

"Who, Willow Jordan?" Nash asks. "Isn't she supposed to be really mean or something?"

"No, not Willow," Ethan scoffs. "*Heena Badahl.*" He points to the magazine next to Willow's, featuring a stunning South Asian woman posing in a similarly dramatic fashion. I recognize her from a poster he kept in his room all throughout college—gross.

Willow Jordan, I think to myself. Fuck, of course, I know that name...*everyone* knows that name. I just didn't connect the dots between "Willow Jordan" and the girl I met on the rooftop of the Empire State Building. She seemed so...real. I guess that's why I didn't equate Willow, the model on the rooftop, with Willow Jordan, one of the most well-known names of our generation.

"And anyway, what do you know about Willow Jordan?" Ethan asks Nash.

"Nothing. Nellie just talks about celebrities all the time." He shrugs nonchalantly. "Riley, why do you look like you've seen a ghost?" he adds.

"Willow's not mean," I say, still in a state of shock.

"You know her?" Ethan balks.

"I met her once. But I didn't know she was *Willow Jordan.*"

Ethan laughs. "Bro, how did you not know who Willow Jordan was?"

"I mean, I know the name. I just didn't recognize her."

"Where did you meet her? Did she look like that in real life?" he prods.

"New Year's party. Stop being gross, Ethan. She was nice."

"So, she wasn't that pretty," he says as a statement rather than as a question.

"She was the best-looking girl I've ever seen in my life," I correct. "Now, drop it unless you'd want her talking about you that way."

"I would kill for her to talk about me that way," Ethan responds. "But, I'd prefer it if Heena did." He practically swoons.

I roll my eyes. "I forgot who I was talking to."

"What'd I miss?" Waylon asks, joining us at the checkout after a quick bathroom run.

"Riley's now famous enough that he knows Willow Jordan," Ethan summarizes.

"I wouldn't say I *know* her," I protest. "I met her once, okay?"

"No need to get so defensive." Ethan smirks. "It's not like I'm trying to steal your girl,"

"She's not my girl, and you're totally trying to steal her."

"Well, if she's not your girl, she can't be stolen, right?" Waylon raises his eyebrows.

"Exactly. Come on guys, enough of this. Let's get back on the bus," I say, leading the way out of the rest stop.

"Someone's touchy," I hear Waylon loudly whisper behind my back.

Chapter 5
Willow

"Name?" the barista asks us after we order coffee and pastries.

"Hee.." Heena starts, realizing her mistake. "Hee–eather." The barista gives her a dubious look but types 'Heather' into the iPad anyway.

Even though Heena and I are wearing sunglasses, scarves, and hats for our January walk with Maple, we're always only one misstep away from being identified by someone. She flips the screen, and three tip options appear: thirty percent, forty percent, and fifty percent.

"Fucking New York," Heena grumbles, even though she types in a fifty-dollar tip. She's big on tipping large at restaurants, calling it her version of wealth redistribution.

"I'm glad I don't have to wear all that," Maple says as we meet her at the end of the counter, waiting for our drinks. Luckily for Maple, her face isn't well-known enough that she needs to disguise herself. Sure, there are a few photos floating around on the internet of our whole family when she was a young kid along with a few recent paparazzi photos of us with

Maple in the background. But nobody really knows what she looks like—at least not enough to recognize her on the street.

While she definitely carries the family resemblance, Maple looks more like our dad than Aspen and I do. Coupled with the fact that she keeps her hair at its natural dark blonde—as opposed to Mom, Aspen, and I's highlights—and her signature dark eyeliner, she certainly has her own look. Every once in a while, someone will tell her that she looks familiar, but no one can really place her. I don't think they're recognizing *her* when they say that…they're probably recognizing one of the rest of us reflected in her.

"You know, Maple, every day I understand more and more why you reject fame," I respond.

"What happened now?" Heena asks.

"Nothing, I'm just sick of the constant eyes on me. I wish I could be normal for a day." I sigh.

"Well, that's our day today, right?" Maple suggests. "Just three regular girls getting some breakfast and then going for a walk in the park. Normal."

"Except for Tito," I say, referencing the 6'5, burly man waiting outside the coffee shop with his arms crossed, staring down every person who passes.

Casual, Tito, I think. Tito has been my personal bodyguard since I was two years old. It's kind of ridiculous that I needed my own bodyguard at two, but as the child of Robert and Isabelle Jordan, my safety was a very real concern. Since I became high-profile, he's been especially needed and now accompanies me everywhere. Tito is practically a member of our family at this point.

"What do you mean, he blends right in," Maple jokes.

"Mhm." I laugh. "He blends in about as well as I do. And by that, I mean he sticks out like a sore thumb."

"Heather?" the barista calls.

We thank her as she hands us our drinks and a bag of pastries, and then we head for the door.

"Any threats?" Maple asks Tito when we meet him on the sidewalk, her voice dripping with sarcasm.

"None," he answers earnestly. Maple chuckles.

I hand him a coffee. "A soy caramel latte, just how you like it."

"Thanks, Willow. How much do I owe you?"

"You know better than to ask that. And here's your plain croissant," I say, procuring it from the bag.

"You know, not too long ago, *I* was the one buying *you* food."

"Then I owe you." I grin. "Take it."

He rolls his eyes playfully before devouring half the croissant in one bite. "Thank you," he mumbles as he chews.

After we separate our pastries, we cross the street and find the entrance to Central Park. Tito trails ten feet behind us.

As soon as we walk into the welcome embrace of Central Park, my backyard, I feel my anxiety-stiffened muscles relax. We amble down a main path, taking in the light dusting of snow that covers the bare branches and dry grass. Most people believe that New York looks best in autumn, but I disagree. It was made for winter. The city never looks better than when it's sparkling beneath a soft blanket of snow. And, as a totally unrelated bonus, the biting cold means that there are fewer people walking the streets, and it's easier to disguise myself underneath layers of cold weather garments.

I've always loved winter, but since becoming a model, January has become my favorite month of all. I get to take most of the month off since February is always jam-packed with work for me. New York, London, Milan, and Paris all have their fall and winter fashion weeks in February. For runway models like Heena and I, February and September (spring and summer fashion months) alone comprise almost half of our yearly work. For example, next month, I'm scheduled to walk in eighteen shows, and that was after I limited myself to only the shows I felt passionate about. Many models often walk in upwards of twenty shows during fashion month.

Therefore, January is for relaxing at home in New York, preparing for the whirlwind month ahead. This year is a little different, though, since my parents took on their first joint film project in LA since before I was born. While we were growing up, my parents would take on projects here and there, but at least one of them was always in New York with us. But now, Maple is sixteen, and my parents were given an offer to co-produce a film that they've been interested in working on for years, with my dad also serving as the director. So, it's just Heena, Maple, and I in the city this month.

"Is it weird having Mom and Dad gone for so long? The longest they've ever left you alone was a couple of days for the Oscars two years ago, right?" I ask Maple.

"Not really. I love having them home, and I do miss them, but I'm a junior in high school, and I can pretty much take care of myself. I wasn't going to let them pass up such a great opportunity for my sake—in fact, I was the one who encouraged them to take it. They were hesitant to leave me, but I have you guys here until February, and then Grandma is going to come and stay at the penthouse with me. Plus, it's only LA. They could take the jet and get here in a few hours if they needed to."

"Really? I didn't know you were encouraging them to go." I glance over at her. "What will you do with all your time now that they're gone?"

"Just because I'm not famous doesn't mean I sit around hanging out with my parents all day," Maple responds, rolling her eyes in a very teenager-y way.

"Well, I am famous, and that's still all I do."

"I also just sit around and hang out with your parents," Heena echoes from my other side.

"Well, unlike you two, I'm going to graduate from high school."

"Hey! We graduated from high school. Or close enough. We got GEDs," I defend.

"I mean *really* graduate from high school."

"And then what do you want to do?" I ask.

"I don't know yet." She pauses. "Maybe something in academia."

"Academia? Wow, you're going to put us all to shame, Syrup."

"I don't know if I could ever put you guys to shame," she says, uncharacteristically bashful.

"You definitely will when you discover the 'Jordan Method' for curing cancer."

Maple chuckles. "We'll see about that."

"If I know anyone who's capable of making a scientific breakthrough, it's you, Maple," Heena says.

"Who says I want to do science?"

"If not science, then what do you want to do?" I ask.

"I don't know. Maybe science," she admits, making Heena and I laugh.

We fall into a comfortable silence for a minute or so before making it to a little stone bridge overlooking a pond, the skyline on full display in the background.

"A view like this never gets old," I say, pausing to admire the scene.

"Want me to take a picture of you and Maple?" Heena asks.

"Or even better, why don't you take one of all three of us, Tito?" I call over my shoulder.

"No problem," Tito says, taking my phone from me. Heena

and I have a silent conversation, debating whether we should take off our disguises or not. Lucky for us, the park is about as empty as it gets, and the few people who pass us are running or walking past without so much as a second look. In unison, we both reach to take off our hats, scarves, and sunglasses.

The three of us line up along the rail of the bridge for a photo, all smiling at Tito, who counts down, "Three...two...one...cheese!"

"Can we do a fun one?" Heena suggests.

"Sure," Maple and I reply. I cross my eyes and stick my tongue out. After Tito says 'cheese,' I reach for my phone and see a girl standing behind him, staring at us.

Shit.

"You're Willow Jordan," the girl says, holding eye contact.

Tito stiffens, subtly positioning himself between us and the girl.

"Oh my God, that's so sweet of you to say. She's gorgeous. That's *such* a compliment," I laugh, trying to play it off.

"And you're Heena Badahl," she continues, turning her shocked face towards Heena.

Well fuck, there's no getting out of this now.

"I am," Heena admits.

"Can I get a photo?" the girl asks, taking a few steps toward us. Tito visually stalks her every move, prepared to lunge.

"Sure, we can take a photo," I permit. Tito relaxes only slightly as the girl's face lights up, settling between Heena and me as Maple ducks out of the frame.

"Thank you so much," she says, hands shaking slightly.

"No worries. It was nice to meet you." I smile, turning toward Tito and Maple, only to see a handful of other people behind them, staring at Heena and me like animals in a zoo.

Like flies to honey, more people keep joining the gathered group to see what they're looking at.

"Should we go?" I ask Tito nervously as the crowd grows and begins closing in on us.

"As quickly as you can," he affirms with urgency.

That's all Heena and I need to hear, running off toward our apartment as fast as our legs will take us. Thank God being models requires us to stay in shape because we have about two miles to go.

We sprint as fast as we can, falling through the doors of my building before the doorman can even fully open them. We catch our breath once we're past the security checkpoint in the lobby and wait on Tito and Maple.

"You're lucky we were able to hold the crowd," Tito scolds thirty minutes later as he and Maple stroll into the lobby carrying our abandoned accessories. "I told you it wasn't smart to go out in New York City with just one guard. Especially when there were *two* models out today. Heena, you should have had your own guard."

"I'm sorry," she apologizes. "Next time I'll bring one."

"Please don't tell my parents," I plead. "There's no need to worry them. Everything was fine. Nobody got hurt, and we didn't even really get mobbed."

"It was a close call." Tito narrows his eyes. "I have to tell them, Willow. For your own safety, you can't do that anymore."

"No, if you tell them, they're going to force me to never leave the house without multiple guards. Please, Tito," I beg. "Come on, you don't want to be stuck with some loser at your side, would you? You work best solo."

"I'd be fine, don't turn this back on me." He wags his finger at me. "I'm sure I could get along with another guard, especially if having him there keeps you safe. The more I think about it, the more I think even two won't be enough." He sighs apologetically. "You might need three at this point."

I blanch. "*Three?*"

"I'm sorry, Willow, but it's for your safety. I have to tell your parents about the incident in the park and make my recommendation. I know they're going to tell you the same thing. Under no circumstances can it just be you and I out together anymore. I need help. I can't fend off mobs of people on my own."

I look to Maple and Heena for support, but they both reflect Tito's apologetic yet determined expression.

"Fine. No more going out with one guard," I mumble, mourning the loss of what little independence I had left.

POP CULTURE PULSE PODCAST

Caroline: Did you see the video of Riley Coleman performing on tour?

Jenna: The country singer? No, I haven't. Speaking of him, I have a really embarrassing confession to make, Care.

Caroline: Which is...?

Jenna: I know Riley Coleman's name, of course. I've heard his name a lot recently and I know he's had a pretty rapid rise to fame in the past few months. But for the life of me, I don't think I've ever seen a picture of this man.

Laughter from Caroline.

Caroline: You're in for a treat then, Jenna. Just look at this guy.

A video plays of Riley wearing jeans and a simple white T-shirt, which is just damp enough from a long show to be slightly translucent as it sticks to the lines of his body. The man is singing into the mic, his lips millimeters from grazing it as his hands climb the stand. He's nodding along to the music and smiling from ear to ear as he stands there draped in red stage lights. He finishes his song with a powerful final strum of his guitar that reverberates through the venue as fans scream. He pulls out his earpiece and somehow smiles even wider as he listens to the cheers of the crowd. He runs a hand through his loose, wavy hair before grabbing the hem of his shirt and wiping his face with it, exposing a six-pack with two defined lines drawing one's eyes below his belt. The fans scream even louder and the film shakes before cutting out, presumably as the fan filming freaks out.

Jenna: Wow. Wooooow.

Caroline: Yeah.

Jenna: He must have like a twelve-pack.

Caroline: And that *smile*. Have you ever seen anything like it?

Jenna: I think the podcast needs to get this guy onto the show, immediately. Or at least go to one of his concerts. For reporting purposes, obviously.

Caroline: Obviously.

Chapter 6
Riley

"They don't have this in North Carolina," Nash says.

"They definitely do not," I concur, staring into the Grand Canyon.

We've been hiking for the better part of an hour, finally reaching one of the most iconic lookout points in the entire park. None of us had ever been to the Grand Canyon before, so we figured it was the perfect use of our day off. We've just finished playing two shows in Arizona, and tomorrow, we leave for San Diego.

"Yeah, I don't know if the Smokies can compare to this. They're beautiful, but this is...otherworldly," Waylon affirms, gaping at the sprawling landscape laid bare before us. Hundreds of hues of red, orange, yellow, and brown are cascading in ribbons along the canyon's rock formations, topped with fluffy green and brown brush. Contrasting those colors is a strikingly blue, cloudless sky, complete with a powerful sun beating down on us. With this sun, I almost regret wearing a jacket despite the January chill.

"I've never seen so many shades of red before," Ethan says. "It's beautiful."

"I bet that's what you say to all the ladies," I tease, clapping him on the shoulder of his 'Eat Pussy, it's Organic,' T-shirt. "So, does the Sex Pest of Appalachia believe in God now?"

"As much as I appreciate the new nickname, you know I don't believe in all that mumbo jumbo. But your mom sure screams his name a lot when we're fucking," he smirks.

"Hey, fuck off, man," I give him a slight shove. "I thought we were having a moment."

"If you want me to yourself, Riley baby, all you have to do is ask," he purrs.

"As if," I scoff.

"You like the red of this canyon? Wait until you see the red of my carpet. Safe to say they match these fiery drapes—"

"Damn, dude, do we need to get you a sex doll or something? You're all horny today," Waylon interrupts him.

"I'm always horny, but thanks for noticing." Ethan winks.

"Maybe you should reapply your sunscreen. Your hair isn't the only thing that's looking red right now," Waylon taunts.

Ethan sighs, pulling a tube of sunscreen out of the side pocket of his backpack and squirting some onto his hand. "Not everyone was blessed with your melanin," he grumbles as he slathers the white lotion haphazardly onto his face.

"Well, I might be mixed, but I didn't get your baby blues. It evens out," Waylon concedes.

"If I didn't know any better, I'd think you two were complimenting each other," I tease.

"Are you feeling left out?" Ethan asks.

"Or do you just hate healthy masculinity?" Nash joins in. I smile to myself, happy to see the friends from different areas of my life meshing so well with each other.

"No, no, don't stop on my account."

"Don't worry, Riley, your green eyes are just as pretty as

Ethan's blue ones," Waylon grins at me, flashing the dimples we share.

"And what about me? I don't have melanin *or* colored eyes," Nash says.

"Yeah, but you've got the brains," Ethan says.

"And that geeky rizz," Waylon adds.

"Geeky rizz?"

"Yeah, like how Riley has country boy rizz. You've got geeky rizz."

"But I'm also from the country," Nash argues.

"Yeah, but that's not where your rizz comes from." Ethan shakes his head. "It's all about the dominant rizz factor."

"And what's yours?" Nash asks.

"Ask your sister."

"You walked into that." I chuckle. Waylon howls with laughter.

"Maybe I'll use my geek rizz on your mom then," Nash tries to fight back lamely. He's not one for this type of banter, and I cringe even more when I realize his faux pas.

"Good luck finding her," Ethan snickers, but I can sense an undercurrent of pain beneath his snide remark. "That crack whore is probably dead in an alley by now."

"What?" Nash asks, taken aback.

"She left me when I was a baby. I lived with my grandparents for a few years, but they were dirt poor, and eventually, CPS took me away when my teachers reported the unwashed, emaciated boy with a spotty attendance record. I was in and out of foster care until I left for App State."

This conversation has taken a very sharp turn, I inwardly cringe.

"Shit man, I'm sorry, I didn't know," Nash concedes, looking genuinely distraught at making an insensitive joke, even if he wasn't aware.

"It's okay, man. How could you have? Enough of this depressing talk. We're at the Grand Canyon! Let's see who dares to get closest to the edge. Winner drinks for free tonight," Ethan suggests.

The other three of us quickly shoot down this idea down.

"Fine. Should we see who can piss the furthest stream down into the canyon?"

"Dude, what are you on?" Waylon shakes his head. "And don't say my mom," he adds quickly.

"Would it be so lame to just stand here and admire the view?" I ask.

"I think that's a great idea," Nash agrees.

"Alright, alright, I guess I'll have to settle for basking in the glory of the natural world." Ethan rolls his eyes playfully.

And so we stand there together, admiring the view, waiting until the sun starts its slow descent to head back.

* * *

"Hey Riley, have you looked through your mail yet?" Nash asks, returning to the gaming area of the tour bus with a stack of envelopes in hand.

"Nope. They're probably just ads and bills." I shrug, my eyes fixated on the screen as Ethan and I face off. "I don't know why my mom bothers forwarding half that stuff to me."

"You might want to look at this one," he says, extending his arm.

"Can it wait until the end of this game?" I ask.

"You're going to want to see this now," he responds. When Nash—a naturally meek guy—puts his foot down, I listen. I pause the game.

"Hey," Ethan whines.

"Sorry, man," I say, grabbing the envelope from Nash. My

heart stops when I see the return address. I look at Nash, and he nods subtly, urging me to open it.

I pull out a black sheet of cardstock depicting a golden gramophone.

"Holy shit," I breathe.

"What is it?" Waylon asks, craning his neck to see what I'm holding.

"It's an invitation to the Grammys."

Chapter 7

Willow

"Are you sure this isn't too skimpy?" Aspen asks me, staring at her ass in the trifold mirror.

We're in a guest bedroom of our parent's rented penthouse in Los Angeles, which has been transformed into a makeshift fitting room in preparation for the Grammys. Despite the fact that no one in our family sings, we've always been invited to the Grammys—along with every other award show in Hollywood.

"Aspen, how old are you?" I ask, staring into her blue eyes, almost exact replicas of mine.

"Twenty..." she says hesitantly. "I'm just worried it's still too mature for me."

"And by 'mature,' I'm guessing you mean 'slutty'?" She nods sheepishly. "I'd worn much worse by the time I was your age," I reassure her. "If it makes *you* feel more comfortable, wear something more conservative. But don't worry about what other people will think." I look over her dress, which is too stunning to be left on the rack. "Besides, they'll only compare you to me, and we both know my style makes you look like Mother Theresa."

"I do really love this dress," she murmurs, smoothing her hands down the transparent blue material that makes up the body of the dress. Beneath it is a matching strapless blue corset bodysuit that covers everything it needs to cover. Truly, I had worn much worse by the time I turned eighteen. "What are you going to wear?" she asks me.

I wave her off. "I'll figure it out tomorrow."

"But the Grammys are tomorrow."

"This entire rack—" I gesture to the rack labeled with a piece of printer paper labeled "WILLOW" "—was made precisely to my measurements. It'll all fit."

"Fair enough."

"Don't worry, Aspen. I'll wear something especially scandalous to keep people from talking about you."

She frowns. "You don't have to do that."

"I want to. If my sister wants to wear a dress without being slut-shamed, she should be allowed to do that. If the press needs a Jordan to shit-talk, let them shit-talk me."

* * *

Surprisingly, my golden dress with both sides left open, save for two measly ties that held it on my body, wasn't press-worthy. At least, not when some pop singer wore a bedazzled G-string and pasties.

As much as I liked the gown that I wore to the main event, I much prefer the bronzed minidress with beaded fringe that I'm wearing on the mini red carpet spread out in front of the hotel hosting the afterparty. I'm also grateful to have my hair down in loose waves rather than in the stiff updo it was in earlier, with bobby pins poking my scalp half to death.

After granting the paparazzi a few photos, Aspen tugs me into the venue: a massive ballroom decorated with hundreds of flickering candles and golden roses. As we walk in, I feel all eyes turn to us. Aspen squirms at my side, walking over to a high-top where some of her friends stand, all greeting her with warm hugs. In contrast, I stare back at the other attendees, taking my time to scope out the crowd. I see some of my parents' friends, who give me kind smiles and turn back to their conversations, some singers around my age who give me more poisonous smiles before slowly breaking my stare, and finally, some wallflowers who seem too stricken to even look at me.

Fame is a weird thing.

I'm beginning to walk to the same table as Aspen when I see a familiar blond-haired man along one of the walls, laughing with another guy who looks about our age.

"Hey, Riley," I say, changing course and sauntering up to them.

"Willow!" he says, looking shocked. "I'm surprised you remembered me."

I shrug. "I'm not as vapid as people make me out to be."

Riley's friend takes that as his hint to cough an excuse and disappear wide-eyed into the crowd.

"No, I didn't mean that. I mean–I don't–you're not vapid at all," he stammers. "It's just that you were pretty drunk, is all. And I didn't think you'd remember someone as inconsequential as me."

"I never forget someone who's kind to me. And you're not inconsequential, Riley. Why would you say that?" Although a small part of me enjoys the power that comes from making him so nervous, the majority of me mourns the sweet guy who had no clue who I was. It was nice to just be another face in the crowd for once.

"Well, I'm sure you know all sorts of important people. I'm probably the least recognizable person in this room tonight.

Well, besides Nash," he says, awkwardly pointing to where his friend was.

"You were invited to the *Grammy's* after releasing your *first* album, and you're currently on a sold-out tour. I don't think anyone would call you inconsequential. So why are you so nervous tonight?"

"Maybe I'm a nervous person," he responds. "How do you know so much about me?"

"You're not a nervous person. And maybe I looked you up." I cock my head, staring him down. He breaks my stare. "I'm serious, Riley. Look at me." He does. "You deserve to be here as much as anyone else. Don't let anyone tell you any different."

He sighs, taking a sip of his beer. "You're right. I guess I just get intimidated being surrounded by people I've been listening to on the radio since I was a kid."

"Well, let's get some air then. It's too stuffy in here anyway."

I gently grab his arm and lead him out of the main ballroom and into the hallway. He doesn't back down from my touch, which surprises me. I walk us down the hallway, opening doors as I go until I find an empty reading room. "Much better," I say, turning on a lamp and shutting the doors behind us.

"Thanks," he says. "I just needed a minute. It's been a long night of being starstruck."

"And I guess talking to Willow Jordan doesn't help, does it?"

"It definitely helps," he says, fixating his eyes on me and giving me a small smile, showing off his dimples. Dimples on top of a face like that? Not to mention his impressive height and stature...I see why so many female fans go crazy for him.

"When I'm not thinking about the fact that you're Willow Jordan," he adds with a chuckle.

"So what tipped you off? You seemed pretty clueless on the roof the other night," I ask, plopping down in one of the worn leather couches.

Riley sits stiffly on the one opposite me, still a bundle of nerves.

"Nash, actually. We saw you on the cover of a magazine. I feel like an idiot for not putting two and two together. You literally told me you were a model named Willow."

I laugh. "I take it as a compliment that you didn't realize who I was."

"Why?"

"Because it means that a part of me is still normal. Every day, I feel like I drift further and further away from reality. It's nice to see that I can still pass for a real person."

"A real person? What do you mean?"

"Someone who's not famous," I say. "I've always had a public presence because of my parents, but it was never anything close to what it became after I started modeling. The past few years, it's become harder and harder for me to seem like, or feel like, a regular girl."

"Well, I'm having the opposite problem."

"You mean you're having a hard time adjusting to fame?"

He nods. "I never aimed to be famous. I just wanted to share my music with people. To be honest, I don't even know *how* to be famous."

"Why don't we help each other?" I ask, without thinking. "You can help me remember what it's like to be normal, and I can coach you on how to be famous."

He smiles at me, his green eyes dark in this dim room. "You mean that?"

Self-consciousness fills me, a feeling I seldom have

anymore. *Was it stupid of me to ask that? Does he think it's a dumb idea? He never even said he needed help, only that he was having trouble adjusting.*

"I mean it," I reply. "But you can say no. I just—I don't have any non-famous friends. Everyone is as famous as I am, and so no one really understands normalcy—"

"I accept your deal, Willow Jordan. Happily." He grins.

His smile is so genuine it sends a spark down my spine whenever it's aimed at me. That smile was how I knew he wasn't accustomed to fame that very first night—famous people's smiles are *much* stiffer than Riley's.

"Okay. I think we should start your first lesson tonight, then. In your opinion, who's the most famous person here?"

"I saw Alex Stehling…" he says, referencing the EGOT-winning, eighty-year-old director.

"Seriously, *he's* your choice?" I can't help but laugh at his bewildered expression.

"Yes? How is he a bad choice? There's not a single person in America who wouldn't recognize that name. He directed *Ephemera*, and *The Blood Meridian*, and *Last Breath*, and—"

"I know, I know," I say, cutting him off. "I'm just laughing because, out of everyone in that room, you chose my godfather."

"You're joking," he deadpans.

"Not joking. Come on," I say, standing.

"And where are we going?" he stands hesitantly.

"To introduce you to Alex Stehling."

Chapter 8

Riley

As we approach Alex Stehling, deep in conversation with the most famous singer of his generation, I clench my hands into fists to stop them from shaking.

"Hey," Willow whispers to me, her hand lightly touching my forearm, which somehow makes my heart race even faster. "It's okay, I won't let him bite you." She smiles mischievously before dropping her hand from my arm.

"He bites?"

"Hard." She smirks. "Hey, Alex," she says, gracefully leaning in to kiss her elderly godfather on the cheek. "I wanted to introduce you to a friend of mine, Riley Coleman. He's a big fan."

"Is he?" Alex's attention turns his attention to me, his hawkish eyes scrutinizing my face before breaking into a smile that easily shaves twenty years off the old man. "Then it's nice to meet you, Riley. Any friend of Willow's is a friend of mine." He holds his hand out for me to shake. "A solid handshake," he says. "You're not dating him, are you, darling?"

"What? God, Alex, no." She turns her head to look at me, mouthing an apology.

"Hey, I'm old, but I'm not blind. I saw that. A shame, though, he seems like a pleasant young man."

"Thank you, sir," I reply.

"Nervous, though," he muses with a slight smile. "Are you new around here?"

"Very new," I respond. "This is my first award show. My debut album was only released a couple of months ago."

"A country singer?"

"How did you know?"

"Your accent gives it away. Country is my favorite genre. Willow, you'll have to give me one of Riley's CDs."

"Do you even have CDs?" she asks me with laughter in her eyes.

"I'm sure there are some somewhere..."

"I'll try to find one for you," Willow says to Alex. "Or better yet, I'll come over to your place before I leave LA, and I can stream it for you. You'd really like it."

"Sounds like a plan. Thank you, Riley, for giving Willow a reason to come visit me." Alex smiles. "Well, I hate to leave you kids, but I promised to chat with Jack Mack tonight, and it's already past my bedtime. Bye, darling," he says, giving Willow a brief hug before walking off in search of the other director.

"See, that wasn't so scary, was it?" Willow asks, turning to face me.

"It was pretty scary." I exhale a breath I didn't know I was holding.

Willow laughs. "You're ridiculous."

"So what if I am? Hey, this is all new to me. Just wait 'til we get you up on a horse, then we'll see who's laughing."

"A horse?" she asks, eyes wide. "That wasn't part of the deal."

"Now it is. Have you ever ridden one?"

"Twice, but I don't know if I could use the word 'ride.' Both times were for shoots, so I just sat there on a standing horse while a handler watched from about three feet away."

I laugh at her. "Yeah, so we're not going to count that."

"Well, if you plan on making me ride a horse all by myself, I'm going to really rip the Band-Aid off for you, too. I'll call the paparazzi on you and make them chase you down the street."

"You're ruthless." I chuckle. "Unfortunately for you, I don't think the paparazzi give a shit about me."

"I think you'd be surprised." She shrugs. "You have a sold-out six-month tour and a number-one song. That counts as paparazzi-worthy."

"Speaking of this database of knowledge you apparently have on me...you've also heard my music? You told Alex Stehling he would like it. That means you've listened to it, right?"

"Don't flatter yourself, Riley. I was just making conversation."

"Oh," I say, catching my smile before it falls.

"I'm just kidding," Willow interjects quickly. "Damn, you make me feel bad for making a joke. You looked like a kicked puppy. *Of course* I listened to your music. I told you I would."

"I just didn't think you meant it."

"I don't often say things I don't mean."

"So, since you think Alex would like it, does that mean you liked it?"

"Slow down there, cowboy, or someone might think you're fishing for compliments. But yes, I did like it. A lot, actually, even though I don't typically like country music."

"Maybe you just haven't listened to the good stuff." I shrug, trying to keep the ridiculous grin off my face from her compliment—and failing.

"You'll have to make me a playlist, then."

"And what'll you make me in return?"

Her eyes light up, then dim a little to cover the glitter of her excitement. "Now, listen, Riley. I mean this in the best possible way, and I love the country look—I think it suits you well, fits your brand," she starts.

"Now *you* sound nervous," I tease her. "You want to revamp my wardrobe, don't you?"

"Yes! There's nothing wrong with it, it's just not wowing anyone. I could keep your same country look while just making it a little more...elevated."

"Sounds like you have yourself a deal." I grin. *Jeez, I can't stop myself from smiling around her....that does not bode well for me or my heart.*

A woman who looks scarily identical to Willow walks up, a glass of champagne in her hand.

"Hey, Willow. And you are..." the woman asks, eyeing me curiously.

"I'm Riley Coleman, nice to meet you..." I pause, extending my hand and waiting for her to fill in her name.

"Aspen Jordan." She smiles. "Willow's sister."

"Ah, I never would have guessed. You guys look nothing alike."

Both sisters laugh at this, a sound so identical and in sync it sounds like one person.

"I like you, Riley, you're funny," Aspen says. "Well, it's nice to meet you. You're new here, right?"

"Is it that easy to tell?"

"Hollywood is kind of a tight circle. It sticks out when you haven't met someone before. Not that it's a bad thing. God knows we could use some fresh blood around here."

"Aspen!" Willow rolls her eyes at her sister but can't contain her laugh. "Don't scare him off by talking like it's some big cult we're in. It's taken him all night to break out of his shell."

"It is sort of a big cult. But, wait, all night? What were you so scared of?" Aspen asks me.

"You guys, I mean, all of the famous people."

"Well, aren't you famous now, too?" Aspen asks.

"That's what I said." Willow nods. "He's just nervous. First big awards night and all."

"Were you nominated?" Aspen asks.

"No. My album only just came out in December. Nominations came out the month before," I answer.

"So you think that you'll be nominated this November?" Willow prods.

"That's not what I meant," I start.

"Don't be humble. It doesn't suit you," Willow chuckles. "I think you deserve a nomination. I mean, six hundred million streams on Spotify is pretty Grammy-worthy to me."

"That's a massive hit," Aspen confirms.

"You guys are conniving together." I chuckle. "Remind me to never get on your bad side."

"Oh, I'll remind you," Aspen says, eying me and then Willow. "Ready to leave, Willy? My single glass of champagne wore off thirty minutes ago, and my feet hurt."

"I don't get why you don't just have a second glass, nobody's going to judge you—"

"I don't like feeling out of control, you know that. What if I do something ridiculous?"

"Nobody would care," Willow starts, then looks at me, seemingly remembering I'm there too, watching them bicker.

I chuckle. "No, please, don't stop on my account."

Willow gives me a knowing smile. "As fun as this has been, Riley, that's my cue to leave. See you around, right?" she says, taking a step to leave with her sister.

"Wait!" I call. "Shouldn't we exchange numbers? What if one of us has a fame-emergency?"

The surprise on Willow's face is quickly replaced by an impressed smile. "Sure. Here," she says, handing me her phone.

I try not to notice all the A-list numbers she casually has saved.

I type my number in, handing back her phone. "Goodnight, Willow. And Aspen. Get home safe," I say, waving as they walk away.

A chuckling Nash joins me, having watched that whole exchange. I lower my hand awkwardly, debating whether I should just cut it off.

Chapter 9

Willow

"What do I say to him?" I ask Heena as our green tea face masks harden.

It's been two days since we were at the Grammys, and we're currently at a spa.

It's become our tradition to pamper ourselves with a full-body spa day before we start the fashion week grind.

"You know," Heena says, giving me a side eye through her mask, "friends don't get anxious about texting other friends."

"I'm not *anxious*. I just don't want to scare him off. Or give him the wrong impression."

Another side-eye.

"Fine, just to prove I'm not anxious..." I say, hitting send on my first message to Riley and showing the screen to Heena.

"'It's Willow'? Really? That's what you went with? What is this, some kind of covert mob deal?"

"Well, you didn't tell me what to say!" I start to laugh before abruptly stopping when I feel my mask crack.

"Because I didn't know you'd start like *that*. I thought you'd say something like, 'Hey, how's LA been treating you?'"

"Then he wouldn't know who was texting."

"How many women does he give his number out to in the span of two days?"

"I don't know, that's his business."

We're interrupted by my phone buzzing.

Riley: Hey Willow, what's up? Still in LA?

"See? *That's* normal." Heena laughs, reading over my shoulder. "And a quick texter, too. That's always a green flag."

I type out a new message, ignoring her.

Me: you know, the first rule of fame is to never trust a new number. you should ask for a photo from me for proof.

Heena laughs even harder as I press send, her mask breaking into a thousand tiny creases. "Willow!" she squeals. "You're the worst flirt I've ever seen."

"I'm not flirting," I insist, laughing along with her. "And besides, it's true. I'm supposed to train him for fame, so that's what I'm doing."

"*Train* him? Like a dog?"

"You know what I mean." I roll my eyes as my phone buzzes again. This time, I hide the screen from her prying eyes as I read his next message.

Riley: But I was the one who gave you my number?? I'm pretty sure it's you.

Me: pretty sure? alright, this is going to make my 40-year-old-living-in-my-mom's-basement life! texting with superstar riley coleman!

He responds immediately, sending me a photo of himself in a tour bus with three other men in their early twenties, one I recognize from the other night.

Riley: Well, here's me.

Me: no, you don't have to send the photo, I messaged YOU. I'M the catfish

"Let me see what you're saying," Heena begs, peering over my shoulder.

"Want to be in a photo?" I ask, showing her the messages.

"Not my best look," she says, glancing down at her fluffy white robe and bare feet. "But, then again, my worst look is anyone else's best." She smirks.

I take a photo of us and send it to Riley.

Riley: You don't look like a catfish to me. You look like an ogre.

Riley: Because of the green I mean

Reading those texts makes me laugh out loud.

Me: thank you for the clarification

"Heena? I'm here to take you back for your mud wrap whenever you're ready," a spa attendant says.

"Don't say anything too embarrassing to him while I'm gone. I still haven't deemed him trustworthy yet," Heena says lowly as she stands.

I nod. "Good to know that you need to approve the people I talk to."

"Well, with the way the media's been desperate for stories on you lately, I'd be cautious, that's all."

"I appreciate the concern, Heena, really, but Riley wouldn't sell me out."

"Just be careful," she says as she walks out, the attendant resting a warm, weighted, lavender-infused pillow over her shoulders.

Riley: Who are you with?

Me: my friend Heena, another model. you might have seen her face around. and yes, i'm still in LA. today is my last day here before i leave for new york for fashion week

Riley: I've heard of her but the green threw me off. What is that stuff anyway?

Riley: That sounds fun. I'm off to San Francisco for a show tomorrow night.

Me: it's a face mask...you've never used a face mask before?

Riley: Um...no?

Me: you need to do one. another rule of fame, everyone does face masks

Riley: Are you seriously telling me your dad, THE Robert Jordan does face masks?

Me: regularly. and botox and filler too. he's a high-maintenance man.

Me: i'm glad to know you did your research on me, too

Riley: Nash told me. I think he's a superfan.

Me: remind me to give him an autograph sometime

Riley: I will literally take you up on that. One for his sister too. Not to be greedy.

Riley: Is the all lower-case a famous thing too, or just a Willow thing?

Me: a willow thing.

Riley: Why?

Me: why not?

Me: but really, i don't know, it makes me feel less intimidating

Riley: You're not really that intimidating

Me: 'not really'

Riley: Well, you are on the outside, but once you get talking you're less scary

Me: i'm scary on the outside?

Riley: I mean you are a supermodel...

Me: you didn't know that when we first met

Riley: You still looked like one. I was still intimidated.

Me: you didn't seem like it when you were trying to take my drink from me

Riley: I was actively shitting my pants

Riley: Not to get graphic

Me: good to know i have that effect on men

Riley: Hahaha

Riley: But speaking of men

Riley: I don't want to be weird and I don't mean this in any presumptuous way

Me: i don't have a boyfriend, no

Riley: Oh, thank God. I didn't want some 7'5 NBA player beating me up for talking to you

Me: don't worry

Me: even if I did have a 7'5 NBA player, i'd make sure he didn't beat you up for talking to me 🙄

Riley: Can't blame a guy for worrying though, right?

Me: nope. you don't have some super strong scary country girl coming to beat me up either, do you?

Riley: Nope. Just a weak country girl

Me: oh

Me: okay, just tell her not to hit my face, it's a precious asset

Me: insured for 1 million

Me: sorry i don't know why i told you that, that's weird

Riley: Is it really???

Me: yep. because it would end my modeling career if my face gets fucked up

Riley: Maybe you could be a hand model

Riley: Or a foot model

Me: is this your way of telling me you have a foot fetish

Riley: HAHA

Riley: No I don't, please don't slander me like that.

Riley: Also, there is no country girl, weak or strong. None at all, just to clarify. I was joking.

"Willow?" a spa attendant calls, entering the spa's solarium. "I'm here to take you back for your algae wrap."

"Oh, sure," I say, shooting off a quick message to Riley before following the woman out.

Me: got to go, spa is calling.

Chapter 10

Riley

"And that's really a real tattoo? You're not playing a joke on me?" I ask the first fan in line at my backstage meet-and-greet—part of the VIP package offered to fans at all my shows for a premium price. My boys are here with me, mostly for moral support since they're just my supporting band. Some people ask for their autographs, which makes my face light up as much as it makes theirs. It's our second and final night in San Francisco before we move on to a show each in Washington and Oregon later this month and then head to Canada before returning to the US.

"One hundred percent real." The male fan smiles proudly as he glances between his tattooed forearm and me. "Do you like it?"

"I love it...really. I'm at a loss for words. This is the first time someone has gotten my lyrics tattooed. Or at least, the first time I've seen it. It's incredible, I like how it—"

"Riley, time to move on," Tracy, my manager, says from behind me.

"Just one more second," I call back to her, shooting the fan an apologetic grimace. "Can I get a photo with you and the tattoo?"

"Riley Coleman asking *me* for a photo? Fuck yeah, man," he says, putting his arm on display between us while I snap a photo.

"NEXT," Tracy calls behind me. The man scurries off, giving me a final wave, which I return regretfully.

"Oh my gosh, Riley, I just can't believe you're real!" a girl says in front of me, drawing my attention away from the receding male fan.

"In the flesh." I grin. "What can I do for you, a photo, an autograph, both?"

"I'd love an autograph." The girl smiles back at me. "Can you sign my..." she trails off, moving her hair to reveal her ample chest, almost bare thanks to her *very* low-cut tank top.

"Um...sure," I stammer, feeling my face flushing. I almost move my left hand to her side to stabilize her as I write, but I think better of it and let my hand fall to my side. No matter how many times I get asked to autograph women's bodies, it never feels normal.

"Got room for a second signature?" Ethan smirks down at the girl from my side.

"No thanks," the girl says before taking a quick selfie with me and skipping away. She must have sensed the sharp eyes of Tracy glaring at her for almost running over time.

"I just wanted to tell you that your album literally saved my life," a young teen girl says, taking the previous girl's place.

"Wow," I say, speechless. "I think that's the greatest achievement my music has ever earned."

"It deserves every ounce of attention it's gotten and more." She smiles. "Can I get a photo?"

"Of course." I don't object as she wraps her arms around me and smiles as Waylon snaps our photo.

"Could I get one with all of you now?" she asks, looking up at me adoringly.

"Definitely, I think you just made their day," I whisper to her while the guys crowd in around us.

Tracy sighs. "We really don't have time for two photos per fan."

"It's my time, and she can have as much of it as I want her to have," I snap back, probably ruder than I should have.

"Last photo, then we're moving on." Tracy scowls, taking the photo for us before shooing the young girl away. As she hurries off, she shoots me one last shy smile over her shoulder.

"NEXT," Tracy calls.

After the last fan leaves, Tracy sighs and looks down at her watch. "Riley, I hate to seem mean, I really do. But when you take longer than one minute with each fan, we run over, and then your whole schedule is thrown off. We're thirty minutes late, meaning I have to tell the stage managers to rush through sound check, making them angry with *me*."

"Listen, I'm sorry, really. Is there any way we could start scheduling more time for the meet-and-greets?"

"Not really." Tracy shrugs. "This is standard for the industry. And it's better for all of us if we rush the fans through. More fans getting to meet you within a smaller amount of time means a larger profit margin for all of us."

"But I don't care about the profits," I protest.

"It's not about what you care about anymore. What about the livelihood of me and the rest of my firm? Or the venue owners? Or the stage, equipment, and security teams? They all make money when *you* make money. And you want them to be able to afford to feed their families, right?"

"Right—"

"Then we need to stick to strictly one minute per fan.

Welcome to show business. We're expecting you onstage in fifteen; don't be late," she says, exiting.

"That was harsh," Nash breathes.

"I mean, I guess it makes sense," Waylon says ambivalently. "As much as it sucks, Riley no longer answers only to himself. He answers to everyone who works to make his shows happen."

"Yeah, but he also answers to his fans," Ethan argues.

"It's a tough spot to be in," I agree. "I just wish I could have more time with fans. Rushing them through in one minute seems so fake."

"One minute is enough to make an impression, though," Nash consoles. "I bet those fans are posting all those photos as we speak or even printing them out to hang on their walls at home."

"When I was really little, I met Dave Grohl at one of these things, and he signed a photo of himself for me. I still have it," Ethan adds.

"You do?" I ask.

He narrows his eyes. "Don't make me regret being vulnerable."

"No, no, I think that's great. Thanks for telling me, Ethan. It makes me feel better about what we're doing here."

"It really is an industry-standard," Nash offers. "No artist gets to spend much time with any one fan."

"Yeah, it just sucks."

"I know, Cuz," Waylon says, squeezing my shoulder. "And I hate to do this, but we really should head to the stage before Tracy eats us alive."

POP CULTURE PULSE PODCAST

Caroline: So now that fashion season is upon us, I thought we could open the episode by discussing our favorite models.

Jenna: Great idea, Care. Are we talking about personality or actual skill as a model?

Caroline: Both. But you could divide it up too and give us a favorite for each.

Jenna: I think that sounds easier for me because picking a single favorite model would be super hard. For personality, I think I'd choose Polina Antonovic because she just seems so nice. Like, I think we would be friends in real life—Polina if you're listening to this, hit me up for drinks sometime!

Caroline: Or to be on the podcast.

Jenna: Podcast, then drinks. On us!

Caroline: I can actually see you and Polina getting along. I think that makes sense. For me, I think my favorite would be either Heena Badahl or Seraphine De Luca. They just seem so femme fatale, and you know I'm obsessed with that energy. Although, I like to think of myself in a similar way, so we'd probably either love each other or hate each other.

Jenna: I can see you getting along with them. I mean, they like each other, right?

Caroline: Yeah, from what I can tell, they seem to be friends, so maybe there's hope for me yet. Who's your favorite in terms of actual modeling ability?

Jenna: I hate to say it but...I think Willow Jordan has a *fantastic* walk.

Caroline: Really?

Jenna: Yeah, for sure. I mean, I've been mesmerized by her in every show I've seen her walk in. Well, technically, they've mostly been videos of shows. I've only actually seen her walk once in person. But she's stylistically mastered both the catwalk and the horse walk.

Caroline: I know this is such an unpopular opinion, but I actually find her walk boring.

Jenna: Boring?

Caroline: Yeah, it's just *too* perfect for my taste. All sultry hips and shoulders, no actual personality.

Jenna: Who is your favorite model, then?

Caroline: Personally, I like Lottie Lawson. She's just so authentic. You can tell she definitely had no formal model training, unlike Willow. Willow seems like she was bred to be a model.

Producer: But doesn't that make her the perfect model?

Caroline: If you like your models basic and cookie-cutter.

Jenna: I see what you mean, but I still find her pleasing to watch. On a different note...

Chapter 11
Willow

"Willow, darling, I need you to stop fidgeting, or I'll take the liberty of pinning your hands to your sides myself," one of the executive designers at Marc Jacobs tells me.

I'm at my final fitting in preparation for their runway this evening, my most anticipated show for New York Fashion Week. Since I'm closing the show, the entire team has been preening over me for the past few hours, making me cleanse, tone, exfoliate, fake tan, and moisturize every inch of my body with products of their choosing. Then, they painted my nails a metallic gold color to match my chain mail bodysuit and ten-foot cape, which connects to my body at the wrists and throat. And after this fitting, I still have to go through a couple of hours of hair and makeup before I'm ready to finally walk.

"Yes, sorry," I mumble. *They shouldn't have had me stand in front of a mirror if they didn't want me fidgeting.*

"You look beautiful," the designer says, seemingly reading my mind.

"My skin feels raw."

"It *should* feel raw. It's remade every show, along with the rest of you."

"You look great, Willow, really," Heena reassures me from the next riser.

She's opening the show in a beautiful long-sleeve golden wrap dress with a matching golden spiked tiara. We're wearing the only two golden pieces in the show. The rest of the models are all wearing neutral colors.

"Thanks, Heena, you do too." I smile at my beautiful best friend. Even with no makeup, she's strikingly, stunningly, drop-dead gorgeous.

That beauty is what got her into modeling the old-fashioned way, by being scouted in a mall in her hometown of Seattle.

"Well, that's to be expected," she says with a wink.

"Stop moving," the woman tailoring Heena's dress snaps. Heena gives me a dramatic, wide-eyed 'yikes' expression. We both turn forward again.

"And," I start, unable to get the sentence out, even though I'm not facing Heena anymore. "I mean, you…" I wring my hands in front of me, earning a dirty look from my kneeling designer.

"Anytime now, Willow, we have all day," Heena jokes.

"You don't think my walk is boring, do you?" I finally blurt out.

"*What?* For fuck's sake, Willow, you have the best walk in the industry! Who the fuck said that?"

"I just saw someone talking about it online…"

"It's not true. It's not even *close* to true. Jesus Christ, jealousy is a disease." I can hear the exasperation in her tone. "Willow, look at—ah! She actually poked me with her pin!"

"You won't stop moving," Heena's woman retorts as my woman laughs.

"Fine, don't look at me," Heena amends. "But listen carefully. You are the best model in the industry right now. And that's coming from someone who thinks very highly of herself. I think you're better than me. I think you're better than every other girl out there. Your walk is textbook *perfect,* and it's why you're the highest paid, most famous one out of all of us—"

"But my family—"

"This has nothing to do with your family, Willow. You have the perfect combination of raw talent, good looks, and charisma that would have made you a world-famous supermodel with or without your family name."

"You don't know—"

"I'm not done yet," she scolds. "You are literally one of the kindest, most beautiful women in the world, and yet you let these fuckwads on the internet get into your head. Just because they're miserable and unsatisfied with their pathetic lives doesn't mean you need to be miserable too. They don't deserve that power over you. No one does. The only person who has the ability to define your self-worth is yourself. And I know you're smart enough to see that you're an amazing, worthy person. So stop letting the incels on the internet get into your head!"

"Wow," I breathe.

"Heena, if modeling doesn't work out, you could become a motivational speaker," her tailor says.

"Oh, shut up," Heena replies, trying to hide her smile. "I didn't say anything that isn't true. So, Willow, start acting like the smart girl I know you are, and stop believing everything you read on the internet."

"But doesn't the internet say that you have a mathematically perfect face?" I tease.

She smirks. "Just because it's not *always* right doesn't mean it isn't *sometimes* right."

"Mhm."

"I'm serious, Willow. Don't believe that shit, or I'll have to hunt down the people posting it, and that would really inconvenience me, especially during fashion season. What would Donatella say if I showed up to her show with a broken nail?"

"Alright, fine. I'll try to stay clear of the stuff people say about me on the internet."

"And to not believe it when you happen to see it," she adds.

"And to not believe it when I see it," I echo.

* * *

I truly feel bad for anyone who has never walked the runway. It's an electrifying feeling, second to none. I'm backstage now, watching the show with Heena at my side, as she's already walked. Even stoic Heena can't wipe the grin off her face resulting from the thrill of modeling some of the most innovative, detailed, and expensive fashions in the world.

"Close your eyes, breathe deeply, and repeat after me," Heena commands, color high on her cheeks from her walk.

"Really? Again?"

"Yes, really, again," she mocks. "Because I'll be damned if I let my best friend close the Marc Jacobs show feeling anything less than the goddess she is."

"Fine." I sigh, closing my eyes and taking a deep breath.

"There you go. Okay, 'I am the most beautiful woman in the world.'"

I crack an eye open and give her a skeptical look.

"They're positive affirmations. Humor me."

"Fine." I close my eyes again. "I am the most beautiful woman in the world."

"Everyone is drawn to me for both my outer and inner beauty. I look amazing and confident because I feel amazing and confident. I am unique, I am radiant, I am a star. I am kind, I am happy, I am strong. I am a goddess on earth, a queen among peasants. And I'm going to close this show like nobody else could, rendering everyone, including Marc Jacobs himself, speechless, possibly even permanently mute."

I echo every sentence as she says it and slowly open my eyes.

"You're up in twenty seconds, Will," Heena whispers, patting me on the arm to avoid messing up our looks. "Break a leg."

I turn onto the stage and hear the familiar clicks of camera shutters. In the words of one of my old modeling coaches, I strut like I'm walking through hell in gasoline-soaked pajamas. I hate to admit it, but Heena's weird affirmations have me feeling more confident than ever before. I stare down the camera at the end of the runway as I strut, hardly even registering the blossoming applause.

I pose at the end, popping out one hip and fanning my cape behind me before turning around dramatically enough to flip my hair as I strut toward Heena. She begins leading all the models back through the circuit in order, with me last. The audience's applause is too loud to ignore now, and it's a feat to keep my face blank as they give a standing ovation even before Marc's appearance. They remain standing and applauding as Marc comes out, and I watch him gleefully walk through the crowd from where I'm perched.

"Wow," Heena says once we're backstage, finding me easily among the other models due to the gold. "You need to do affirmations before every show. That was *incredible*. I've literally never seen a standing ovation start before the designer comes out."

I nod, smiling ear to ear. "It was a great collection."

"Yes, but they were applauding for *you*. Not the collection."

"Well, maybe they just liked my outfit the best."

"Not your outfit, *you*," she says, finally pulling me into a hug, throwing caution to the wind despite our extremely valuable and delicate outfits. She beams as she pulls back. "Willow, what a way to shut up the people who say you can't walk."

Chapter 12

Willow

After walking seven shows in New York (and playing a central role in each), my 'unwind' is the redeye flight to London. Which isn't proving to be much of an unwind at all. Despite my past week of grueling fourteen-hour days, a full-length bed, three melatonin gummies, chamomile tea, and an eye mask, I still can't sleep. The seven other models I'm sharing this chartered flight are sleeping soundly. I sigh and turn on my phone, a beacon on the otherwise dark flight, and cringe, hoping it won't disturb anyone else.

I see a message from Riley, sent an hour ago. It's a screenshot of my own Instagram post of me on the runway in my Marc Jacobs look.

Riley: You look really cool here.

Me: thanks. i like that you sent me a screenshot of my own post, that's funny.

Me: and thanks for the like :)

To my surprise, he replies almost immediately.

Riley: Of course. I know you needed that 4,869,012th like

Me: i really did, that's the new benchmark my manager wants me to meet these days

Riley: Luckily my manager has not mentioned any social media benchmarks

Me: let me look you up

Me: 4.1 million followers!

Me: look at you!

Riley: Like 3.9 million of that is from the past six months. It's still weird to have such an audience

Riley: Although, I guess that's probably not much of an audience to you lol

Me: no, that's still a very big crowd…feel perceived yet?

Riley: Very.

Riley: Want to be the 4,100,0001st person to perceive me?

Me: sorry i only follow my family and Heena… it avoids drama to only follow the same 5 people

Riley: I'm kidding, Willow, you don't have to follow me. I only follow you for your sick outfits, anyway

Me: taking it as inspiration?

Me: speaking of which, i sent your label's office something for you

Me: i didn't know how to find your address on the road. i figured they could get it to you

Riley: A bedazzled cowboy hat????

Me: no?? is that what you want though, because i could make that happen

Riley: …no

Riley: So what is it

Me: you have to wait and see! but just know i've been using fashion week as an opportunity to make good on my side of our mini-deal

Me: speaking of which, where is my country playlist??

Riley: Don't laugh but I actually made you 3 different ones because I wasn't sure which vibe you wanted

Riley: All of the songs I really like, but one playlist is more pop-y which I thought would be good to ease you into the genre. One is my current favorites in the Americana/outlaw genre which is more my style. And the last one is my all-time favorites, but I didn't know if you'd be interested...they're all a bit older.

Me: i'll happily take all three, but if i have to choose one, i want your all-time favorites

Riley: Here are the links to all three :)

Me: wow and personal access to riley coleman's secret spotify account! i am starstruck!

Riley: Stop making fun of me, a person who ACTUALLY gets starstruck by people

Riley: Including you

Me: still?

Riley: To be fair, I don't think I'll ever NOT be starstruck by you, Willow Jordan

Me: maybe exposure therapy will help. i'm prescribing you to keep texting me, for science... i can't sleep

Riley: Me neither, but you don't need me. You must have a million other people texting you

Me: not really. the only people who text me regularly are my family and Heena. again, i keep a pretty small circle

Riley: And yet you hardly know me and are begging me to text you

Me: okay, i never BEGGED. i'm just bored half to death and everyone else is asleep

Me: and aside from our deal which realistically necessitates some texting, you have trustworthy vibes and you're not the worst company in the world...so far, at least

Riley: Fair enough. Well, now that I know you sent me something, I feel like only sending you a few playlists is slacking on my end of the deal. But you have my word that the next time we're in the same city, I'm taking you to a dive bar. That's my first order of business in making-Willow-normal...speaking of which, where are you now? I'm in Vancouver, CA.

Riley: And thank you, I'll use that as the epithet on my gravestone "Here lies Riley Coleman: trustworthy vibes"

Me: you have to cite me as the source though

Me: it would be even funnier if you did something to betray me and then i murdered you

Me: would be ironic

Me: i'm on a flight to London.

Riley: Are you threatening me?

Riley: London sounds fun, I've never been

Me: london is boring and gray and the food is terrible lol. i'd rather be in canada!

Me: and i'm not threatening you...yet

Riley: See why I'm not comfortable around you yet?

Me: haha

Riley: Can I ask you something slightly more serious though, as part of your duty to help me be famous

Me: sure

Riley: I feel like I never actually have time to talk to my fans...how do you deal with not being able to really connect with them?

Me: ah, yeah that's hard

Me: you just come to accept it

Me: try when you can, always make an effort, but at the end of the day, you just don't have the time to have a meaningful conversation with every fan you run into

Me: doesn't mean you can't try though :)

Riley: It just sucks. It's weird to mean so much to people and not be able to give them the attention to make them mean something to you, too

Me: yeah, unfortunately in the world of fame you're vastly outnumbered by fans

Me: just have to accept it for what it is and try to take time to talk to them when you can

Me: that part never stops bothering you

Me: all the old famous people i know still complain about that...i think it's part of human nature to want to connect with and care for the people who care for you

Riley: You're very wise

Me: nah, i've just been in the public eye a long time

Me: by the way, how old are you?

Riley: 23. Don't worry, I'm legal babe ;)

Riley: Your online stalking of me didn't tell you that?

Me: probably but i forgot

Me: i'm 22, you're older

Riley: 🙄

Me: what's your zodiac sign

Riley: I'm a cancer

Me: you would be. i'm a sagittarius

Riley: I don't know what that means but I'll ask my

sister. She's into all that, too. I hope being a cancer is a good thing, when you say it like that...

Me: it is!

Me: you have a sister?

Riley: Yeah, she's older, 26

Me: any other siblings?

Riley: Nope, just Olivia. And I know you have Aspen.

Me: i have another one too, Maple.

Riley: Remind me to yell at Nash for not telling me about that when he gave me the rundown on you

Me: i am slightly unsettled by the amount of knowledge this guy has on me

Riley: He claims his sister is a big fan. But don't get creeped, the amount he knows about EVERYTHING is unsettling. He's like Wikipedia on legs. Never talk to Nash if you want to feel smart.

Me: noted!

Riley: So what's Maple like? Is she as close as you and Aspen?

Riley: Also I'm just making assumptions, you seemed close at the Grammys but I could be wrong

Me: no you're right, Aspen and Heena are my best friends

Me: Maple is 16 and deep into the teenage rebellion phase

Me: but that girl is a force to be reckoned with, way more world-changing potential than Aspen or me

Riley: Hey, I think you're both doing a good job. You're putting yourselves out there. Just because you haven't changed the world in a big way doesn't mean you haven't changed it in a million small ways through the impact you have on your fans

Me: who's wise now?
Riley: I wouldn't call it wisdom, just my 2 cents
Me: what is wisdom if not people's 2 cents?
Riley: Okay, professor
Me: haha
Me: what's Olivia like?
Riley: She's so much cooler than me. And smarter. And prettier lol. She's in veterinary school, definitely the pride of our family
Riley: My dad is a mechanic and my mom was a stay-at-home mom, so neither of them got any schooling after high school. They saved all they had to send us to college. Liv actually made use of it unlike me
Me: you're making use of it plenty. you're very successful
Riley: Not in any way that compares to Liv...she was summa cum laude, top of her class in everything
Me: and you're world famous super star riley coleman!
Riley: I like that you don't capitalize my name, makes me feel super famous indeed <3
Me: Riley Coleman **
Riley: Lol
Riley: But yes, we are all very proud of Liv
Me: and i'm sure she's very proud of you too
Me: you should invite her to a show sometime
Riley: I don't want to distract her from school, or make her feel like she has to come. Maybe one of my ones in Florida, where she goes to school
Me: i think she'd like that, you should
Me: anyway, i should probably make another attempt at falling asleep now. first day in london starts

in a few hours and i don't want any designers yelling at me for my eyebags

Riley: Oh I didn't realize it was such a tight turnaround. Sorry for keeping you up. Goodnight Willow!

Me: goodnight!

Chapter 13

Willow

I ended up getting two hours of sleep on the plane before being ushered around from the fitting session to the glam station, to rehearsal, to photographs, and then to the runway. It was nothing short of bone-achingly exhausting.

I walk into my hotel room, shut the door behind me, and take a deep breath as I inspect the space. I haven't even been here yet—an assistant ran my bags here while I was led straight into the depths of fashion week. It's nice, though. A king-sized bed, a huge bathroom, a kitchenette (when do they envision me having time to cook?), and a cozy living area. I grab the chocolates left on my pillow and bite into one as I push the curtains open a crack to look out the window.

I'm met by a fantastic view of London, and I can hear the Londoners' lively shouts and car horns from my room. I smile faintly, knowing I'm in for a good night's sleep with the street noise. It almost sounds like home.

I debate going to the gym before bed, as I haven't had time to work out in three days, pushing me way off schedule. But I quickly shut the idea down, as I can already feel myself curling up in the hotel's luscious silk sheets and fluffy pillows. It's been a struggle to keep my eyes open all day, and I've gotten more than a few disapproving looks from makeup artists and designers who saw me before their concealer expertly covered my eye-bags. As I head into the bathroom to scrub the elaborate makeup off my face, my phone rings.

Just what I needed, I sigh. I walk back into the bedroom and see Aspen's face light up my phone. She's one of the few people I would pick up for right now.

"Hey, Aspen, what's up?" I say, trying to hide the drowsiness from my voice.

"Hey, Willow. Not much. Are you busy?" she asks in a weird, indecipherable tone.

"Not at all," I say. If I sit on this bed for a second longer, I will fall asleep. So, I stand and start pacing just to keep sleep's pull at bay.

I hear Aspen inhale a shaky breath.

"Aspen, what's up?" I reiterate my question with a little more urgency this time.

"You swear you're not busy?" she asks again. Now I can discern her tone better...my sister is on the verge of tears.

"No, I'm not busy. I promise. What's wrong?"

"I just—" she laughs, a sad, pained sound. "I'm losing it a little right now."

"Why?" I prod gently.

"*Fairview Ridge* is wrapping in a few months, and I have no idea what I'm going to do without it. I know most leading actresses on those teen shows leave the second they find fame and go their own route. But I never did that."

"Nothing's wrong with seeing a project through, Aspen," I say.

"No, it's not because I wanted to see the project through. I know that's what I tell everyone, but that's not it *at all*. Unlike those other actresses, I'm not talented. I have the Jordan name and that's it. I'm so scared to leave this show, Willow...I'm so scared," she whispers, suddenly overcome by the tears she had kept at bay for the first minute of the call.

"Aspen, you're not untalented, not in the slightest. I mean, look at me. All I do is 'prance around in my underwear,' as Maple says. You actually have a gift. You are a fantastic actress. Why do you think *Fairview Ridge* even wanted you in the first place? Why do you think they kept you as their lead role all this time?"

"Because I'm Aspen Jordan!"

"Exactly, because you're *Aspen Jordan*. One of the greatest young actresses alive."

"Willow, please, stop," she cries before pulling her phone away from her ear, muffling the sound of her tears.

"Aspen."

No response.

"Aspen!"

"What," she answers with more despair than I've ever heard from her. The sound makes my chest physically hurt.

"Where are you?" I ask gently.

"I'm in LA at my house."

"Would you be okay if I sent Maple or Mom or Dad over to see you? They could bring you that mac and cheese from that place you like. Or a milkshake or something."

She sniffles. "I don't want anyone here right now."

"It might help to have some company—"

"Willow, don't. Please don't send anyone over. I just want to be alone. I look fucking pathetic, and I really couldn't handle anyone seeing me right now."

I pause, moving to run a hand through my hair before feeling it stiff as stone with what must have been an entire bottle of hairspray.

"Can I at least order some food to be delivered to you?" I ask her.

"No, Willow, don't. I'm sorry." She moves the phone away from her face again, but I still hear her muffled sobs. "I'm sorry for bothering you. Don't worry about me, really. I'll be okay. Please, don't send anyone over. I want to be alone. I might just go to sleep," she says, even though it's only early afternoon in LA.

"Aspen, are you sure you don't want to talk it through more? Really, I'm free for the night. I can talk longer."

"No, Willow, I'm okay. You've been a great help. Sorry for bothering you," she repeats, her voice wavering.

"Okay. But Aspen, please call me if you need anything. I'm always here," I implore, not wanting to push her but also knowing she's bullshitting.

"Goodnight," she says, hanging up the phone.

I walk back into my bathroom, debating what to do as I wash my face. If I send someone to check on her, I know it will break her trust in me. But on the other hand, she is *clearly* having a breakdown, and it feels so wrong to leave her alone.

I settle on ordering her food before washing the hairspray out. As I do, I can't shake the feeling that I really should call someone to check in on Aspen. I mean, I've *never* heard Aspen cry uncontrollably like that. For God's sake, she's an actress. She's pretty much mastered the fake smile. I could tell she was trying to cover her emotions up, only for them to crash down on her, too strong to be hidden.

Although I hate myself for betraying her trust, I know I would hate myself infinitely more if something happened to her.

"Is everything okay, honey?" my mom's voice asks through my phone. "Shouldn't you be sleeping? It's late in London."

"I'm fine, Mom. But I don't think Aspen is. She called me

really upset, and I think someone needs to check on her. I know you're in LA. Would you mind?"

"Would I mind?" my mom asks disbelievingly. "Willow, I'm out the door as we speak."

Her words lift the weight off my chest. "Great, thank you so much, Mom."

"Baby, don't ever thank me for taking care of my kids. That's my job. I'll take care of it, okay? Get some sleep, and I can call or text you in the morning with an update."

"Okay. I love you."

"I love you too, Willow. Go get some sleep," she says, hanging up the phone.

I lie back against the pillows and am out cold in seconds.

Chapter 14

Willow

The next morning, my mom called me and told me Aspen was fine, just upset. They ate the food I ordered and fell asleep to *Notting Hill* together. Despite the good news, I continued to worry about Aspen all week during the cracks in the long days. Between the exhaustion and the worry, London Fashion Week was an absolute blur. Then, I was whisked away to Milan for their fashion week, which is notoriously even crazier than London's.

It's my first full day here, and I'm currently in a dressing room, sitting with gold under-eye masks (none of the other models were given these...message received). A team of three has just begun working on my hair when my phone buzzes. Facetime from Riley. Shit, I haven't contacted him at all since leaving New York.

"Hello?" I swipe open the call.

"Hell—what's on your face?"

"Eye masks. Hey, sorry for not messaging for a while..." I say, clicking through my phone and seeing three missed texts from him over the course of the past week. *Fuck, I'm an ass.*

"And I'm so sorry I missed your texts. Really, I'm just seeing them now. I've been *so* busy. London was crazy, and the—"

"Willow, it's okay." He smiles like he's amused at my anxiety. "Seriously, it's fine. I know you've been busy. Don't stress." His accent is like honey coating my worn-down nerves.

"Well, you've been busy too, and you still made time for me."

He grins. "Now you make me sound whipped."

One of the hairstylists behind me snorts.

"Did he just laugh at me?" Riley asks.

"I did," the hairstylist responds plainly.

"I'll get some earbuds. Hold on a second," I say, bending to reach into my bag, earning grunts of protests from my hair team. "Sorry, guys," I say, popping in the earbuds. "And sorry they're making fun of you," I say to Riley as his audio flows into my ears.

"No problem." He laughs. "Nothing I haven't heard already from my friends."

"They say you're desperate, too?"

"Well, nobody said *desperate*, damn." He laughs as my face reddens. "But, yeah, I may be desperate. But they're not the ones Facetiming Willow Jordan, now are they?"

I wince.

"Sorry," he says. " I didn't mean it like that. I'd talk to you no matter what your name was or what you looked like. In fact, I'm not even into blondes."

I raise my eyebrows.

"I do—I mean, I am into blondes. I don't know why I said that. I've only ever gone out with blondes. You're definitely my type. That's not what I meant. But, that's not what I meant either...ah shit, I'm fucking this up, aren't I?" he asks, running a nervous hand through his hair.

"You're doing fine, Riley." I laugh. "Better than most, to be honest. Most people would be too afraid to call me in the first place. Big bad Willow and all."

"You're neither big nor bad. I'm really not that afraid of you."

"But you're still a little afraid?"

"A little." He pauses. "How are you doing, Willow? You seem..."

"Seem what?"

"Withdrawn," he finally says.

"I'm just tired." I wave off his concern. "So where are you, anyway?"

"If you say so. But just know you can talk to me about anything. Who am I going to tell? And I'm always on this damn bus. I have nothing better to do than listen to you rant."

I laugh. As sweet as Riley is, there's no chance in hell I'm telling him about my personal issues. "Are you on the bus now?"

"Yeah. We're driving through Canada, from Saskatchewan to Winnipeg."

"What time is it there?" I ask, just realizing that since it's late morning here, it must be really early there.

"Four in the morning." He grins lazily. "But see, with my trusty built-in reading light here, you'd never know."

"So why are you awake?"

"I don't know. Couldn't sleep."

"Aren't you going to wake up your band with your talking?"

"Nah, they all sleep like the dead. Except Nash, but he has his earplugs in."

"He sleeps with earplugs in?"

"Well, Ethan snores. It's a whole thing."

I laugh, "Sounds like it. But you don't snore?"

"Not that I know of. Do you?"

"Riley! You can't ask a woman that. It's rude."

"Sorry."

"But I do," I chuckle.

"You do?" he asks, laughing way harder than merited. "Willow Jordan snores!"

"Oh shut up, that's not that bad. And you better keep it down, or else you'll wake everyone up, including Nash and his earplugs."

That only seems to make Riley laugh harder, which makes me laugh too.

"Willow, if you don't stop shaking, I'll hang up that phone myself," the hairstylist snaps at me.

"Someone's grumpy," Riley says between laughs as I try to control myself.

"Riley! Stop saying stuff like that and making me laugh, or I'll be forced to hang up."

"Fine, fine, I'll behave," he says with a wink that I know would make thousands of other girls swoon.

"Good. So, how is Canada?"

"It's good. I've never been here before, so it's interesting to see how similar it is to the US. Except for the accents. Everyone asks where I'm from here. I guess a Southern accent is a novelty."

"To be fair, it's a novelty in New York and LA, too."

"So you think I'm a novelty, then," he asks, raising a brow and the corner of his lip.

"I never said *I* did." I shrug but can't hold back my smile. "So, you've never been to Canada or London, right? Have you been to Italy? I'm in Milan right now. I don't know if you knew that."

"I saw your post last night in your hotel room with the location tagged. Nice robe, by the way." Again, he flashes that roguish grin.

Despite myself, I feel my cheeks reddening. "It is a nice

robe. Slightly thicker than this one," I say, looking down at the black silk dressing robe I'm currently wearing. "No mention of the cleavage or bare legs, though? I guess next time, I'll have to do better."

"Sure. Though, you could just send that photo to me personally." He smirks.

"Please tell me you're not about to scold me for 'leaving too little to the imagination' and posting it online for everyone to see."

"What? No, never. You're doing everyone a favor by showing off. I mean, fuck, if I looked like you, I'd walk around naked all the time."

I snort. "I'd love to see that."

"You would?"

"Not literally," I say, putting a quick stop to that train of thought. "Just friends, remember."

"Right. But to circle back to your Italy question, no, I've never been. This is actually my first time out of the country."

"You're joking."

"Nope. I know it must seem lame to you, but my family never had much money when I was growing up, so our vacations typically consisted of a road trip to Myrtle Beach or—"

"Riley, I don't think that's lame at all. I think it's great—you have so much left to see. Although, I guess I also have a lot to see, in a way. Sure, I've been all over, but I've never really *been*. As a kid, I was carted around by my parents to wherever they wanted to go. As an adult, I'm pretty much only traveling for work. I never really go anywhere for fun."

"Well, I hope you get to change that soon."

I grimace. "After fashion month."

"Yes, after that," he confirms as the hair team leaves and the makeup team begins prepping my face, removing the eye masks. "Who is this now?"

"The makeup team," I answer while tightening my robe.

"That sounds fun."

"Usually it is, but I think I'm missing the top two layers of skin off my face from how many times I've had my makeup done and removed in the past three weeks. But on a more positive note, I've been listening to your playlists this past week."

"You have? Do you like them?"

"I love them. You're right, I think I just had never heard any *good* country music. You might have just turned me into a fan."

"Any favorites standing out so far?"

"I really love the breakup stuff, to be honest. Something about hearing people vent their negative feelings makes me feel better about my life." I laugh. "Also, anything by George Strait or Keith Whitley. I may or may not have taken a deep dive into them..."

"You like George Strait and Keith Whitley?" Riley asks, eyes crinkling from smiling so big. "That's awesome. They're two of my all-time favorites, too. Wait, so what kind of music do you normally listen to? I realized that I'm a dick, and I never even asked."

"Did you just assume I listened to pop music?"

"No."

"Be honest," I pry.

"Yes."

"Well, I do like pop music, to be fair. But my favorite will always be 90s and early 2000s hip-hop."

"Old hip-hop? You're full of surprises," he says, shaking his head with a smile. "I hope you know I'm gonna need a playlist of that from you. It's only fair."

"But I gave you the shirt!"

"Yes, and I love it. Thank you. But I still need a playlist."

"You got it?"

"I texted you a thank you when I got it," he adds.

"I must have missed that, sorry."

"No apologies. You were busy. But speaking of which, go look at my Instagram."

"Okay...holy shit! It fits perfectly! I had to guess on your proportions but it looks like Marc did his job. It looks fantastic."

"You *guessed* that? I was assuming it was either a coincidence or you got my measurements from my manager."

"Nope, I guessed. Fashion is my job, in case you forgot."

"No, I know that, but...holy shit, you're good. Have you ever thought of designing anything yourself?"

"Um, other than that shirt?"

"*You designed that?*"

"Yeah," I say nervously. "It's not that big of a deal. It's just a shirt."

"Willow, it's embroidered with the most beautiful flowers and greenery I've ever seen, snaking up the sleeves and across the chest in a way that makes me look like Vin fucking Deisel when I wear it, complete with matching embroidery and fringe on the back shoulders. It's fucking incredible."

"You like the fringe? I wasn't sure, but I thought it would be fun," I start.

"Even Ethan couldn't give me shit for that, it looked so cool. Who knew fringe could be so badass? Sorry, I'm just in awe that you *designed* that."

"It wasn't that hard. I drew it up in like five minutes."

"Willow, stop flexing, Jesus. Some of us are mere mortals without an ounce of your raw artistry."

"Okay, and some of us are tone deaf and can't string two coherent notes together, unlike you, especially that run in 'Three a.m. in Asheville.'"

"So you listened to my album? And *that's* your favorite song? Not 'Moonlight and You'?"

"Yes and yes. I like the breakup stuff, I told you. Sad and angry always hits harder than happy, for me...hence the nineties hip-hop. By the way, who eviscerated your heart like that?"

"Ahhh, long story. She's ancient history, though."

"Doesn't sound like it since you wrote a whole album about her..."

"Hey, only *most* of it is about her, not all of it, if we're really getting into the nitty gritty. I'll tell you the whole story sometime, but yeah, we're done for good."

"Noted. I really like this photo of you, by the way. The one you posted in the shirt I sent you."

The photo is an action shot of him leaning the mic stand away from him, holding the mic in his opposite hand. The fringe on the back of the shirt is visible since the shot was taken in motion from the side, and his face is cast in the most beautiful partial silhouette thanks to the stage lights. A sea of hands is reaching for the stage, and Riley's smile is so genuine, you can see his eyes crinkling.

"Thanks. I think the shirt makes it, really."

"Mhm, nothing to do with the tall, ripped, blond country boy having the time of his life onstage."

"Tall and ripped? I'll take that. Happily."

"Willow?" one of the makeup artists starts from behind me, and I turn my head to look at him. "I'm going to need you to hold still for this last part. We have to do the lips and eyeliner."

"Sure, one second," I say before looking at Riley again. "I hate to do this, but I have to go. They have to do the detail work on my makeup, and then I have a show."

"No worries at all, do your thing. But remember to make me that hip-hop playlist whenever you have time."

"I'll send it over the second I get some free time," I promise.

"Bye, then. Good luck at your show."

"Thank you. Good luck at yours today or tomorrow or whenever you have one."

"Thanks." He smiles as I hang up.

"Thank you, sorry about that," the makeup artist says, gently angling my head so he can do my eyeliner.

Chapter 15

Riley

Early afternoon, we finally reach Winnipeg and have the day free to explore the city. But before we wander around downtown, we beg our driver to drop us off at a gym. After two days of being cramped on the bus, we're all desperate to get some energy out.

"Starting with cardio?" Waylon asks me after we pay for our day passes.

"Yep," I respond.

"I might start with weights and end on cardio. I need to push some heavy shit," Ethan says.

Nash nods. "Same."

"Want to run around the city?" I ask Waylon.

"Perfect," he says.

We throw on our layers and place our gym bags into lockers before setting out.

"So, how are you holding up?" Waylon asks me as we exit the gym and begin jogging toward the waterfront paths.

It's cold as shit here, I think, pulling down my beanie to fully cover my ears.

"You mean, how am I doing, being away from home?" I ask.

"Yeah," he says. Even his brown skin is looking pale in this cold.

"Are you asking because of what happened when I went away to college?"

"No..."

"You liar, you totally are. In my defense, it was the first week, and I wasn't used to being away from my family. But I'm not eighteen anymore, and I spent *four years* away from home at App State. I'm fine, Waylon."

"To be fair, you called home every night of your *first month*, not week, there. And App State really isn't even that far from home. It's like a two-hour drive."

"Hey, come on, some kids did worse, like actually driving home every weekend. At least I wasn't one of *those*. And I only called that much during the transition period. After that, I found my rhythm."

Waylon makes a little hum that could either be affirmation or skepticism.

"Pick up the pace, Way, I'm freezing my ass off," I snap.

Waylon laughs and gains speed. Definitely skepticism.

"How are *you* doing?" I ask him. "That's the real question. You're not even done with college yet, you baby. Did you know your mom made me promise to keep you safe? At least my mom trusts me to be an adult."

Waylon scoffs. "My mom made me promise to keep you safe too. You know her, she worries too much. I'm doing fine, but then again, I'm not the one with my face on the side of a tour bus, signing boobs every night."

"Are you implying that I'm *complaining* about that?"

"No, but it's a big change for anybody, especially for a

country boy who'd never been West of the Mississippi before this tour."

"Hey, not all of us can afford to summer in Europe," I quip.

"You can now." He winks. "You could afford to take the whole Coleman family on our first European vacation."

"Keep wishing, bud." I roll my eyes, even though I've already started brainstorming ways to repay my parents for all they've done for me over the years—even though no amount of money could ever make a dent in the amount of love and support they've shown me. "You're getting paid. You can afford your own ticket."

"So, you're doing well with the fame, then? You seem to be handling it all pretty well."

"I'm making my way. It's just crazy to me that I can sell out shows across the country or in countries I've never even *been to* before," I say, gesturing around us at icy Winnipeg. "And it helps that I've made some friends in the business to help me adjust," I add casually.

The second that escapes my mouth, I regret it. After seeing Willow on that magazine at the beginning of the tour, I haven't mentioned her to any of my friends and made my mind up to keep it that way, even swearing Nash to secrecy about seeing her at the Grammys. If they knew about our friendship—or worse, how infatuated I am with her—they'd tease me incessantly about it.

"Who?" Waylon asks.

"Willow," I say, running a little faster, hoping to avoid the conversation by keeping us both out of breath.

Waylon huffs, not letting his lack of breath deter him from asking, "Willow *Jordan*? I didn't know you were still talking to her. I thought you just met her briefly at New Year's."

"Well, at some point, I guess we exchanged numbers."

"At some point? When else did you see her?"

"At the Grammys."

"You're seriously telling me that you're friends with Willow Jordan?"

"Yeah, why not?"

"Because she's...Willow Jordan. I didn't even think she'd talk to someone like you."

"Hey, what's that supposed to mean?" I scowl at him as we continue to practically sprint around the waterfront.

"Nothing—I didn't mean that in a Claire way. It's just that she's *Willow Jordan,* and you're from the backwoods of North Carolina."

"Again, why not? She isn't Claire."

"I know she's not." He looks sidelong at me, sympathy in his eyes. God, I hate that look. "No, it's just... I don't want you to get hurt again. I mean, if I were her, I'd be talking to NFL players, award-winning actors, famous rappers, billionaire business moguls, maybe even an F1 driver or two—"

"I think I get the point," I cut him off. "I guess I'm lucky you're not her."

He looks disgusted. "Ew, I wouldn't flirt with my *cousin.*"

"Well, I'm not *her* cousin. And anyway, she doesn't flirt with me. We're strictly friends. She's made that pretty clear."

"Ouch."

"Better a friend than nothing. And she's pretty great too. She's so sweet and genuine. Not anything like you'd expect her to be," I say, thanking God that we're coming up to the gym again, completing our loop.

"Just be careful, Riley. We don't want you heartbroken again, no matter how good that album you wrote about Claire was."

"Don't worry." I shudder, not just from the cold. "She's no Claire."

Strike a Pose

* * *

"So, did y'all know Riley is friends with Willow Jordan?" Waylon asks the group that night in a diner booth.

I try to catch his eye to glare at him, but he's conveniently focusing on his cheeseburger. Nash's eyes widen slightly.

"No way," Ethan says. "I thought you just met her once."

"I saw her again, and we've been texting on and off since. No big deal."

"Dude, that's a *huge* deal. Could you have her put in a good word with Heena for me?"

I raise an eyebrow at him.

"What? They're like best friends," he says. "A video of her is literally on Heena's story as we speak."

"Dude, you need to chill with the Heena shit," I finally crack, laughing at him. "She's tough, she wouldn't even *talk* to you."

"We'll see about that." Ethan smirks. "So will you? Put in a good word for me?"

"I won't do Heena that disservice." I grin. "Let me see the video of Willow."

"Why would I show you now, you dick?"

"Fine, I'll just look it up myself," I say, finding Heena on Instagram and hitting the follow button before watching her story.

Willow is dancing around what looks like a rehearsal space in one of the shortest dresses I've ever seen—definitely high fashion, judging how weird its mixture of tartan and black tulle is. She's moving her lithe body to the beat of some rap song while she skips down a "runway" outlined in tape on the floor, barefoot. She looks so radiant, laughing as she twirls at the end of the runway. Heena can be heard laughing behind the camera.

It's such a relief to see joy on her face, especially after our last call. I can't explain what was off specifically, but she definitely didn't seem like herself—which is saying something since her base state seems to be fame-tortured and hyper-vigilant.

"Hmm," is all I say.

"Hmm?" Waylon echoes, looking at me, eyes wide.

"She looks happy," I add.

"She looks like a fucking *dream*." He laughs. "Riley, you're in deep if you won't even admit that much."

"She's pretty," I say noncommittally.

Even Nash laughs at that.

"Guys, stop." I groan. "Can't we find something better to talk about?"

"Probably not, but I think we can at least try," Waylon concedes.

Ethan plants his chin on his hand. "But aside from the literal masterpiece Riley is 'friends' with, nothing else is going on."

Masterpiece...that could work in something, I think, jotting the thought down in my notes app under the table.

"We are on tour in Canada. I, for one, think that's pretty cool," Nash says. "I still haven't bought one of those Kinder eggs with the toys in it. I promised my siblings I'd bring them each one from Canada. I don't know why *that's* what they associate with Canada—"

"What are you doing?" Ethan asks with a wolf's smile as he sees me.

"Nothing," I say, clicking off my phone.

"Doesn't look like nothing to me. Are you writing a song?"

"No."

"You're lying."

"Fine, maybe I am. What does it matter?"

"Nothing, I'm just curious what it's about."

"It's not about anything. It's just something I'm working on."

"Not about anything? Or anyone?"

"Nope."

"Let's see it then," he says, holding out his hand expectantly.

I look to Waylon and Nash for help, but they seem just as interested as Ethan.

"Fine, but you're paying the bar tab tonight." I eye Ethan. I'd make him pay for dinner, but that's covered by my label. Nights out, however, are not.

"Deal." He shakes my outstretched hand. I unlock my phone and hand it over.

She puts Helen to shame,
    Makes a Monet look plain
    You'll forget about anything in a Louvre frame
    She stole my heart and its keys
    But I got away with the masterpiece

"Jesus, Riley, you're fucking *sick* for this girl," Waylon exclaims over my shoulder, reading the lyrics.

Ethan just laughs maniacally. Nash's eyes jump back up to the top, rereading the lyrics.

"It's not about Willow. I just told you that," I say.

"Whatever helps you sleep at night." Nash shrugs, earning a round of laughter from the other two.

"You too, Nash?" I ask.

"I'm sorry, man, but this is just...damning evidence."

"So you think I shouldn't record this?"

"They're pretty great lyrics. We just think you're delusional," Waylon says.

"Hey, I'll let you guys believe what you want to believe, and I'll know the truth," I say, knowing damn well that they see right through me.

"Alright, man, whatever you say," Ethan responds. "Can we put this to music and play it live one night? See how the people like it?"

"Yeah, nobody else will know who it's about," Nash echoes. "And the lyrics are really good. You can just *feel* the pining." He smirks.

"Fine, but also fuck you guys," I laugh. "Now, let's find the nearest bar and rack up a huge tab for Ethan."

POP CULTURE PULSE PODCAST

Jenna: My first object of business today is this video of Riley Coleman playing an unreleased song.
Producer: Playing it now.

A video of Riley sitting on the edge of the rehearsal stage, strumming his guitar and singing the first verse and chorus of "Masterpiece," before sheepishly smiling and cutting the video.

Caroline: Who's he talking about?
Jenna: I don't know. He's not publicly dating anyone so it could be about some old girlfriend or no one in particular.

Caroline scoffs.

Caroline: Jenna, "She stole my heart and its keys, but I got away with the masterpiece"? That is *definitely* about someone in particular.
Jenna: Well, who?
Caroline: I don't know. But I'd love to figure that out. Guys

—listeners—can you please do some snooping into Riley Coleman's love life and report back to us?

Jenna: That's a great idea! Give us anything, big or small. Elaborate theories or just photos/references. We're dying to know. I know you Pop Culture Pulsers won't let us down.

Caroline: Yeah, seriously. For my part, I'll try to find him on Raya to see if he's single.

Jenna: No fair, I want to find him on Raya, too.

Caroline: Then you better beat me to it. Moving on...have you seen the video of shirtless Charlie Carraway surfing?

Jenna: No. The hot Connecticut Senator?

Caroline: That's the one.

Jenna: Pull it up, I'm already drooling.

Chapter 16

Willow

"You listen to some dark shit, girl." Riley laughs on what seems to have become our weekly call.

I'm in Paris, squeezing in a workout before my first fitting this morning. I'm trying not to get too out of shape during fashion month, lest I give my trainer a stroke when I return to New York.

As much as I love fashion month, I'm excited for it to wrap up in a few days. There's nothing I need more than some rest, relaxation, and privacy after this whirlwind of a month—fashion week, yes, but also worrying about Aspen.

Aspen and I have been playing phone tag all week, and although we're both incredibly busy this time of year, I can't help but worry that my breach of trust has caused an unspoken divide between us.

I shake my head as I jog my warm-up on the treadmill, returning to my conversation with Riley. "Hey, I warned you. Those rappers say everything I think but just can't say myself."

"What do you mean 'can't say'?"

"You've seen what the press says about me just for existing.

Can you imagine what they'd do if I publicly complained about them?"

"I think you should try it. It seemed to work out pretty well for Eminem." I can hear Riley's grin through the phone.

"Well, I'm no Eminem. He has thicker skin than me, I think."

"I don't know about that. You seem pretty tough."

"I liked your music, too. I think you've converted me into a country fan. Especially Willie Nelson and Keith Whitley."

"No way. I think this is my crowning achievement in life, introducing someone to the kings of country."

"Coming from a prince himself." I smile.

"Hey, you said it, not me." He laughs. "Can you post that online or something? Try to make it catch on. I like that title."

"Oh, shut up." I laugh. "I will absolutely *not* post about you, Riley Coleman. And I certainly will not post that you're a prince."

"Fuck, now I have to take down my 'Willow Jordan is my princess, all hail Willow Jordan' post."

I laugh again.

"You have such a cute laugh," he says through a smile. "In a platonic way, of course," he adds.

"Thank you, platonically."

"Platonically, what are you doing after fashion week? It ends this week, right?"

"I'm going to Kiawah Island, South Carolina, for a few days to celebrate my mom's birthday, and then after that, I'm not sure. Probably going back to New York for a few days. I have a Sports Illustrated shoot in Turks and Caicos at the end of March. Oh, and a Vogue makeup routine video to shoot at some point in the next few weeks."

"Casually dropping the fact that you're a Sports Illustrated model," Riley notes.

"I thought you could use the reminder." I smile even though he can't see me. "Why, what are you doing? Where's your tour headed in March?"

"I'm actually getting a two-week-long break starting in a week. And Kiawah is only a short flight from Asheville...I think you should come visit me at home."

"Riley, I don't think that's a good idea—" I start. Fuck, I never should have let an ounce of flirtation out. I can't date Riley. The press would tear me to shreds—and him to shreds by proxy. They'd rip him apart right when he's starting to gain his footing with them.

"Just as friends," he cuts me off. "It would be strictly a 'turning Willow into a normal person' visit. Let me fulfill my end of the deal. You've done way more for me than I've done for you."

"I don't know..." I trail off.

"Please? No funny business, I swear it. You can sleep in my sister's room. She's at school. Come on, I could take you to all my favorite haunts. Nobody keeps up with celebrities in my town—I mean, I didn't recognize you, right? Nobody would know who you are or bother you, I promise."

"I just don't want you to get the wrong idea."

"Willow, I swear I won't. Purely professional. It could be a super quick trip for you—only a couple of days. Let me show you a good, normal time. You sound like you need it."

"Is it that obvious?" I laugh dryly.

"A little," he admits. "But working for a month straight would run anyone down."

"You've also been working the past month straight," I point out. "But fine. Before I have the chance to overthink it and say no, I'm saying yes now."

"You're saying yes?"

"Yes."

"Great! Do you want me to pick you up from Kiawah, or would you rather fly?"

"I'll fly. I don't want you to have to drive all the way down to get me."

"Really, I wouldn't mind. I love driving my truck. I haven't been able to drive for myself in a while, it would be nice. We could play some Eminem," he offers.

"As tempting as that sounds, let me talk to my family about the plan with the plane and get back to you. I don't want you to drive all the way if I could easily just use the plane."

"You have a plane?"

"Um...no," I say innocently.

"You're ridiculous. Okay, just let me know, Willow Jordan."

"Okay, Riley Coleman, superstar. I'll let you know. I should probably get off the phone now. I'm about to start lifting, and I don't want you to hear my heavy breathing."

"I'd love to hear that," he offers.

"What happened to strictly professional?" I laugh, turning off the treadmill.

"I'd love to hear your heavy breathing in a *strictly professional* sense."

"Maybe next time. Bye, Riley," I purr as I hang up the phone, chuckling to myself. I can just see him rolling his eyes at me.

Chapter 17

Willow

The next day, Heena and I surprisingly both finish our last shows in the late afternoon, meaning we have the entire evening to spend as we please in Paris before we go back home in a few days. We find ourselves sitting side-by-side at an outdoor cafe, looking out onto the bustling street in front of us.

Since even supermodels are rarely allowed to keep the clothes we model, we've changed into our own outfits. I'm wearing a black pleather trench coat with knee-high black boots, a black minidress, and a white scarf and beret...because when in Paris, right? Heena is wearing wide-leg grey trousers with a matching vest and blazer. Neither of us are bothering to disguise ourselves tonight—because we have a collective six bodyguards here with us, including Tito and my recently promoted permanent guard, Justin—which is garnering a lot of attention from passersby.

"Hello," our wide-eyed waiter says as he approaches our table, obscuring our view of the street. "What can I get for you two ladies?"

"*Nous prendrons deux martinis expresso, s'il vous plaît,*" I say, dusting off my French skills, thanks to my childhood French au pair. The waiter's eyes somehow widen *more*.

"And some truffle fries," Heena adds. I see she's taking advantage of being away from her nutritionist.

"Coming right up," the man says through his thick accent.

"Merci." Heena winks. The man nods quickly before walking away, fisting his trembling hands.

"That's pathetic," Heena says to me with a laugh, as the man passes over the threshold and disappears into the cafe.

"Heena, don't be mean," I scold. "He was probably so nervous already. You didn't have to wink."

"It's not my problem he's nervous. Why should he be? We're just people," she scoffs. "It's not my fault he can't handle a wink."

"Do me a favor and look in the mirror. Then tell me that again."

"Oh, I can't do that. Last time I looked in the mirror, I was stuck, entranced there for a full day."

"It must be hard, being so jaw-droppingly beautiful."

Heena nudges me with her shoulder. "You would know."

"So, you're coming with us to Kiawah next week, right?" I ask, changing the subject.

"I wish I could." She groans. "But I already committed to a Versace fragrance shoot in New York next week."

"That can't last more than a day. You could come with us for a day or two."

"Yeah, but that's a lot of traveling. To be honest, I'm already burnt out from fashion week. I think I'll just hold down the Jordan fort in the city, if that's okay with everyone."

"You don't even have to ask. I'm just sad you can't come with us."

"You don't need me. You'll have your sisters to keep you company," she says as the waiter returns, delivering our martinis and fries while impressively avoiding eye contact with us.

"Excuse me?" Heena asks the retreating waiter with a predator's grin.

"Yes?" the man asks.

"Could we get some ketchup?" she asks, blatantly looking the waiter up and down.

"Sure," he says shakily before practically *running* away.

"Heena," I scold.

"Let me have my fun," she waves me off.

"It's not very funny to him. The poor guy looked like he was about to piss his pants."

Heena laughs. "Now *that* would have been a sight."

"And anyway, French people hate ketchup. You know that."

She shrugs. "But *I* don't hate ketchup."

"You're horrible." I laugh, taking a sip of my martini. "Holy shit, these are better than the ones we had in Milan." I take another sip.

"Really?" Heena takes a sip of hers. "God, you're right, these are incredible. I'll have to tell Vittoria. She'll have a stroke."

"You just live to piss people off."

"That's why you love me," she croons in a tone that would bring a man to his knees. "So, you're coming back to New York after Kiawah, right? I have prime tickets to the opera."

I pause, knowing she won't like that I'm going to see Riley.

"Come on, they're doing *Carmen*, your favorite," she prods.

"Actually, I'm going to visit Riley in North Carolina after Kiawah."

"What? Riley? The country singer?"

Our waiter delivers the ketchup quietly, without being tormented by Heena, for once. She has bigger bait now.

"Yeah. He told me that no one would recognize me, and

he'd take me to do a bunch of normal people stuff. You know, like dive bars."

"You want to go to *dive bars*?"

"Why not? I think it'll be fun. It'll be nice to have a break from the public eye for a few days."

"Okay." Heena shrugs. "I can understand that. But just...be careful. You know, with whatever this situation is."

"It's strictly platonic," I clarify.

"I know. Just stay on guard. I don't want you to get hurt."

"Riley's a nice guy."

"I believe you, but I also have zero trust in men." She eats a fry before adding, "I want to meet this guy. Not that he needs my approval, but I still want to vet him."

"Oh God, I don't think I'd ever subject him to an interview with *you*."

"What does that mean? I'd play nice," she says, even though she's laughing deviously.

"I don't think you *can* play nice, Heena."

"Probably true. But if he can handle the heat, he'd probably get my approval."

We each sip on our martinis, falling into a comfortable silence while the sun slowly sets over Paris.

"To answer what you said before...about no man of mine needing your approval," I start.

"Mhm," Heena hums, looking at me.

"Of course they would need your approval. You're my best friend. If the man I'm dating isn't approved by you, they're gone."

"Hey, if they impress you, they'd impress me." Heena shrugs. "I'm not as tough to win over as people think. If only they'd stop being paralyzed by fear."

"Most people are different from you, Heena. They don't have your innate self-confidence."

"Well, I don't see why not. Everyone should be their own champion. If you don't take pride in yourself, who will?"

"Sometimes it's easier said than done."

"Willow, you take plenty of pride in yourself. You've never met someone you were afraid to walk up to and strike up a conversation with."

"I guess that's true," I muse. "I think it manifests in different ways with me."

"Like feeling insecure because the press shits on you every chance they get? That would affect most people, Will. Not that anything they say about you is true."

"Like that I'm a spoiled, talentless, nepo baby?"

"Okay, except the nepo baby thing," she teases. "But I've told you, you have so much talent and charisma that you would've made it big whether you were a nepo baby or not. It's just their favorite insult to hurl because this isn't that alternate universe where you weren't born famous, so there's no way to *prove* that you could have made it on your own. But look at some of the other nepo babies in the industry—none of them are consistently opening and closing for the biggest designers in the industry. Designers want *you*. Not your name."

"That was inspiring," I say, rendered a little speechless.

"You know I'm always here to give you a pep talk. Let my excessive arrogance actually do something for someone else for once. And besides, speaking of my excessive arrogance, would I, Heena Badahl, be *best friends* with a spoiled, talentless, pathetic excuse for a model?"

That cheers me up. "No. Only the best for Heena."

"Exactly. Remind yourself of that," she says, tipping her glass at me.

Chapter 18

Willow

"Welcome, Miss Jordan," the lead bellman says, actually *bowing* to me as the chauffeur helps me out of the black car. Since I refused to charter my own jet all the way from Paris to Kiawah, I flew into New York on one I shared with about ten other models, including Heena. Then I transferred to a chartered plane for the last leg of the trip from New York to Charleston, and then I had a driver take me the last hour out to Kiawah. Safe to say, I'm exhausted and jetlagged.

"Thank you." I nod politely to the man and sneak a cash tip into the hand of the chauffeur after he passes my bags to the bellman who spoke to me. There are two other bellmen out here, staring at me from behind their podium. "Is my family already here?"

"Mr. and Mrs. Jordan are here, along with Miss Maple. Tim will show you to your room," the man says, waving over a tall, dark-haired young man.

Tim steps forward, practically tripping over himself, and clears his throat. "It would be my pleasure."

I smile at him, and we walk through the huge double doors

and into the lobby. I pause in the large foyer, taking a moment to look around. Straight ahead is a large sitting area, the wood floors covered with sectionals, coffee tables, and oriental rugs. The wall behind has plenty of large windows and glass doors to highlight the great, unnaturally green lawn and the ocean beyond it. To the left of the sitting area, across the grand walkway, is a dark bar room decorated with comfortably worn leather armchairs and model schooners. To the right is the same room mirrored, but with tea tables replacing the bar, coupled with pink wallpaper and fresh bouquets. When my gaze sweeps back to the center of the lobby, I realize everyone, guests and staff alike, is frozen in their tracks, staring at me.

Why didn't my parents just rent a house? Staying at resorts is always so uncomfortable, no matter how private or exclusive they claim to be. People stare, no matter what. It makes my family seem like zoo animals.

"You must be very popular," I muse to Tim.

He barks a surprised laugh, furrowing his eyebrows as he looks at me. "I guess my SoundCloud career is finally taking off," he plays along.

"So, where's my room?" I ask, feeling the weight of dozens of eyes on me but unsure which direction to head down.

"Technically, you can get to it either way," he answers. "Your family is in the President's Suite, which is right above us —" he points upward, " —three floors up."

"Then let's go this way," I say, headed to the right, past the pink room. "I like flowers more than boats."

"Fair enough," Tim responds, overtaking me to lead the way to the elevator.

"Why is it that the dark, masculine room gets the bar while the feminine room gets tea? Seems like a bit of a message there," I find myself saying, the sleep deprivation loosening my tongue.

"I don't know, but it's been that way as long as I've been here," he answers.

I angle my head sideways to look at him as we reach the elevator and he presses the button. He really can't be any older than me, judging by his youthful face. But he has a shadow of a beard—probably from missing a shave—and a built body. Around twenty or twenty-one years old. He's tall—about 6'2—and handsome with a very symmetrical face. He could definitely model if he wanted.

"But, I could bring it up to management," he adds awkwardly.

"Sorry, I didn't mean to stare," I respond. "I haven't had a good night's sleep in a week, if that's any excuse."

"No worries. I'm sorry for staring at you, too. I mean, when you first pulled up. We get celebrities here pretty often, but rarely someone as huge as you, and—"

"Huge?" I laugh. "I know I'm tall, Tim, but no woman likes to be called huge."

"No, no, that's not what I meant at all," he says, face reddening.

"Relax," I say as the elevator dings. "I know what you meant." I step in and he follows, clicking floor three. "I know it must be hard for you to have to talk to me," I half-joke. "Thanks for taking one for the team and showing me up."

"It's my pleasure, really. You're much nicer than I thought you'd be," he adds with a smile.

"I'm glad. Prepare yourself for Aspen, though. She's a diva," I joke.

His face pales a little as we exit the elevator. "Really?"

"Not at all. I like to think that all of us Jordans are pretty nice and normal once you actually talk to us. But I know we might seem a bit daunting."

He nods, stopping in front of a door and knocking. "Just a little."

My mom opens the door, squealing and pulling me into her arms in a tight hug. "Willy! I'm so glad you're here," she says into my ear, still gripping me tightly.

"I'm glad I'm here too, Mom." I grin as she finally lets me go. "You look good."

Something indiscernible flickers in her expression before it melts off into joy again. "Bobby!" she calls behind her. "It's Willow!"

"Enjoy your stay," Tim says from the doorway. I give him a quick wave as he exits, letting the door softly close behind him.

"Willow! How were your flights?" my dad asks, pulling me into another bone-crushing hug.

"They were good. Lots of travel. I'm happy to finally be here."

"Well, you just need to take it slow for the next couple of days. I know fashion month is hard, and you need some time to recover. We all have a spa day reserved tomorrow, which should help."

"That sounds perfect. Thanks, Mom. Where's Maple?"

"She's taking a walk on the beach," my dad answers. "But she'll meet us for dinner. Speaking of, would you rather stay at the restaurant in the hotel or ride across the island and go to the one on the golf course? We have reservations at both, so it's up to you, Will."

I plop down on the surprisingly firm couch—ow. "Let's just stay here. I'm exhausted."

"Perfect," my dad says, clapping his hands in a distinctly dad-like way. "I'll call now to sort it out. Want to hit the bar first?"

"Honey, she's tired. Let her rest," my mom answers for me.

"No, it's fine. I'll go with you, Dad. Just give me an hour or so to nap." I sigh, glancing down at my sweatpants. "And then another fifteen to change into something a little more presentable."

"Of course, take your time," Dad answers. "They haven't even brought your stuff up yet. I'll tell them to just leave it outside your door."

"Thanks," I mumble, heading toward my room.

Chapter 19

Riley

The video I took the other day of me singing my song-in-progress was originally only intended for me. But, on a whim, I figured I'd post the video and see what my audience thought of it—I never expected the video to go viral. I got a call the next day from my label, raving about the song and asking if we could all come into Nashville to record it before we started our break.

Even though my label promised it would only take one day, none of us were too pleased to hear that our breaks were being cut into. After two months on the road, we were all craving a good night's sleep in our own beds at home. Waylon personally called them back and said he would only go if they gave us free meals for the day. Surprisingly, they agreed. And when Ethan caught wind of that, he persuaded them to give us each $500 in cash to fund a night out on Broadway, which they also somehow agreed to.

So that brings us to where we are now, walking into a honky-tonk in downtown Nashville. I've become my worst nightmare, the dick that wears sunglasses to the club. And despite the sunglasses, eyes are immediately drawn to us the second we walk in. Optimistically, I think that maybe it's just because we're all fairly attractive men in general.

"Oh my *fuck*, is that Riley Coleman?" I hear a girl hiss, shattering my illusions.

Fine, sunglasses off then if they're not doing any good anyway.

"*It is*," her friend squeals back.

I lead our pack deeper into the place, aiming for the bar. The crowd parts for me like I'm Moses—I don't think I'll ever get used to that.

"Four shots of Jameson, please," I say to the bartender, who's dropped everything to tend to me.

"Actually, make that eight,"

Ethan says, sidling up beside me, his blue eyes looking a devilish black in this dim lighting. He's wearing one of his favorite shirts tonight—it has cartoon wedding rings on it and reads, 'I'm Saving Pegging for Marriage.'

"Sure thing," the bartender responds, diligently lining up eight shot glasses and filling them to the absolute brim. I turn to my other side and see Waylon and Ethan beside me, the entire section of the bar clearing out reverently to let us stand there. We take our shots and then figure we might as well order beers, too.

I extend my card to the bartender, but he waves me off. "On the house."

"We'll drink you dry," I warn. "Come on, take the money."

"Really, on the house."

"If you insist." I shrug, taking my beer and returning to the depths of the crowd, my friends following me.

"Excuse me?" I hear a voice ask me. I turn towards it and see no one until I look down and see a petite, dark-haired girl by my side. "You're Riley Coleman," the girl says as my eyes meet hers.

The bravest person in the room, the only one to come up

to me, is this tiny girl who can't be over 5'2, who keeps getting jostled by the crowd like a buoy floating in the harbor.

"I am." I nod, letting her take the lead, curious about where she's going with this conversation.

"Who's your new song about?" she asks, a hint of a smirk playing on her lips. And the look in her eyes, it's like a cat setting eyes on a mouse. I almost feel bad for any other guy she sets her sights on tonight.

"No one in particular," I respond, returning her shadow of a smirk. "Why do you want to know?"

"No reason in particular," she mirrors my response, laughing with her eyes. "Worth a shot." She shrugs, taking a sip of her drink. "Do you want to dance with me then?"

"Sure," I say, as the intriguing girl grabs my hand and pulls me deeper into the pulsing crowd, towards the band.

And so we dance, my hands never touching her besides an occasional brush against her arms. But, it's as though the dam broke with that girl coming up to me. *Everyone* now wants to dance with me. The crowd tightens around me with people passing me drinks and someone even stealing my sunglasses from where they were hanging from the collar of my shirt.

People pass me more cans of beer, and I happily pop the tops and drink them, delighted by the foam that spills over the top and onto the sticky floor. I'm lost in the music for God knows how long, occasionally sweeping my eyes over the dance floor until I spot my friends, making sure they're also having fun. Judging by Nash nodding along to the music from his spot on the edge of the crowd, Waylon jumping to the beat in the heart of the dance floor, his curly hair bouncing with him, and Ethan gripping some brunette's waist with a lazy grin as she grinds onto him, I'm satisfied.

"Riley Coleman," the band's vocalist purrs into the mic in between songs. I look up, and everything blurs for a minute before the world stills and I see him staring down at me from the stage. "I've been watching you all night, waiting for you to come up on stage with me, but it seems like you've been hiding. Get your ass up here and sing a song for us."

The crowd cheers, practically pushing me towards the stage.

"I don't know about that," I respond.

"Alright, guys, he's getting a little shy, so let's use some good old-fashioned peer pressure. Cheer with me, Ri-ley, Ri-ley," he starts, the crowd joining in with deafening volume.

I laugh and give in, making my way to the stage.

The vocalist smiles and pulls me into a handshake-hug, handing me the mic when we separate.

"Hey guys." I grin out into the crowd. The fraction of my remaining rationality after all those drinks is screaming at me that getting up here while shit-faced is probably not a good idea…but the rest of my brain ignores it. "First order of business: I want my sunglasses back. So whatever little thief stole them, could you please pass them up to the stage? I promise I won't get mad. Look, I'll even turn around while they're returned," I say, turning to face the band rather than the crowd. I hear some murmuring before I sense something clatter by my foot. I turn back around and grab the sunglasses, putting them on. "Thank you. Now that that's settled, do you guys know 'Vicious'?" I ask the band. The crowd cheers when they hear the name of one of my most upbeat songs. "Then let's get rockin.'"

* * *

The next day, I wake up with a pounding headache, extremely disoriented, before I realize I'm in a hotel room. I turn frantically to face the other side of the bed. Empty, thank God.

On the nightstand is a glass of water, a few Advil tablets, and a note in Nash's handwriting that reads: *Thought you could use this. Don't worry, you didn't do anything too embarrassing. Give me a call when you're up, and we can go get something greasy to eat.*

I groan and take the Advil before going back to sleep for a few more hours.

I'm not ready to face the world until afternoon, when we all head to a diner before parting ways. I'm still donning the sunglasses, glad for the excuse that they're protecting my privacy, not easing my hangover.

Waylon grins from the opposite side of the booth. "Dude, you were *awesome*."

"I was shitfaced."

"And you were *awesome*," he reiterates. "Look at this video of you I saw online this morning." He pulls out his phone and shows me a video of myself onstage, sunglasses on, beaming and dancing like a drunken fool while singing. At least I don't sound half-bad.

"I can't watch that," I say, pushing it away, "I just hope my label isn't mad." I groan. "That's seriously so embarrassing."

"It wasn't so bad," Nash offers.

"Yeah, Riley," Ethan goads. "I actually really enjoyed that. How come you don't dance like that for me in private?"

"Stop," I plead half-heartedly, and they all laugh but drop the subject.

POP CULTURE PULSE PODCAST

Jenna: Okay, so real Pop Culture Pulsers already know that we're obsessed with Riley Coleman.

Caroline: It's so bad that our producers have told us to find something else to talk about, but we still find a way to bring him up at least once per episode.

Jenna: But today, it's actually for a good reason.

Producer: Mhm.

Jenna: I'm serious! Apparently, he made an unexpected visit to Nashville a few days ago while he was on break from the tour. And when I say he *visited* Nashville, I mean he was literally on Broadway all night. There are hundreds of videos of him from that night floating around on the internet now.

Caroline: I think we need to play some, just to really illustrate what we're talking about.

Jenna: Well, lucky enough for everyone, I sent our producer some specific videos earlier after suffering through *hours* of Riley video content for you guys.

Producer laughs.

Producer: Since you went through so much for us, fine, I'll play a few.

A video plays of Riley in a sea of people, fairly easy to spot because of his height. He's wearing sunglasses, but they're diagonal over his face, hanging off one ear. He's dancing around to the music, running a hand through his hair, shouting along to the lyrics of the country song the band is playing.

Jenna: Okay, now play the one of him onstage.

A video plays of Riley onstage, ripping the mic out of the mic stand and taking it with him as he walks to the side of the stage, climbing about ten feet up the scaffolding. He holds out the mic for the crowd to sing the chorus of one of his songs, smiling as they chant every word.

Jenna: Is that not just iconic?
Caroline: What I wouldn't give to have been there.

Jenna sighs dreamily.

Jenna: I know right.
Caroline: Was he spotted there with anyone? The internet has been suspiciously quiet as to the identity of his mystery girl.
Jenna: No, only his male bandmates. But word on the street is he left alone. And even though he danced with plenty of women there, he kept everything really above-board.
Caroline: Damn. Hopefully he and this mystery woman will crack soon and make a public appearance.
Jenna: Or even better, they'll break up.

Caroline laughs.

Caroline: That too. Anyway, this isn't the Riley Coleman show—
Jenna: But maybe it should be
Caroline:—so we're going to move on.

Chapter 20

Willow

It turns out *everyone* decided to come to the bar—even Maple.

"Only a Shirley Temple for you," my dad scolds her after she orders a whiskey neat. "What do you want, *adult* ladies?" he pointedly turns to Aspen, my mom, and me.

"But Aspen is only twenty," Maple protests.

"Fine, in solidarity with you, Syrup, I'll just have a Shirley Temple too."

"Well, *I'll* have a French 75," I tell him.

"I'll have the same." My mom shoots me a smile. "She has good taste. Thanks, Bobby," she says as he walks away toward the bar to order.

"I'll help him carry everything," Maple suggests, trailing after him.

Since I barely had time to put on simple makeup and change into my dress—an elegant, strapless, bodycon light pink silk minidress with the only decoration being a large bow on the small of my back—I haven't had time to check in with Aspen, yet.

"I'm fine, Willow," she says, as if sensing my thoughts. "And

Strike a Pose

I'm not mad at you. I mean, I was, but then I put myself in your shoes. If we had switched places, I would have called Mom too after a call like that."

"Good. It was a tough decision, but...I just couldn't live with myself if something happened to you."

"I know." She nods. "Same for you."

"I'm just glad you two get along so well." Mom grimaces. "Me and Aunt Jenna fought like cats when we were younger."

"To be fair, you were stuck in a trailer with each other. Luckily, Aspen and I usually have a continent of space between us," I joke.

"Oh please, you two never even fought as kids. You would have been fine," my mom dismisses.

Aspen reaches for my hand and squeezes, adding, "Seriously, Willy, we're fine."

Dad and Maple return with our drinks, and we all clink glasses in the center of our two-couch setup, toasting to family. Even though we're in the darkest corner of the bar area, everyone is looking at us. At least nobody's taking pictures.

"So, how was fashion month?" Aspen asks me.

"It was good. Heena and I were able to walk in a lot of shows together. She wished she could be here, but she's doing some shoot in New York," I reply, taking the first sip of my drink. "Oh, Mom, Jean Paul Gaultier said to tell you hi. And he's sending you a leather jacket or something?"

"He's too much." She waves her hand dramatically despite the smile she's failing to hide. "But I appreciate it, nonetheless."

"How's LA? How's the project there going?" I ask.

"It's going well," Dad answers. "We've just finished planning everything and are preparing to start shooting the film in two weeks when we get back."

"And you're both producing it, right?"

"Yes, and your father is directing and starring in it," Mom adds. "I'm just there for moral support."

"Iz, don't sell yourself short. You're doing *all* the work behind the scenes, helping with the casting, hair and makeup, costumes, and the shot lists."

"Wow, Mom, that's huge, congratulations!" Aspen says. "Remind me to start looking for an Oscars dress."

"For yourself or for us?" Mom returns the smile. "We can't forget about your big accomplishment, Aspen. Shooting your final season of *Fairview Ridge* is huge, and we can't *wait* to see what you'll do next."

"I can't wait to see what I'll do next, either," Aspen says sullenly.

"Something will come up," Dad reassures her. "You've proven yourself. Now is the easy part, when you just count the days until producers come to you, begging you to be in their movies."

"This isn't the nineties, Dad," Aspen retorts. "And I'm not on the top of anyone's list."

"You don't know that," my mom says. "Nobody's approached you because they know you already have a full-time gig. Once you're available, the offers will come."

"Here's hoping."

"How's school, Maple?" Dad asks, wisely changing the subject.

"Not as exciting as producing a movie, or walking the runway in Paris, or starring in a hit TV show. But it's good."

"Well, do you want to do any of those things?" Mom prods her delicately.

"No. But when we're sitting here swapping updates, my life pales in comparison."

"Do you want to come to LA with us? We could get you tutors," Dad suggests.

"I like New York. And I like being in school. I like that I'll be the only Jordan, besides Dad, to have actually graduated from high school," Maple says. "Then, I don't know, maybe college."

"I think that would be great," Mom says. "You can be the scholar of the family and put us all to shame." She squeezes Maple's knee reassuringly.

Maple smiles. "I don't know what I would major in yet..."

"That's okay, you have a few years to figure it out," I respond. "And I'm sure having a famous family gives you tons of trauma to write about in a college essay," I joke.

"Hey," my dad faux-scolds. "Your mother and I didn't rule nineties film for you kids to have to write about *trauma* to get into college. Your name should be enough."

"And if it's not, we could always donate a building," Mom adds.

Maple hoists an eyebrow. "I'll keep that in mind."

Chapter 21

Willow

The past few days have been chock full of eating, sleeping, and lazing—the perfect vacation. Tonight is our last night, and our parents have reserved the private back room of the island's nicest restaurant for us to dine in before parting ways tomorrow. Before we head out, Aspen, Maple, and I are cramming in some extra time together by all getting ready for dinner in my room.

"Willow, you never wear the color cantaloupe, right?" I hear Aspen ask from behind me, sorting through a stack of hanging dresses.

I scoff. "God, no. It makes me look sick."

She sighs, showing me a long, strappy, pastel orange dress. "I knew it—we have the same coloring and I think it looks awful on me. I don't know why my stylist put this in here."

"That would look great in black," Maple offers.

"I know, it's such a waste of a dress. Maybe Heena could wear it. It might look good on her."

"If anyone could pull it off, it would be her," I agree. "Have it shipped to the penthouse. She can at least look at it."

"Sure," Aspen says, setting it aside. "My only other option

for tonight is this navy one." She pulls out another long dress. It's a very simple halter cut but has a low back featuring a thin accent tie.

"I like that." I nod. "It's sort of similar to mine." I look down at my floor-length baby blue satin dress. Like Aspen's, it's a halter-top style with an open back but with a plunging V-neck meeting at the top in a neck scarf á-la *To Catch a Thief*. "What are you wearing, Syrup?"

"This," Maple answers, holding up an off-the-shoulder black mini-dress paired with long black gloves. I should have known. Maple's wardrobe is 90% black.

"I *love* that, especially the gloves," I respond. "Please tell me you're doing a dark lip and really leaning into the whole Morticia Addams thing."

"Duh," she responds.

Satisfied, I turn back to face the mirror to resume doing my makeup.

"I'm so happy we're all together," Aspen says. "I really needed this."

"I'm glad we are too," Maple agrees with uncharacteristic earnestness.

"Me too. I love you guys, you know that?" I say.

"We love you back," Aspen answers, slipping into her dress.

"I wish we could all be together more often," Maple laments.

"Me too," I say, tactfully applying fine glitter to the inner corners of my eyes. "But it just makes the time we are together all the more special, right?"

Maple sniffs. "Yeah."

"Are you *crying*?" Aspen asks, shocked.

"No, there's something in my eye," Maple defends, dabbing her eye with the limp glove hanging in her hand.

"Oh my God, Maple, you're totally crying," I say. "I never thought I'd live to see the day."

"Shut up," she says, her voice breaking even though she's smiling. "I'm just so...happy. I missed you guys. It gets lonely around the house without you."

"Aw, come here, you big softie," I say, getting up and pulling her into a hug. "You too, Aspen," I say, extending an arm for her. "We're all only a phone call away," I assert into their hair.

"And we'll all be together again soon," Aspen adds. "I don't know when, but we'll make it happen."

"Sisters from cradle to grave," Maple adds, squeezing us once before separating. "Now get off me before you smear your makeup on my dress."

We finish getting ready quickly and hustle to meet our parents at the restaurant on time. The main dining space is dim and romantically lit, with real candles flickering in wall sconces. The walls are painted a midnight blue color and decorated with paintings of sailboats and seascapes. The hostess leads my sisters and me to the private room in the back, where my parents are waiting for us. We also have our own private waiter, who is incredibly attentive and punctual. The four-course meal is so rich and delicious that by the end of it, I'm leaning back in my chair, well on my way to a food coma.

My mom clears her throat as the waiter takes our dessert plates. "So, girls," she begins in a tone serious enough to make me sit up straight again. "There's...something we want to tell you."

The waiter exits quietly with the plates, giving us privacy.

Maple groans. "Please tell me you're not having a baby."

"What?" My dad furrows his eyebrows. "No—No, we're not."

"I—" my mom starts. My dad rests his hand over hers on the table, seemingly giving her the strength to continue.

"Before I say anything," she begins again, eyeing all of us in turn. "I want you to know that everything will be okay and that we both love you very, *very* much."

It feels like the temperature drops forty degrees. Just seconds ago, I was half-asleep, and now I'm well-awake, a shiver running down my back.

"I've been diagnosed with stage three lung cancer," she finally blurts out.

And suddenly, I don't feel like I'm in my body at all anymore. Time freezes, and I'm an outsider looking in. My mom's mouth moves again, but I don't process anything she says. She looks at me expectantly.

"Willow," she says, loudly enough that I know it wasn't her first time saying it.

I shake my head. "You *what?*"

Chapter 22

Riley

"Riley!" my mom cries, pulling me into a bone-crushing hug the second I walk through my front door. "I can't believe you're finally here."

"I've only been gone a couple of months, Ma." I laugh, as though I didn't miss my parents as much as they missed me. "I was gone for stretches that long in college."

"It feels different when we know you're across the country instead of in Boone, though," Dad adds, pulling me into another hug the second my mom lets go.

"How was it? You're a world traveler now," Mom says, looking me up and down like she's assessing for injuries. "Are you hungry?"

"I ate on the road." I chuckle bemusedly at her fussing. "And I'd hardly call myself a world traveler...I just went to the West Coast and Canada. That's hardly the world."

"Hey, it's more than we've been to," Dad says.

"Fair enough. It was cold." I shrug. "Nothing compares to West Carolina."

"Mhm. You don't have to make us feel better, son, we know

it's not much," Dad says, gesturing to the cozy two-story home I grew up in.

"I'm serious. I missed this place. Oh, Mom, I saw your flowers out front. They look great."

"Thank you! I've been giving them a new fertilizer, and they seem to be responding well. They're blooming pretty early, but hopefully they'll last another month or so at least."

"Mind if I cut some?"

"To bring to your little friend?" she asks, cocking a brow.

"Yes, my *friend*."

"Sure, go for it. I'm sure your *friend* will appreciate it."

"How come you never give Nash any flowers? Seeing as he's your closest friend and all," Dad joins in.

"He's allergic."

"What about Waylon then? I know for a fact that boy's not allergic to daisies. My sister would have told me."

I groan. "Fine, forget the flowers."

"No, no," Mom clucks. "Don't let us bully you. Bring her flowers. I'm sure she'll love the gesture."

"If I do, will you stop teasing me?"

Dad laughs, clapping me on the shoulder. "Oh, son, you know we can't promise that."

We spend the evening catching up. I tell them all about the places I visited, funny stories from the tour, and the crazy 'I'm a celebrity now' moments. We eat a home-cooked meal—the best meal I've had in months—and finish the night with a double feature of *Mission Impossible* movies.

After I go upstairs for the night, I make sure to tidy up Olivia's room, where Willow will be staying. Then I sleep like the dead on my own mattress, which is infinitely better than the cot I have on the tour bus.

* * *

I've been to Charleston a few times, but I've never been to Kiawah. And I realize why, as I drive by house after house that could really only be described as mansions. After passing through *two* gates, I finally reach the giant, looming hotel Willow and her family are staying at. I pull up to the front and shoot her a text, letting her know I'm here. When I look up from my phone, I have the shit scared out of me by a guy standing at the passenger side door.

"Welcome. Need any help with your bags?" he asks through the open window with a friendly smile.

"No thanks, I'm just picking someone up," I say, stepping out of the car and walking around the front to face him and the front doors. "She should be down in a minute," I add, feeling a little uncomfortable loitering around such a nice place.

"Holy shit..." the uniformed man breathes. "You're Riley Coleman."

"Yep." I nod, still struck by the shock of being recognized by strangers. "And you are..."

"Tim," the man answers quickly. "This is just...insane," he says, staring at me before shaking his head. "Sorry, I'm just such a huge fan, this is...insane. I literally play your songs all the time. I have them all memorized vocally and on guitar. This is just insane."

"So you've said." I laugh, feeling put at ease in this ridiculously fancy place by Tim's earnestness. "No worries, Tim, it's nice to meet you too."

"I'm so starstruck right now." He chuckles. "I can't *wait* to tell my friends that I met you. They're gonna be so jealous. We're actually going to your show here in a few weeks."

"No way! That's awesome. I'm so glad you're coming. I'll have to give you a shoutout on stage. Really rub it in to your friends."

"That would be *incredible*," he says as I lean against the truck. "Is that a '69 Ford F250?" he asks.

"Damn, you know your cars. Yeah, I bought it from an old neighbor of mine when I was in high school. It had been just sitting in his garage for years, so he gave me a really good deal on it. Still, I had to save up for a year to buy it, and then I worked day and night for a few months to get it into driving shape again."

"It's such a beauty," he says, admiring it. "I wish my neighbors had cars like these to sell to me."

Over his shoulder, I see the doorman open the door and Willow gracefully thanking him as she walks out, my heart stopping at the sight of her. She somehow gets more and more beautiful each time I see her. Her long golden hair is free, cascading loosely down her back and around her face. She's wearing light wash daisy dukes and a white top made up of two panels that tie at her chest, leaving a stretch of her abdomen exposed. She looks so flawless and ethereal that I wouldn't be surprised to discover that she's an angel walking the earth, sent here to remind us all that God exists through her utter perfection.

Her eyes lock on mine, and I stop breathing as her schooled expression melts into something akin to relief. And I forget about the wealth, forget about Tim, forget about *everything* as I pull her into my arms.

Chapter 23

Willow

I don't know what the normal reaction is when you find out your mom has cancer, but I'm pretty sure it's not going numb and then vomiting up your guts all night like I did. I was so sick that the little sleep I did get was on the bathroom floor.

I feel about as shitty as I look today, despite showering, running a brush through my hair, and putting on a little makeup. I was debating calling off this trip with Riley, but my mom insisted that I go. She jokingly promised that she wouldn't die in the few days I was gone, which I didn't find very funny at all. She knew how excited I was for a little bit of normalcy (and to see Riley, whom I'm ashamed to admit that I miss terribly, considering I've only met the guy twice) and would not take no for an answer. So, here I am, leaving the hotel and my family and hoping I can hold it together for Riley. I don't want to ruin his break with my shitty mood.

I walk through the front doors of the hotel and see an old-fashioned, dark green truck waiting for me at the end of the porte-cochère. Riley's casually leaning against the side of it, facing me with his arms and ankles crossed, talking to Tim, the bellman. As Riley sees me approach over Tim's shoulder, he offers me an easy smile. Prompted by Riley's reaction, Tim turns, offering me a smile of his own.

I don't know if it's from the weight of last night or the strain of the past month, but something about seeing Riley's casual, boyish grin loosens a bit of emotion from me, and before I know it, I'm picking up the pace and practically running the last few feet to him. He straightens from the truck and reaches for me as I fling my arms around his neck, hugging him way tighter than I probably should.

"Thank you for coming to get me," I murmur into the space between his neck and shoulder, the tears that never came last night finally welling in my eyes.

Jesus Christ, Willow, get your shit together.

He voices a response as I slyly dab my eyes with my arms still around him, hoping he doesn't notice. He graciously lets me hug him for as long as I need before I eventually pull away. I look up into his pale green eyes and am again struck by how tall he is—I mean, he makes *me* feel small.

"You can just stick her bags in the back," he says over my head to the bellman trailing me with a cart full of my suitcases. "You pack heavy," he adds, smiling down at me. Realizing we still aren't more than a few inches from each other, I take a step back.

"I'm high-maintenance." I shrug, silently begging my emotions to stay at bay.

"I can see that. I have something for you...well, two things." He reaches into the open passenger-side window and pulls out a bouquet of daisies wrapped in brown butcher paper and a medium-sized box.

"Riley." I gasp, smelling the flowers. "You really didn't have to bring me anything."

"Yes, I did." He smiles, his dimples alone tugging at my

heart. "To pay you back for the exclusive Willow-Jordan-designed shirt. I made a *ton* of money off that on eBay," he jokes.

"Shut up." I feel my face morph into a smile, something that seemed impossible just seconds ago. I open the box and see gorgeous, golden, bedazzled cowgirl boots. "Oh my God, Riley!" I squeal, hoping the excitement in my voice sounds sincere. If I wasn't feeling so hollow, I'd probably be literally jumping for joy right now at both the actual shoes and the gesture. "These are *amazing.*"

"I figured you probably didn't have any boots like that. Plus, I thought you'd like the gold. They reminded me of your Grammy dress. They're not designer or anything but—"

"Stop, they're perfect, Riley," I interrupt as I kick off my sneakers and tug on the boots. They fit like a glove. "How did you know my size? You never asked."

"Surprisingly, that's public information," he answers as I smile down at my shoes, admiring how the sunlight lights them up.

"Alright, you two are all set to go," the bellman says, bringing us back to reality.

"Ready?" Riley asks, holding the passenger door open.

"Ready," I confirm, grabbing his outstretched hand and climbing into the seat.

Once I'm settled in, Riley walks around and gets into the driver's side. As he turns the key, I remember that *anyone* could have seen us here together—my thoughts have been so scattered that I didn't even consider it. People have been gawking at my family all weekend, and even though Riley and I *aren't* together and did nothing more than hug, the press blows things out of proportion all the time.

And from the outside looking in, the tight hug combined with the gifts, combined with me driving away with him would seem pretty suspect. I look out the window anxiously as Riley shifts into drive, scanning the front of the hotel. Thankfully, I only see the two bellmen.

Tim makes eye contact with me and gives a small smile, running his thumb and forefinger across his lips and throwing away the metaphorical key. I return the smile and relax against my seat as we drive away, knowing that no tabloids will be reporting what very well could have been twisted into a cover story.

"How was the weekend with your family?" Riley asks once we've pulled away.

"It was...good."

"You don't sound so sure."

"It was good," I say more definitively.

Stay strong, I tell myself. *Mom's right. I'll see her in a few days, and nothing's going to happen to her in the meantime. I've been looking forward to these next few days for a while and moping around won't help anyone. I just need to relax and stay in the moment. Riley and I will have fun. Mom will be okay.*

I add, "It was nice to spend some time with everyone. I haven't actually seen my family since the last time I saw you."

"It must be hard to go so long without seeing them."

"Well, you're going through the same thing." *But not exactly,* I add in my head.

"It's tough, yeah. But getting to share my music with people is worth it. I'm sure you feel the same, right?"

"Definitely." I nod candidly. "I don't know what I'd do without fashion. It's been my passion for as long as I can remember."

"Have you ever thought of designing your own line? I mean, that shirt was incredible, not to keep bringing it up. I'm just so impressed."

"Maybe one day. You know, like when I'm thirty and thus an old lady as far as runways are concerned."

He looks sidelong at me, his wavy golden hair tousled by the wind flowing through the open windows. "I don't think runways would *ever* get tired of you."

"So you're saying that at eighty, people will still want me walking in their shows?" Despite myself, I stifle a laugh at the mental image.

"I really think they would," he says. "Maybe at that point, you'd have your own seniors-only line to model."

"Sure, and you could open the male show for my line."

"I don't think I'm model material," he says.

"What, is modeling too feminine a profession for you?" I half-joke. You'd be surprised how many men actually believe that.

"Not at all." He shakes his head. "I just don't think I have the look they want."

"You're right. No one would want a tall, fit, blond, green-eyed, symmetrical man. I guess you'd be more of a burden to my show than anything."

"You know, nowhere in there did you say I'm attractive." He grins in a way that makes my stomach flip.

"Do you want me to?"

He shakes his head in disapproval. "Well, now it just feels like pity."

"Isn't the entire internet obsessing over you enough?"

"Nope." He smiles, looking at me again. His eyes are the same earthy green color as the marsh we're driving past. I find myself thinking that if I were a painter, he'd be something I'd like to paint, especially with this background. "But nice to know you pay attention to who obsesses over me or not."

"You're reaching." I smile, rolling my eyes playfully.

"Wishful thinking."

"So, you still live with your parents?"

"It's sort of complicated. When I graduated college, I had no clue what I was doing with my life...my music career had taken off in a small indie way, but not in any real way. So I started apartment hunting in Charlotte, planning on rooming with Ethan and getting a job in business. I mean, at that point, I had a degree in communications, and my music minor wasn't paying the bills.

"But then, before we could settle on a place together, one of my songs went semi-viral on the internet, and the next thing I knew, I had a record deal. So, I had to quickly scramble to get a place to stay in Nashville while I wrote and recorded my first album. And then I only had a month or so between the release of my album and the start of the tour....anyway, long story short, I have my own small, temporary place in Nashville. But yes, I live with my parents when I'm home in North Carolina."

"I sort of do the same thing. I keep small places in London and Paris, but when I'm in LA, I stay with Aspen, and when I'm home in New York, I stay with my parents." Realizing the path I've started down and quickly pivoting the subject, I throw the conversation back to him. "Do your parents know I'm coming?"

"Of course."

"But do they know *I'm* coming?"

"They didn't ask, so I didn't tell. I didn't know if you'd want them to know. I don't think they'd recognize you, so it's up to you."

"Hmm," I say, watching my hand float along in the wind through the side mirror. "If it doesn't come up, I don't see why I'd tell them. But I won't lie either, if they do somehow recognize me."

"Sounds like a plan."

"Do you live close to Nash, Ethan, and Waylon?" I ask.

"Nash and Waylon, yes. Ethan, no. He lives about two hours away, near Charlotte. "Why? Do you want to meet them?"

"Maybe. Is it weird that the person I most want to meet is Nash's sister? I feel like she knows more about me than I know about myself."

"Not at all. I was going to take you out to this bar in town one night. We could invite them. It'd be fun."

"So, you don't listen to your own music in the car?" I ask, changing the subject and taking note of the George Straight quietly flowing through the speakers. I'm slightly impressed with myself for recognizing his voice.

Riley laughs. "What? No, that's ridiculous. It's like how nobody likes to listen to their own recorded voice played back to them."

"Wait, you genuinely don't like your own voice?"

"I can acknowledge that I can sing well without actually liking to hear recordings of myself singing. I mean, I guess I don't *dislike* it...it's just weird. And anyway, I've been singing those songs ad nauseam on tour. I think it would do me well to go a week or two without hearing them."

"Interesting," I murmur, looking at his side profile.

He turns to look at me. "Do you know people that listen to their own songs?"

"I don't personally know many musicians very well, but I once briefly dated this rapper who exclusively listened to his own music."

"No way." Riley gapes. "Who?"

"Arm$trong."

"*You dated that guy?*" He laughs himself into a fit.

"Hey! Don't make fun. I was seventeen, and to be fair, his music is pretty good."

Riley keeps laughing so hard I don't know how he's staying in his lane. "Willow," he croaks out.

"What," I say, laughing—really laughing—at the sight of *him* laughing.

"Nothing, I'm just learning a lot about you," he says, finally gaining some semblance of composure.

"What, just say it," I insist.

"It's just...that guy is like one-hundred and thirty pounds soaking wet and covered in *full-color* tattoos."

I shrug.

"You're not even going to try to defend it?" he laughs again.

"How can I?" I chuckle. "He's ridiculous. But his music is pretty good. I stand by that."

"Apparently, he thinks so too."

Chapter 24

Willow

"We're almost there," Riley assures me after about four hours of driving. During the long drive, we've been talking nonstop about anything and everything, from childhood crushes to his brief basketball phase to my postcard collection. I played all of my favorite Keith Whitley songs, and he played all of his favorite 2Pac songs. All in all, my mood has lightened significantly since I got in the car what seems like mere minutes ago.

"No worries at all, I'm having fun. It's a pretty drive," I say, admiring the curvy mountain back roads. "Thank you for making this drive twice in one day. I can't even imagine how draining that is. And on your break, too."

"Please." He waves me off. "I love to drive. I don't mind."

"So, what are your parents like? Will they be there when we get to your house?"

"Probably. My mom is one of the kindest people you'll ever meet and a really good judge of character. She's also one of the best cooks I've ever met. My dad is more extroverted. He's never met a stranger."

Warmth flows through my chest. "Sounds familiar."

He looks at me. "Something tells me you don't meet many strangers either, Willow Jordan."

I shrug and change the subject. "So, any tips to impress your parents?"

"They'll love you just as you are," he says, pulling into a long, private driveway that leads to a modest two-story house. He parks out front and helps me get my bags out of the back. As we struggle to get everything, the door opens, and a friendly-looking middle-aged brunette woman appears.

"You guys made good time," she says cheerfully in the same drawl Riley has. "Here, let me help," she says as a similarly aged, salt-and-peppered man steps into view behind her.

"I've got it, honey," he says, walking past her to reach us. "You must be Willow." His smile is almost a mirror image of Riley's.

"Yes." I smile back, shaking his outstretched hand. "It's so nice to meet you two."

"Riley's told us so much about you," his mother says, approaching us. "But *wow*, he failed to mention how absolutely gorgeous you are." She raises her eyebrows, looking from me to her son.

Riley groans as I feel my face heating. "*Mom!*"

"Sorry, honey, I didn't mean to embarrass you. Here, hand me that," she says, reaching for the bag in my hand.

"It's okay, I can carry it. I don't want to trouble you any more than I already am."

"I insist, you're our guest," she says.

I figure it's probably ruder to fight her, so I hand her the bag.

They lead us into the house with my bags in tow. The foyer opens to a staircase and a dining room to the left. The floors are worn, sun-bleached hardwood, and the beige walls are lined with photos of their family. They set my bags at the foot of the staircase, promising to help me bring them up when I'm ready and lead us into the kitchen, where there's enough food to feed an army spread out on the counter. I slyly remove the bottle of wine I brought from one of my bags as I follow.

"I don't know if y'all are hungry or not, but I made a little late lunch just in case." Riley's mom smiles, gesturing to all the food.

This is little?

"Oh my gosh, that looks *amazing*," I gush, truly meaning it. "Mr. and Mrs. Coleman, you didn't have to do all this for me, truly."

"Please, call us Dave and Laura," Riley's dad says. "And it's our pleasure, really. Any friend of Riley's is a friend of ours."

"Well, I'm grateful, nonetheless. And to thank you for letting me spend some time here, I brought you this as a small thank you," I say, holding up the bottle of 2012 Romanée-Saint-Vivant Pinot Noir.

"Willow, darling, you really didn't have to do that," Laura says, but the sparkle in her eyes doesn't lie—she's thrilled. "Romanée-Saint-Vivant,'" she reads. "I don't think I've heard of that."

"It's a pinot noir from Burgundy. I was just on a little trip to France, and I brought back some bottles for my family, too. It's really good—I mean, if you like reds," I ramble.

"I *love* reds. Thank you so much," she says. "And the effort you went to getting it for us is…wow. Thank you."

"Yeah, thank you so much," Dave echoes. "I guess we'll save this for another time unless anyone wants some mid-afternoon wine?"

Riley and I laugh, both politely passing.

"Fair enough," Dave says, setting the bottle on the counter. "We'll come back to it. Thank you again, Willow, it looks delicious."

"It's the least I could do."

We get our food and settle around the table to eat.

"You know, Willow, you remind me of someone," Laura muses as we begin eating.

"Oh," I say. Riley gives me a concerned look, but I just nod. "Who?"

"Like a young Izzy Michaels, back in her early days." I stiffen at the mention of my mom, but luckily no one notices. "We used to go see *all* her movies when they came out. Do you remember that, Dave? How I dragged you to those?"

"I remember," he muses. "I remember how we went to those movies, but then you'd have to go back to see them again with your friends because we always—"

"And I think that's enough," Laura says, cutting him off.

"Ew, guys." Riley wrinkles his nose in disgust. "Really?"

"Really," Dave confirms with a wink.

I laugh.

"But really, you look *just* like her, Willow. Doesn't she, dear?"

"Mhm." Dave nods again. "It's the eyes, I think."

"Yeah, they're so blue. Really beautiful. It's a compliment, don't worry. Izzy Michaels was—still is—gorgeous."

"Thank you." I smile. "She's uh—she's..."

They all look at me expectantly, Riley's eyes still dripping with concern, telling me through his gaze that I don't have to say anything. But it just feels wrong not to at this point. I hope they don't treat me any differently because of it, but I know that they will. Everyone does.

"She's actually my mom?" It comes out as more of a question than a statement.

It seems I caught Dave mid-sip, and he coughs on his water.

"She's...what?" Laura asks.

"She's my mom. That's why I look like her. I'm Willow Jordan. The daughter of Robert and Isabelle Jordan."

"Holy shit," Laura whispers, her eyes widening.

"Sorry to drop that on you. Maybe I shouldn't have mentioned it. I just thought it would be better to be honest instead of dancing around it," I start rambling again.

"But she really wants to keep it private and just have a low key weekend," Riley adds. "So please don't mention it to your book club or anything, Mom."

"Of course not. Thank you for telling us, honey," Laura says, recovering herself. "My lips are sealed."

"And don't worry, we won't gawk at you all weekend," Dave adds. "Well, Laura and I won't, at least," he teases, eyeing his son.

"Y'all," Riley says exasperatedly. "You promised me you wouldn't make this weird. I told you, we're just friends."

"Obviously." Laura snickers. "She's way out of your league."

I laugh again and realize that I've done enough laughing today that my abs hurt—despite last night's terrible news.

"Mom!"

"Last one, I promise. I just had to get it out of my system." Laura grins deviously, subtly revealing her crossed fingers to Dave and me.

I think the Colemans and I are going to get along just fine.

Chapter 25

Riley

After dinner, my parents and I help bring Willow's bags upstairs to Olivia's vacant room. They leave us up here and head back downstairs, where they'll presumably stay for the rest of the night since their bedroom is down there.

"So," I say, leaning on her door frame but not quite stepping into her room.

"So?"

"I texted Nash and Waylon, and they're both free for the bar tonight if you still want to do that. And Nash's sister is free, too," I add. "He just told her I was asking, though, we didn't want to spoil the surprise."

"God, I hope I don't give the poor girl a heart attack."

"So you're in?"

"I'm in," she affirms. "But I'd like to humbly request a nap before we go. I didn't get much sleep last night...jet lag."

"For sure." I take my cue and turn to leave. "Just knock when you're ready. My room is the one directly across from yours."

***

Around 8 p.m., I hear a faint knock on my door. "Come in," I call from where I'm sitting on the edge of my bed. I was strumming on my guitar, trying to work out a melody that's been stuck in my head all day.

I hear the door creak open and see Willow looking straight out of a Southern man's fantasy. She's wearing bell-bottomed jeans that hug her curves and a plain white T-shirt, tight enough to be a second skin. I didn't realize my gaze had drifted so far down her body until I noticed the golden boots I gave her poking out from beneath her jeans. I snap my eyes back up to her face and see her smirking. Suddenly, it's a hundred degrees in here.

"Take your time," she jokes, shaking her newly curled head of hair at me. "I'm guessing I nailed the country girl look?"

"You look great," I manage to say.

"Perfect. So when do you want to head out?"

"Now's good with me." I stand, setting my guitar on its stand, trying not to think about what her jeans would look like on my floor—and failing miserably. "Nightlife starts a bit earlier out here than it does in New York. If you're cool with it, I'll text Waylon to come pick us up so we can both drink. He lives just down the street and is driving anyway."

"Great," she says, leaving me in the dust and heading downstairs. I grab the worn leather jacket off the back of my desk chair, mainly for Willow in case she gets cold, and my favorite cowboy hat.

"Sure, I could have a bite," I hear Willow saying from the kitchen.

My mom must be offering her more food. It's one of her love languages, as well as mercilessly making fun of the people she cares about.

As predicted, Willow's standing by the counter eating chocolate cake as my mom admires her hair.

"Is it natural?" Mom asks, lightly playing with a lock of Willow's hair in awe. Willow laughs, a sound infinitely better than any song.

"It's highlighted, but other than that, yes," Willow answers. "I used to keep it trimmed short so designers would have the choice of keeping it short or adding extensions and making it long, but I stopped doing that. I like it long—if they want it short, they can give me a wig."

"Amen, girl," my mom echoes. "If I had hair like this, I'd never cut it either."

Willow looks up and sees me, offering a bite of her cake to me on her fork. I take it.

"Oh good, you're here, Riley. I was just about to tell Willow about how beautiful your hair was as a baby." She turns back to Willow. "It was so gorgeous, a platinum blond that not even a nice salon could get you. So I left it long on him, not wanting to cut it. But then everyone would come up to me and compliment me on my beautiful *daughter*." Mom laughs. "So eventually, I felt forced to cut it."

Willow laughs again as I roll my eyes. "She forgot to mention that I was in *first grade* when she finally gave in. The other boys in my class teased me mercilessly."

Willow grins, looking at my mom. "I would love to see photos of that."

A car honks outside, and I silently thank God—and Waylon—for saving me from the humiliation of my baby photos.

"I'll get his whole baby album out for you to flip through tomorrow," my mom promises Willow as she walks us to the door. As Willow walks in front of me, I notice the large red stars on either back pocket of her jeans, before quickly averting my eyes. I'm starting to think that I accidentally got in way over my head by inviting Willow to visit.

"You guys have fun," my mom calls as we climb into Waylon's old pickup. I open the door to the passenger seat and offer it to Willow, but she shakes her head and climbs into the back.

"Goodnight, Mom," I call back.

"Goodnight, Laura," Willow echoes.

"First name basis, wow," Waylon says as we buckle in.

"You must be Waylon," Willow says from the middle seat, leaning her head between Waylon and mine. "Nice to meet you."

"You too. What's your name again?" he asks, crinkling his brow at her with feigned confusion.

"Waylon," I chide.

Willow just laughs. "I like you," she says to him, leaning back into her seat as we reverse out the drive. We swing by Nash's house on the way so he and his sister, Nellie, can drink with Willow and me.

"Is it true that you guys really had a—" Nellie clamors as she approaches the car before stopping dead in her tracks at the sight of the blonde head in the backseat. "Shut the fuck up," she starts. "Nash, *shut the fuck up*," she repeats, still frozen in her tracks. Her face has lost all its color.

"I didn't say anything," Nash murmurs.

Waylon is cracking up like he's watching a new *South Park* episode. Willow raises her hand meekly, offering Nellie a warm smile through the window.

"Are you getting in or what?" Waylon calls to them, cranking the volume of the rap music he's playing loud enough to shake the car.

"Come on," Nash says, dragging his awe-stricken sister toward the truck.

"I promise I don't bite." Willow grins as they get in on either side of her.

"Nellie, meet Willow. Willow, meet Nellie."

"I can't believe you dicks didn't tell me she was coming!" Nellie says, roughly punching each of our arms in turn. "Sorry," she apologizes to Willow. "It's a pleasant surprise, I promise...I just would have done my hair or at least not have worn my old high school jeans."

"No worries, I just hope I don't disappoint. And as for the jeans, they have that 'fashionably worn' look—you know, like Yeezy or Vivienne Westwood. I like them." Willow winks.

We pull into the nearly full parking lot of the bar a few minutes later. Willow hops out, and Nellie's jaw drops. "You're *tall!*"

Waylon snorts as he leads the way to the bar. "Not everyone is barely over five feet, pumpkin."

"I appreciate it," Willow diplomatically responds.

I catch my arm extending toward the small of her back, but I quickly pull it away.

Get it together, Riley. You're just friends. She doesn't want you touching her.

Chapter 26

Willow

The first thing I notice when I walk into the bar is the reek of stale beer. And the peanuts crunching under my boots. And the giant wooden dance floor full of people doing all sorts of different dances; some are doing a partner-switching thing, some are doing a swing dance, and others are doing the type of individual dancing you'd see in any nightclub.

I beam up at Riley beside me. "I love it."

"Let's get some drinks, then I'll teach you." He nods to the dance floor before leading me to the bar.

"Woah, woah, woah. I don't know about that," I respond, trailing after him.

"Why not?"

"Because I can't dance."

"Then consider it a challenge, Willow Jordan. You know, normal people dance," he adds. "It's practically written into the contract of our deal that you have to learn." He grins as he catches the bartender's attention. "A beer, whatever's coldest is fine, and..." he trails off, looking at me expectantly.

"I'll have the same," I panic-order.

The bartender slides us two bottles, and Riley clinks his against mine. "Cheers," he says, taking his first sip, which should *not* have made my heart race. "What's wrong?" he asks, nudging the arm holding my glass.

"I don't drink beer," I admit.

Riley throws his head back laughing so hard his shoulders shake, drawing a few stares.

"What," I whine, embarrassed by all the eyes on us.

"Of course you don't," he says, clearly delighted. "And so why, pray tell, did you order a beer?"

"Because I didn't know what to order! I usually order cocktails, but I figured they wouldn't make those here, and I don't know the names of any wines they'd have—"

"It's okay," he assures me. I can tell he's struggling to contain another bout of laughter. "I get it. I'm going to be so, so honest with you, though, Willow...I would not order wine here. Do you like any mixed drinks? You know, like rum and Coke or something?"

"Um..." I hesitate. "I like tequila."

He loses his internal battle and laughs deeply again before flagging down the bartender. "Two shots of tequila, please," he says, swiping the beer out of my hand.

The bartender fills the shots until they overflow onto the sticky bar top. Riley expectantly raises his eyebrows at me. Not one to back down from a challenge, I take both of the shots. He nods approvingly, chugging one of the beers before grabbing my bottle.

"Now that you've had some liquid dance lessons..." he prompts, looking longingly toward the dance floor.

"I don't think anyone calls it that, but even if they did, I haven't had nearly enough," I say as the boys and Nellie settle in on our sides, ordering their own drinks.

"And another two shots of tequila," Riley throws in. My jaw

drops. Four shots back-to-back would make me *drunk*. "Don't worry, one is for me." He grins, seeing the surprise on my face.

"Tequila, huh?" Nellie asks. "I thought your go-to drink was a Sauv Blanc with one ice cube." She covers her mouth like she can't believe what just came out of it. "Oh my God, I did *not* mean to say that."

"Don't worry, I'm impressed, if anything." I laugh. "Usually it is, but Riley told me not to drink the wine."

"Smart," she says, catching the beer the bartender slides to her and drinking down half of it in one go. "Sorry, I'm just so nervous right now," she admits. "I've never met a celebrity before."

"You've met me," Riley protests.

"Shut up, you don't count," she quips. "I meant like a *real* celebrity."

"I *am* a real celebrity," Riley huffs. Waylon slaps his shoulder in male solidarity.

"Yeah, yeah, call me when you get to the big leagues," I join in on teasing him.

Nellie cackles. It's so refreshing to meet someone who knows who I am and actually *likes* me for it. I have the feeling that if I told Nellie I killed someone right now, she'd help me hide the body without so much as blinking. It's a good feeling.

Riley just shakes his head in exasperation as the bartender pours our shots. "Drink up, then we'll see if you're all bark and no bite on the dance floor."

"You hear the way he talks to me?" I ask his friends, despite the grin on my face.

"He's despicable," Nellie agrees. "But I am partial to dancing."

"Fine," I say, reluctantly permitting Riley to drag me onto the dance floor.

"How do you plan on dancing with a beer in your hand?"

He holds eye contact as he drains his second beer, setting it on a table on the sideline. "Happy? Don't worry, Willow, we'll do something easy," he adds, reading the hesitation in my face.

"I'm holding you to that," I say, feeling the first hints of alcohol flooding my system.

"Okay. First things first," he declares, gently taking each of my hands. "Take a step in toward my left shoulder, and I'll take a step in toward yours."

"You're sure this is easy?"

"Trust me," he answers. "Now we flip our arms up behind each other's necks..." he garbles out a list of instructions, walking me through it slowly. "And then we can do this," he finishes.

He chuckles at the small yelp that escapes me as he spins me back into him. He grabs my free hand and dips me slightly.

"See?" He smiles. "You're not so bad. Now let's try that again."

I remember the steps well enough that he doesn't need to prompt me this time.

"Good girl," he says as I rise from the little dip. "Now let's add a few more steps onto this..."

After about an hour, we take a quick break to grab more drinks from the bar.

"How come I'm the only one without a hat? That's not right," I say as we walk back onto the dance floor. After more shots of tequila, both of us are properly drunk by now.

"Next time, I'll have to get you a hat to go with the boots."

"What if I just..." I reach for the hat on his head with my free hand.

"I wouldn't do that if I were you," he cautions.

"Why not?" I ask, freezing my hand in midair. "You're not sweaty, are you?"

Riley laughs. "I love that that's your main concern. No, not sweaty." He leans in close to whisper in my ear over the pounding music. "But they say if you take a cowboy's hat, you have to ride the cowboy."

I raise an eyebrow in response as I slowly, deliberately pluck the hat off his head and set it on mine. Riley raises his eyebrows in return and grabs me, and I'm swept into another dance. And the minutes blend into hours as we dance the night away, everything a blur of boots, hats, and neon lights.

It must be well past midnight when we attempt a really wide spin, and I fall flat on my ass, bumping into another man on my way down.

"I'm so sorry," I say to the man as Riley helps me up, insisting it was his fault.

"Clumsy bitch," the man grumbles, rolling his eyes.

"Excuse me?" I ask, genuinely unsure if I heard him right, with the way my head is spinning.

"I said you're a clumsy bitch," the man spits, turning back to his partner. "And apparently deaf, too."

"Oh fuck no," Riley says, grabbing the man's shoulder and forcefully spinning him back around to face us. "Apologize to her."

I suddenly feel much more sober.

"I don't think so. But she sure does have you by the balls, doesn't she?" he sneers. Riley's glaring at the man with pure malice, a look I've never seen him even *close* to making before.

"Riley, it's okay, really," I say, trying to diffuse the situation. "I've been called worse."

This only seems to infuriate Riley more, and he grabs the man by the collar, forcing him onto the tips of his toes. He's still easily a head taller than the guy. "I won't repeat myself again: Apologize. To. Her," he growls.

The man clearly has no self-preservation instinct, as he says, "Or what, you'll—"

Riley punches him in the face before he has a chance to finish the sentence.

"Riley, stop." I try to separate them as the man swings back. Riley dodges but not quite fast enough, and the man's fist grazes his jaw. Riley twists his arm back to throw another punch, but luckily, Waylon runs up and restrains him just in time. Well, restrains him well enough to keep his arm from swinging. Nash comes up not two seconds later and helps, the two of them fully able to hold Riley back.

"I don't know what you did, but I'd probably get the fuck out of here if I were you," Waylon advises the man, who wisely grabs his date and pushes his way toward the back exit, but not without a final sneer in our direction.

"Come on, let's get you home," Nash says to Riley, gently releasing his arm.

"I saw that from across the room," Nellie says, appearing out of nowhere. "What the fuck did he do, Riley?"

Riley spits blood on the floor in answer.

"It was my fault. I knocked into him, and he said something nasty and—"

"Ah. I figured he deserved it. I've never seen Riley throw a punch in his life." Waylon turns his head and looks at a security guard who's slowly approaching us. "But either way, I think we should split before we get kicked out."

"Agreed." Nellie nods, taking advantage of her small body to nimbly cut us a path through the crowd.

* * *

"Where's your first aid kit?" I whisper to Riley as we pass through the threshold of his house, not wanting to wake his parents.

"I think there's one in the upstairs bathroom cabinet," he answers, his first words since he punched that guy.

I lead the way upstairs and enter the narrow bathroom, Riley following. "Willow, it's okay. I can do it myself."

"I want to do it. Let me help you."

He breathes a sad, tormented sigh. "I'm sorry."

"Sit on the edge of the tub," I direct, my emotions so tangled I'm afraid to pull on any thread by saying more.

"I swear I don't have anger issues or alcohol issues or whatever else you're thinking right now. Before tonight, I'd never punched anyone in my life," he laughs mirthlessly.

"I know you don't," I assure him, locating the red pouch in the closet. "You just got...worked up. It happens."

"You deserve better," he says as I turn back to him and meet his eyes. They look even greener than usual since the whites of his eyes are slightly reddened by the alcohol. The despondency that shines through is too much for me to bear right now, so I break eye contact.

I gently lift his right hand and inspect it. "Riley, don't say that. It's okay, really. I forgive you." Just bruised, not broken, thank God. His face, however, is another story. His lip is busted, and his jaw is already slightly discolored.

"Better than me, yes," he continues. "But I really meant better than the way people treat you. When you were so unphased by that guy—when you said you've been called *worse*. I don't know. Something in me just snapped. And by trying to stop the people who bring you down, I ended up becoming one of them. I ruined your night."

"Riley, stop," I demand, lightly dabbing his split lip with an alcohol-soaked pad. He winces, either from my words or the alcohol seeping into his cut. "I had a great time tonight. Some dick calling me a bitch doesn't change that."

"You shouldn't have to put up with that shit."

"As I said, I'm used to it. It hardly phases me anymore."

"That makes it worse."

"Maybe, maybe not."

There's a brief pause while I pack the supplies and put the kit back in the cabinet.

"I don't regret it," he says lowly.

"What?"

"I don't regret hitting that guy. I only regret that Waylon and Nash stopped me from beating him to a pulp."

"Riley," I scold. "That's not you."

He stands. "Maybe it is."

"It's not."

"Maybe it's me around you."

"What does that mean?"

"I don't know." He sighs. "I think I should go to bed before I dig myself deeper."

"Are you sure you're okay?" I ask.

"Are you?"

"Yes. I'll see you tomorrow, Riley," I respond, leaning in to lightly brush my lips against his cheek. "Goodnight."

Chapter 27

Willow

I sleep in the next morning, finally crawling out of bed just before noon. I check my phone and see nothing from Riley, but there are two other texts.

Heena: Your parents told me the news about your mom. I'm so sorry, Will. Want to talk about it? I'll be in LA when you get there tomorrow.

Mom: How's the trip with Riley going? I love you!

I ignore both. I can't think about that right now. Instead, I take a quick shower and throw on a flowy white minidress paired with an oversized denim jacket and the boots Riley gave me. At least I look the part of a normal girl, even if everything except the boots is custom-made couture. No one needs to know that, though. I add a few layered necklaces and rings and a Yankees cap—not quite a cowgirl hat, but it'll do. I'm just finishing up my quick makeup routine when there's a gentle knock on my door.

"Willow? It's Riley," he adds, as if I wouldn't recognize his voice.

I open the door and see him in a similarly country outfit—worn jeans and a sherpa jacket layered over a dark hoodie. My eyes make their way up to his face and catch on his discolored jaw, a dark purple color made even brighter by the midday light streaming in through the blinds in my room.

"I just wanted to see if you were awake. And to apologize again."

"Riley," I say sternly. "If you apologize to me again, I'll *actually* be mad at you. You have nothing to apologize for. I mean, seriously, isn't it every girl's dream to have a big, angry cowboy defending her honor?"

"Well, it's nice to know city girls aren't immune to the country boy charm." He grins back, looking like a weight was lifted off his chest.

"So, what's on the docket for today?" I ask, waving him into the room as I plop down on the side of the bed. He remains standing but takes a few steps into the room.

"I believe I promised you horseback riding," he says. "And as much as I love that dress, I don't think it would be conducive to riding," he adds, daring a look at the lacey hem of the dress, which rode further up my thighs when I sat down.

I smirk and pull the hem up over my hips. Riley quickly averts his eyes at the motion, the tips of his cheeks reddening almost imperceptibly.

"Willow," he warns. "What are you doing?"

"Riley." I laugh. "Look." He does no such thing. "Riley, I'm wearing shorts."

Finally, he looks. An unreadable emotion washes over his face. "See, I can wear this. Perfectly appropriate."

"You have a twisted sense of humor," he answers. "But fair enough. Ready to go, then?"

I nod and we head downstairs. We greet his parents and grab a hasty breakfast, although I suppose it's more of a lunch, before heading out the back door toward the stables. The view from Riley's backyard is *incredible*. There's a large green field dotted with little white flowers, and beyond it lies miles and miles of mountains. I count at least seven different peaks, all reaching up toward the fluffy white clouds. Despite it being March, it's pleasantly warm thanks to the radiance of the sun today.

"Did you grow up riding horses?" I ask as we walk into the stables.

"Yeah, for as long as I can remember," Riley says, leading a chestnut-hued horse out of its stable and starting to tack it up. "This is Lucky. I got her for my tenth birthday." Lucky snorts in response, seeming to affirm the truth of his statement.

"Lucky?"

"Hey, it seemed like a pretty badass name at the time."

"I can't believe you were one of the kids who *actually* got a horse for their birthday," I tease.

"You're one to talk, Willow Jordan." He rolls his eyes good-naturedly. "What did you get, a yacht?"

"Okay, I don't know if I would call it a *yacht*. I mean, it only had a three-person crew."

"Willow."

"I'm kidding!"

"Are you?" he asks, tightening the saddle on Lucky.

I catch myself following the path of his veins from his hands up his forearms before disappearing under his sleeves. I look away, fixing my gaze on Lucky instead.

"Well, it was really more of my dad's gift to himself than a gift for me," I deflect. "I mean, what can an eight-year-old do with a yacht?"

Riley chortles. "You're ridiculous. What was it called, *The Willow?*"

"No, I got to name it. It would have been really weird if I named it after myself."

"Go on," he prompts as he leads out another horse, this one white with tiny brown spots. "What did you name it?"

"*The Seashell Princess*," I mutter.

"What was that?" He definitely heard me. He just wants me to say it with my full chest.

"*The Seashell Princess*," I say louder.

"That's the best thing I've heard in a long time." You'd think all this laughter would hurt Riley's bruised jaw and split lip, but apparently not. "Where is *The Seashell Princess* these days? I think you owe me a trip in return for this one, right?"

"Last I heard, it was being rented out for tours of the Mediterranean. But if you really want to go on it, I could make some calls, I guess." I shrug, trying to see if he's bluffing or not.

"Don't worry about it." He waves me off, giving me my answer. I knew he couldn't give less of a shit about my money. "I think all your luggage would sink such a small boat anyway," he adds with a smirk.

"If my bags didn't, your attitude might," I quip. "Best to leave the poor boat alone and afloat."

"Smart choice. Alright, Duchess is all ready for you. She's my mom's horse, super docile. You'd have to *really* fuck up to have her buck you off." He smiles deviously, patting Duchess before leading both horses out of the stables and into the sunlight. They look beautiful all lit up, Duchess' white coat glowing golden and Lucky's chestnut coat glowing red. Even Riley looks beautiful, his green eyes and blond hair glinting in the light.

"That's reassuring…" I say, walking out toward him and Duchess. She's tall.

"You'll be fine, Willow. I won't let anything happen to you," Riley promises, noticing my trepidation. He helps me into the saddle before mounting Lucky. "First things first—" he instructs "—sit up nice and tall, making sure your weight is balanced. You hold the reins like this." He shows me how he's holding his leather straps in loose fists with his thumbs pointed toward the sky.

I copy him.

"Perfect. Now, to get her walking, gently squeeze her sides with your feet. And to steer, just lightly pull on either side of the reins, depending on which direction you want her to go in. And to stop, just pull back on both sides."

I do as he says, but Duchess doesn't move.

"Why isn't she moving?" I ask.

"It probably has something to do with your iron grip on the reins. Lighten it up a little."

I do as he says and squeeze her sides again. This time, she begins walking after Lucky and Riley towards the woods.

"There you go! You're a natural." He smiles as I catch up to them. "I had a feeling you'd be an exceptional rider," he says in a suggestive tone.

"Riley!"

"Hey, we couldn't have gone horseback riding without me making *one* joke about it. But now it's out of my system."

"Mmhm," I say, not trusting that for a second.

We ride for a few minutes in comfortable silence as I acclimate to the new skill. We trod up a mountain trail, going around a few large curves, up and down a couple of small hills, and even through a shallow stream.

"So," I start, unsure if I should broach the subject but decide to against my better judgment. I've been curious about it since he briefly mentioned it a few weeks ago. "You mentioned that a lot of your album is about an ex."

He groans beside me. "Oh God."

"We don't have to talk about it if you don't want to," I

quickly interject. "Sorry, I don't know why I asked. It's not my place."

"You can ask anything you want to know about me, Willow," he responds. "It's just not the most pleasant topic, is all. But yeah, most of it was about Claire, my ex-girlfriend. We started dating our junior year of college. She's...an interesting character."

"What do you mean?"

"She was very pretty. I mean, clearly no competition to you." He lifts a corner of his mouth.

"Riley."

"But she was very pretty," he continues. "She was from Charlotte and the only child of two really successful, wealthy business people. And she had such confidence and conviction. Like, when Claire said something, people *listened*. She had tons of friends and was even the class president of our entire year at App State."

"Okay."

"And she was super interested in me. So I started going out with her. Why not, right? But then, after a few months, things started getting pretty serious. We were always together, and I couldn't go anywhere social without her, or else she'd freak out."

"That doesn't sound healthy," I comment.

"It wasn't. At the time, I just thought we were in love or some twisted version of it. I had never really had a real girlfriend before, only little flings. So I thought this was just how it went.

"But then she started going to things without me. In fact, several times, she would bring other men along as her 'dates' to events. Like, I remember her bringing someone else to her dad's company Christmas party and again to a debutante ball in her hometown. She told me that these guys were just friends and that she just didn't want to trouble me with going back to Charlotte with her for these events...and I believed her. Even though she would have *never* let it fly if I had tried going somewhere without her, much less with a date."

"That's awful."

"It gets worse. Then she started getting drunk and saying shit to me. The first time she said anything really mean was one night when we were out with a pretty big group, and she called me 'white trash' in front of all of them and then laughed it off like it was a joke. Then, another night, she admitted she didn't bring me home because her parents would be ashamed of her for dating me. Then, she started saying this stuff while she was sober. She said that my accent made me sound stupid and tried to convince me to train it out. Once, she acted genuinely surprised that I knew how to read because I was raised in the country. And she had seen me read many, *many* times. I mean, we were in *classes together*."

I'm surprised my skin hasn't literally caught fire with the way my blood is boiling. "She sounds like an absolute cunt," I say, unable to piece together any other words.

Riley chuckles and raises his eyebrows at my language. "Yeah, maybe she is. I was blind to it for a long time, though. I kept making excuses for her behavior. That she was drunk, she didn't mean it. The list of things I'd tell myself was a mile long. But yeah, that's the story. I'm sure you're so glad you asked," he adds drily.

"I'm glad you told me," I say as our horses climb a mild incline. "And I'm sorry that you had to go through that."

"It's alright. I got a hit album out of it, right?" he jokes, trying to add some levity to the conversation.

"Still. You didn't deserve a single second of that. She shouldn't have taken advantage of your good heart like that. She abused your kindness."

"No, but it's alright," he dismisses.

"I know nothing I can say about it would make much of a difference...but I think it speaks volumes about your character that you were able to stay kind and trusting, even after an experience like that. It only reflects poorly on her character, not yours. It takes strength to remain soft."

"Thank you, Willow. It means a lot," he says candidly.

"How long were you with her?"

"A year and a half."

"God, if I ever meet her, it's *on sight*," I seethe.

"She'd probably try to befriend you. You being famous and all. In fact, she's texted me a few times since my music career took off, trying to get back together."

"I hope you blocked her."

"I did one better. I changed my number."

"Good for you."

"We should probably head back," he says, and we turn back the way we came. "I have something else planned for us tonight." He grins deviously.

"No riding involved?"

"Probably not, unfortunately." He laughs.

POP CULTURE PULSE PODCAST

Caroline: We have some breaking news to report on today's episode, guys.

Jenna: Yeah, it's really sad, so prepare yourselves.

Caroline: Today, the Jordan Family's representative released a statement reading: "It is with a heavy heart that we share the news that Isabelle has been diagnosed with stage three lung cancer. She is doing well and in good spirits, beginning aggressive treatment within the week. She and Robert will remain based in LA for the time being to complete the film that they're currently producing, at the request of Isabelle. The family asks for privacy and prayers during this sensitive time, and they will hopefully return to you soon with better news."

Jenna: That's awful. Have any of the individual family members spoken on it?

Caroline: Nope. Radio silence.

Chapter 28

Willow

After dinner with Riley's parents, the two of us climb into his truck and begin our drive to an unknown location.

"You really won't tell me where we're going?" I ask about thirty minutes into the drive for the millionth time.

He glances sideways at me, smiling. "Nope."

"I really hope you're not about to murder me."

"I wouldn't murder you." He furrows his eyebrows. "You're way too high profile. Somebody would come looking for you, for sure."

He pulls the car over into an unlit turnoff.

"This really seems like a murder spot."

"You're ridiculous," he says, hopping out. I follow suit, meeting him at the back of the truck, which is full of blankets and pillows.

"This has taken a sharp turn from scary to romantic," I say as he helps me climb up.

"I thought you might want to see the stars without all that light pollution, city girl," he says. "But if you don't want to, that's fine. We can do something else."

"No, sorry, I'll stop whining. Let's stay," I say, settling into the blankets and looking up at the sky. "This is incredible," I breathe, awestruck by the thousands of stars I can see, not to mention the literal belt of the Milky Way. I don't think I've ever seen the night sky like this in all twenty-two years of my life.

"It's one of the best spots in the country for stargazing, light pollution-wise," Riley says, reading my mind. He climbs in next to me, keeping a respectable distance. "My parents have been taking us here since we were kids."

"I can see why."

We lie in silence for a while before Riley finally breaks it. "What are you thinking about?"

"I'm wondering if anyone else is staring back at us," I answer.

"Like in a God way or in an alien way?"

I chuckle lightly. "I guess both. But I meant in a God way."

"What do you think?"

"I like to think someone is looking out for us. I don't know, though. If there is a God, I can't help but think he must be a pretty sick fuck."

"There's still plenty of good in the world," Riley presses.

"But sometimes it feels like there's just as much bad, if not more," I reply. "What about you? Do you believe in God?"

"Most days."

I feel inclined to agree. I turn my head away from the stars and toward him, taking in the beauty of his profile. He does the same. His hair is slightly tousled, and maybe it's the dim lighting, but his face seems extra-chiseled right now, his nose and cheekbones looking like they were carved from marble. His bottom lip is slightly swollen from where I know a bruise lays on his jaw, obscured by the near-dark. Even with a punch to the face, he's obscenely attractive.

"Can I ask you something?" he asks, tenderly brushing a piece of hair out of my eyes and behind my ear. "You don't have to answer, but I feel the need to ask." He lets his hand linger a second longer than necessary before he pulls it back.

"Sure," I whisper, already missing the contact of his fingers against my skin.

"I heard about your mom earlier today. Are you okay?"

I pause. I don't know what I was expecting, but it wasn't that.

"How could I be?" I sigh after a few seconds of silence. "I don't know. I haven't really unpacked it yet."

"Do you want to?" he asks gently.

"I don't know—maybe." I turn back toward the night sky. Riley does the same, tucking his arms behind his head, giving me the time to piece together my thoughts. "I was researching all night when I first learned about it. They say—they say it's more deadly than breast cancer, colon cancer, and prostate cancer combined. But, they caught it fairly early, the tumor is pretty small, and it's only in one lung."

"That's good," he offers.

"She hasn't had any severe symptoms yet. And I'm planning to be there for her surgery tomorrow to remove the tumor and chemo to hopefully wipe out the rest...but even then, the survival rates are low. It said—" I take in a shaky breath of pine-laden fresh air. "It said she has a one in three chance of seeing another five years."

Riley inhales sharply next to me. He must not have known the prognosis was so bad. "One in three isn't unheard of. She'll pull through, Willow," he assures me with a steady voice. "She will."

"And if she doesn't?" I conjure up the nerve to ask.

"Then you'll cross that road when you come to it. But no

use worrying over something that may not even happen, right? You'll just drive yourself crazy."

"Yeah."

We sit in silence for a few minutes before a thought pops into my head, and I start laughing uncontrollably. A nervous Riley turns to face me, concern written all over his face.

"The funny thing is—" I continue laughing, "—she never smoked. *She never smoked a single fucking cigarette.*"

The laugh quickly turns into a sob, and to my horror, I don't even have half a mind to be embarrassed. I can't think of anything except the fact that my beautiful mother, my role model, my likeness, is slowly dying from the inside out.

"Willow," Riley says, his voice cracking as he sits upright and pulls me tightly against him. "I'm so sorry," he whispers, stroking my hair as I cry into his chest.

"It's not fair," I cry.

"It's not," he agrees.

He holds me like that until I finally seem to have cried myself dry.

I sniff and sit up, realizing that a section of his hoodie is now soaked through with my tears. "I'm sorry," I say as I try to rub it away. Riley grabs my hand in his to stop me.

"Don't apologize," he says. "I'm always here for you, Willow."

"I ruined such a beautiful night," I say.

"You didn't," he insists, wiping a rogue tear off of my cheek. Neither of us has let go of the other's hand.

"This is like the exact same argument we were in last night, but with the roles reversed," I comment as I study his face.

"I guess we're predictable," he replies.

"Thank you for the great trip, Riley, really. It was just what I needed." I take a centering breath, trying to collect myself.

"Thank you for coming. I just wish you didn't have to go so soon."

"I wish I didn't have to, either. Maybe I'll come visit you on tour. See if you can actually sing live." I force a smile, trying to lighten the mood.

Riley chuckles, his face dangerously close to mine. "I'd like that."

I tip my head a little, angling my lips millimeters away from his.

"Willow," he cautions. "Are you sure this is a good idea?"

"No," I answer. "But I want it anyway." As if weighing all the outcomes in his head, he doesn't move. "Please, Riley," I whisper. "Distract me."

"Fuck it," he mumbles, closing the distance between us.

Our lips meet slowly, tentatively. I feel a spark travel from my lips and down my body—that's never happened to me before from just a kiss. My hand moves to rest on Riley's shoulder, and his moves to the back of my neck, pulling me closer. The kiss quickly becomes more desperate, as if he feels the same need that I do. Despite the chilly air, my skin feels like it's on fire. I slip off my jacket one arm at a time, keeping a hand on Riley at all times for fear of what will happen when I let go. He takes advantage of my motion, sliding me fully horizontal beneath him with one fluid motion. I run my hands through his hair, down his back, and back up again as he rests one hand on my waist and uses the other to hold his weight above me. And we make out like a couple of kids, neither of us pushing for more until I eventually come to my senses and reluctantly pull back.

This was *a bad idea. Because I don't think I'll ever be able to kiss anyone else again after knowing it could be like this. For me, kissing is usually just something you do before sex. I've never actually enjoyed it as though it's the main event. Like I just felt kissing Riley....*

"Riley," I pant. "We shouldn't be doing this."

He chuckles lightly, resting his head in the crook of my neck. "I know," he says.

"I have too much going on right now. I can't...I can't commit to anything with you. And I don't want to give you the wrong idea."

"I know," he repeats, rolling to the side and lying beside me. His eyes are semi-glazed, sated from the kiss. "No pressure."

"I think we should just stay friends for now. At least until things calm down a little. I mean, with me traveling all the time, you touring, and my mom sick—"

"It's okay," Riley assures me. "I understand, really, I do. You have enough on your plate right now. We're just friends, Willow Jordan."

"Just friends," I agree, my lips tingling in protest.

Chapter 29

Riley

*H*oly *shit*. I was up half the night replaying that kiss...I feel like a teenager again, obsessing over the tiniest bit of contact. But I can't help it when I just had the best kiss of my life by far. I mean, the second her lips met mine, I was instantly hard, using every ounce of self-control I had to keep my hands from roaming all over her body. Even now the thought of her still has me feeling some type of way.

But I knew I was working on borrowed time last night. Willow's not into me, and she has made that very, *very* clear any time something even remotely romantic happens. I mean, she broke away from the greatest kiss I've ever had to tell me that it was a mistake. I get it, though. Why would she be into me when she could have literally any man on Earth? I'll just have to do my best to swallow my feelings for her.

The morning after the kiss, Willow and I wake up early to head for the airport. It's a short drive, and we arrive just as the sun begins to peak out above the horizon, coloring the sky in vibrant shades of orange and pink. I pull up to a back gate where we're waved in and directed to pull up next to her family's jet.

A bodyguard is already at the side of our car, helping Willow out.

"I'm going to miss you," I say as I exit the car and help the guard get her bags out the back.

"I'm going to miss you too, Riley," she says, her light hair reflecting the orange-hued sky. "But we'll text. And call. And I think I owe you a luxurious, fame-soaked weekend, right?"

"Right." I laugh. "As long as it's aboard *The Seashell Princess*."

She fights a grin. "I never should have told you about that."

"You really shouldn't have. I'm not going to let you live that down. And you better come to one of my shows, too. Normal people go to concerts."

Willow laughs. "No arguing with that. I guess I have to, then."

"I'll see you soon," I say, pulling her into my arms. She hugs back tightly, holding on for a few seconds longer than is standard. Not that I mind.

"Soon," she echoes as we separate, running a hand through her long hair absentmindedly, completely unaware of the effect it has on me. "Thank your parents again for me, will you?" she asks as she begins walking backward toward the plane.

"Of course," I say as she turns her back to me, fully walking away now. I watch as she climbs the stairs to the jet. As if she feels my eyes following her, she turns and gives me one last smile before disappearing inside.

* * *

"Son." My dad peers over the top of his newspaper as I walk into the kitchen. "You could have mentioned that your little friend was *the daughter of Isabelle and Robert Jordan*."

"I'm sorry. I would have told you, but I didn't know if she

wanted you to know or not. She's understandably a little wary of telling people who she is."

"Oh, Riley," my mom says, sitting beside my dad, "you know we wouldn't have treated her any differently. But I understand."

"I know you wouldn't have. But still, I left it up to her to tell you. I'm sorry."

"There's nothing to apologize for. Well, besides the near heart attack I had when she said her mother was Isabelle Jordan. But truly, she was absolutely lovely," says Mom.

I laugh, grabbing a seat at the table and loading some pancakes onto my plate. I'm not surprised that they made a whole feast while I was busy dropping Willow off.

"Sorry about the shock. I'm impressed you recognized her, though."

"She's the spitting image of Isabelle. Anyone who read tabloids in the nineties would have noticed."

"You're very astute, honey," Dad says, kissing her on the cheek.

"So, you're not having sex, are you?" my mom asks me suddenly. I almost choke on my pancakes.

"No, we're not. Gross, Mom."

"Did you just call Willow Jordan *gross*?"

"*No*, I called you prying into my sex life gross."

"Good, I was about to get your eyes checked," Mom replies. Dad is staying tactfully quiet throughout this exchange. "So, why *aren't* you having sex? You two sure seemed all over each other..."

She gives my dad a knowing look. I roll my eyes. They must have been talking about us before I walked in.

I shrug, taking another bite. "She's not interested in me."

"I think she is," Mom counters. "The way she looks at you...that's how I looked at your dad."

"*Looked?* Past tense?" My dad quirks the corner of his mouth. "I'm pretty sure you still look at me like that. In fact, you had that look last night when I was—"

"*Ew*, guys, stop." I scrunch my face in disgust. "I'm trying to eat here."

My mom cackles. "Riley, don't be such a prude. She likes you. I think you should go for it."

"I've tried...well, not anything big, but I've made little moves. She pushes me away half the time, and the other half she clarifies that we're just friends...repeatedly. So I'm taking that as a pretty big hint that she's not interested."

"It sounds like she's trying to remind herself of that more than she's trying to remind you."

I sigh, getting up from the table. "Don't give me false hope, Ma."

"Where are you off to?" she asks.

"I'm going on a long, long ride to erase this entire conversation from my memory. See you later," I say as I slip out the back door.

Minutes later, Lucky and I trot toward the mountain trail I took Willow on, the same trail I first learned to ride on years ago. I didn't even bother to put a saddle on her today, which Lucky seems thrilled by. She's a good sport with saddles, but she really prefers to go without one.

"I've missed you, Lucky," I tell the horse as if she can understand. To her credit, she swishes her tail behind us as if she missed me too. "It's weird being on tour. I mean, singing my songs every night is amazing. And literally every venue has been sold out. I'm living every kid's dream. I'm living *my* dream. But it's just a little...I don't know. It's lonelier than I thought it would be. I don't know why I'm complaining.

"I have great friends, tons of fans, and an incredible career. But I miss this. I miss you, I miss the mountains, I miss the general store, I miss the accents, but most of all, I miss the people."

I take in a deep breath of the forest air that I woke up thinking about while on tour.

We veer off the trail, sneaking down a back entrance to the giant apple orchard a few miles from my house. Lucky speeds up until we're galloping through the rows and rows of trees, just like we used to do when I was in high school. I throw my head back and laugh, stretching my arms out between the giant trunks while riding bareback, maybe just to prove to myself that I can still do it. I missed *this*.

Eventually, we slow down and head back toward the trail. I hop off and stretch my legs, giving Lucky a chance to take a drink of water from a stream. I lean against a tree, admiring the way the dappled light makes her chestnut coat glow.

For some reason, that horse has a crazy affinity for stream water. As if she can read my mind, she makes a snort of approval as she drinks and I laugh, snapping a photo of her.

"I really like her," I muse, my mind wandering to the joy written on Willow's face yesterday when we were riding. "And a small part of me dares to think that maybe there's a tiny possibility that she might like me back. I mean, she did ask me to kiss her...she was so upset, though. Maybe she would have asked anyone." I pause. "But that *kiss*. It was so good. But I don't think she felt the same. But how could she not have felt that? What do you think, Lucky?"

No answer. I don't know what I was expecting.

"Maybe her being busy is an excuse. I mean, the two of us will always be busy with the nature of our jobs. She was probably just letting me down easy. But, to be fair, she's dealing with a lot of personal stuff right now, so I can definitely see that truly being an issue for her, right now specifically." I sigh. "Or maybe I have false hope, and the truth is that she's just not that interested in me. I'm not surprised that she isn't. I mean, I'm sure the girl is used to dating billionaires, models, A-List actors, and all-around high-class guys. That's not me. We're not very evenly matched. But that doesn't stop me from wishing."

Snapping me out of it, Lucky lifts her neck from the stream and gives her mane a shake.

"Ready to go?" I ask. To my surprise, she walks over and gently drops her head onto my shoulder, melting my heart. She stays there for a few seconds before she chuffs and walks away, giving me a look over her shoulder that says, *If you tell anyone I missed you, I'll kill you.*

I chuckle. "I missed you too, Lucky."

Chapter 30

Willow

I arrive at the hospital in LA around 11 a.m. Tito meets me at the hospital entrance and escorts me to my mom's room. My mom's surgery is scheduled for 2 p.m., so I have a little time to spend with her before she goes under.

I open the door and am pleasantly surprised by the size of the private hospital room. It doesn't feel too crowded despite being occupied by my parents, sisters, and Heena.

"Willow, thank God you're here." My mom rises from her bed as I enter. "They're hovering over me like I'm a newborn baby."

"Hey, Mom," I say, giving her a tight hug. "How are you feeling?"

"Not you too." My mom groans. "They haven't cut into me yet. I've heard that the feeling-bad part comes *after* the cutting-me-open part."

Behind her, my dad rolls his eyes affectionately.

"Hey, Will," Heena says, giving me a hug. My Dad, Aspen, and Maple follow suit.

"How was your trip?" my mom asks. "I looked up your little

singer this morning. You didn't mention that he looks like he belongs on the cover of GQ."

"Mom! It was fun. But we're just friends."

"Why? He's unnaturally attractive, Willow. Do we need to get your eyes checked?"

Despite myself, I laugh. "He's very cute, yes."

"Then what's the issue? Does he have a girlfriend? Surely you're prettier than her," she tsks. Heena laughs, and my mom grins at her. "See, Heena gets it."

"No girlfriend, Mom. We're both just so busy. He's on tour, and I'm all over the place anyway."

"That didn't stop your father and I," she responds. "When we first started dating, I was a full-time model, and he was a big-time director." She pauses before adding, "You don't think he's...small...do you?"

My dad coughs, but the rest of us laugh. Words can't even describe how grateful I am to see that she hasn't lost her usual good spirits.

"I wouldn't know, Mom." I touch my chin reflectively. "But I hope not."

The color leaves my dad's face as the women laugh.

"Then what's wrong with him?" Mom demands.

"Can't we have this conversation when you're not about to have surgery?"

Mom sighs dramatically. "But there's nothing else interesting to talk about, and I have hours before they'll take me back."

"Mom, I think Dad will actually combust if we start talking about boys in here."

"There's too much estrogen in here as it is," my dad jests.

"See?"

"Fine. But I want you there when I wake up, Willow. To continue this with your poor, sick mother."

"Mom," Aspen scolds. "Don't say that."

"Don't worry, honey, I was just joking. I plan on beating this thing with record speed."

"Good," Maple says.

"So, Aspen. Any boys on your radar?"

* * *

All of us handle the wait while my mom's in surgery differently. Aspen is pacing the hospital room. Maple is writing an essay for school. My dad is pouring himself into his work, making phone call after phone call. Heena left the hospital entirely, saying she needed to go on a drive and blast some music. And I am social-media-stalking Riley. I've never done it before, so it's a treasure trove for killing time.

I start with his Instagram since that seems like his favorite way to stalk me. First up is a photo of Lucky drinking from a mountain stream, posted earlier today. I guess he went on a morning ride after he dropped me off—cute. Next up is a photo of him on tour, looking exceptionally attractive. I zoom in on his bare arms and try not to stare. The next post is where things get interesting. I put my earbuds in to listen to the video, one of him singing backstage, hunched over an acoustic guitar.

"*An angel in the flesh, enough to still Da Vinci's brush,*" he begins the first verse. I listen to it all the way through, then replay the video. The chorus ends with, "*She stole my heart and its keys, but I got away with the masterpiece.*"

Holy shit was I wrong to doubt this man's live vocals. He sounds phenomenal, somehow even better than his studio versions.

Am I vain to hope that this song is about me? I mean, as far as he's told me, the only other alternative is Claire. Unless he has someone else? I feel a twinge of jealousy pang through my chest at either possibility. There's no way it's about Claire. And he would have told me if there was someone else, right? Especially since I asked him to kiss me. I open up the comments.

Janie_Whelan: WHO'S THIS ABOUT???

Riley.Coleman.Fan2: RILEY MARRY ME UR SO HOT

thee_vegan_baker: "SHE STOLE MY HEART AND ITS KEYS BUT I GOT AWAY WITH THE MASTERPIECE"???!!! OKAY SLAY KING

EthanBoone: thanks, I need to change my panties now.

I laugh out loud at the last one. I recognize his friend Ethan—Riley has mentioned him often enough. Apparently, he's quite the ladies' man, and I can see why. He's funny.

I keep scrolling, passing more tour and songwriting photos, eventually returning to his pre-fame college photos. There's one particular photo of him grinning boyishly in a backward baseball cap at what must be a frat party. I'm ashamed to admit what frat-boy-Riley does to me. No wonder Claire was into him—despite apparently hating everything else about him. That bitch.

I glance to the top of my phone to see the time—I've been stalking him for almost an hour—when I see he's *live right now*. Without thinking, I click on his live.

He's sitting at his desk at home, a guitar in his lap, seemingly doing some Q&A thing with the 18,000 or so fans who've joined. Someone must have noticed me pop in because all the comments are now reporting to each other that I've joined the video.

"Willow Jordan has joined?" Riley asks, reading the chat. "Who's that?"

I think the stress of my mom's surgery has gotten to me, as I find myself typing, "Did you ever find the right rash cream?"

Riley laughs, seeing the chat. "Okay, whoever Willow Jordan is, you're funny," he says.

The chat goes crazy, some people claiming we're friends or dating while others are exasperatedly trying to explain to him who I am. Then they start asking about my mom. Mercifully, Riley changes the subject, strumming on his guitar and asking the fans what song they want to hear. I remain for the rest of the stream, too enraptured to exit, but don't say anything else.

After the livestream ends about an hour later, I make a post with some B-Reel photos from fashion month, keeping myself occupied by scrolling through my camera roll.

Tired of staring at my phone and hearing Aspen's incessant pacing, I decide to kill two birds with one stone. "Aspen," I say, and she instantly stops. "Want to go grab some food or a coffee or something with me? I'm sick of being cooped up in here."

"Sure," Aspen says, seemingly relieved to be given something else to do, as if she didn't even consider that not-pacing-for-hours was an option.

We head down to the cafeteria and scan the options. Luckily, most people are too distracted by their own health concerns or those of relatives to pay much attention to us. Except the actual hospital staff, who—to their credit—are trying hard not to stare. We both end up buying fruit cups before sitting at a window table.

"How are you doing?" I ask her.

"I'm good," she says, giving me a smile that's clearly fake—I'm fluent in Aspen's facial expressions.

"How are you really?" I ask again. "And don't say you're fine because I'm pretty sure you just wore the tread off your shoes in there."

"I'm okay." She shrugs. "I mean, Mom getting sick isn't

helping my nerves or anything. But I have a therapist now, and she's been helping me through a lot of it. She told me to try focusing my energy on the future and lining something up for after *Fairview Ridge* wraps up. So I've been sending out feelers to different producers and directors, trying to see what else is out there."

"That's great! So you like her, she's good?"

"She's good." Aspen moves a strawberry back and forth in her fruit cup. "She's nice and funny but definitely has her shit together. She's young, like mid-thirties, so I think she understands a lot of what I talk to her about. And she has little kids at home, so she does most of her work over video call, which is great for my schedule." She pauses. "I'm sorry again about scaring you the other week."

"Oh please, you know you're always free to call me about anything."

"I know." She gives a small smile. "But I still feel guilty for doing it."

"Don't. Are you thinking of doing more TV, or do you want to pivot into film?"

"I'm thinking film," she says. "It's not as big of a commitment, and it's something new."

"I think that would be great for you," I say earnestly. "I want a ticket to all of your premieres. And Oscar ceremonies."

Aspen laughs. "As if we're not always invited to the Oscars anyway because of Dad."

"It would be different if it was for you. I bet you could beat Dad's record, too."

"You mean, get more than three Oscars?"

"Yep. There's at least ten with your name on them."

"You're delusional. I'd be happy to even get one."

"Hey, you already have an Emmy. It shouldn't be that hard to get an Oscar."

She waves me off. "An Emmy for lead actress on a drama series is hardly an Oscar."

"Aspen, you're ridiculous. I wish you could hear yourself talk, sometimes." I shake my head, grinning. "*I only won an Emmy for Best Actress*," I mock.

"What," she protests, knowing exactly 'what.' "Enough about me. How was your trip with Riley?"

"It was so much fun," I gush. "We went to a dive bar, horseback riding, stargazing, and I got to meet his parents and some of his friends. It was nice to be a regular girl for a couple of days, you know?"

"Believe me, I get it. That must have been so great." Her mouth morphs into a smirk. "You like him."

"I don't."

"You do. I can read Willow as well as you can read Aspen," she says, fully smiling now. "You're smiling. You totally like him!"

"I'm only smiling because you're crazy. I don't like him."

"Fine, you don't. But would it be so bad if you did?"

I sigh. "Aspen, the press would tear him to shreds, you know that. They hate me."

"They don't *hate* you."

"They hate me. I'm like their 'mean girl' scapegoat or something."

"They're just jealous."

"Then why do they love you? If they're jealous of me, they'd be jealous of you. We have practically the same face."

"Because you're a world-famous supermodel, and I'm just an actress on a shitty teen drama."

"Aspen."

"What? It's true."

"Your 'shitty teen drama' is one of the highest-grossing TV shows of all time."

She shrugs. "Either way, they're just jealous of you."

"And either way, they'd turn their backs on Riley if we started dating, and you know it."

"You could keep it secret."

"That seems like hiding, and I don't think either one of us would want to do that. I mean, we'd be in a *relationship*, not robbing banks. We shouldn't have to hide it."

"Then don't. Maybe they'll be better to Riley than you think."

"Nah. No way."

"Maybe you should let Riley make that decision himself. If seeing you is worth the media scrutiny. You might be surprised by his answer."

"But what if *I* don't want him to go through that? The media loves him right now, and I can't be the one to shatter that. I know what it's like to have the entire world shit on you, and Riley is one of the least-deserving people of that on the planet. He's been through enough already," I add quietly. Aspen raises her eyebrows in interest, but I wave her off. "Not my place to tell."

"Fair enough. I see what you mean. It's something to think about, though, at least. Anyway, we should probably head back up. I think Mom should be coming out in a few minutes."

"Sure. She'll be okay, Aspen," I voice as we stand.

"I know." Aspen smiles tightly.

We both throw out our uneaten fruit cups on the way back up.

Chapter 31

Riley

After I strum the last note for sound check, I turn to the band and take out my earplugs, about to say something when I hear someone clapping and whooping from the pit. The lights turn down, and my eyes land on...my eyes—well, Olivia's eyes, but they look pretty identical to mine.

"Holy shit! Liv!" I call, jumping off the stage and running to meet her, engulfing her in a huge hug that lifts her off her feet. "When did you get here? *How* did you get in here? Why didn't you tell me you were coming? Are you staying for the show?" I ask in rapid succession.

"Slow down." Olivia laughs. "And set me down," she adds, patting my arm for emphasis.

I set her down, and *wow*, I almost forgot how much shorter she is than me. I mean, Liv's not necessarily short, but she's certainly not tall. She likes to joke that I got all the height genes since she only comes up to my shoulder.

"One: I got here like twenty minutes ago. Two: Nash helped arrange for me to come and surprise you. And three: yes, dummy, I'm staying." She rolls her eyes lightheartedly. "My

Strike a Pose

little brother is on a sold-out national tour. I needed to come and see what all the hype is about."

"Well, I'm glad you could make it." I smile. "Come on, let's head backstage. I have a pre-show meet-and-greet starting in fifteen." We walk to the entrance of the backstage area, where I abruptly stop. "Oh shit," I curse, clapping my hand on my forehead for emphasis. "Did Nash get you backstage tickets?"

"Uh," Olivia starts. "I don't think so...?"

"Shit, then you can't come back here. You'll just have to wait out there for a few hours until the show starts."

Olivia looks stricken. "Are you serious?"

"Yeah, Liv. I'm so sorry. I'd sit out here with you, but I have that pre-show meet-and-greet I need to get to."

"Oh," she says. "Oh, okay then, I guess I'll just catch up with you after the show, then," she offers, trying (and failing) to cover the disappointment on her face.

"I'm just kidding. Jeez, Liv, I'm the star here," I tease. "Of course I can bring you backstage."

"You *dick!*" she cries, hitting my arm. "I thought you were serious."

"You should've seen your face. You looked so sad. It *almost* made me feel bad for lying. It's nice to know you want to hang out with me, Liv."

"Please, I just want to see the backstage setup. I couldn't care less about you," she stabs back, strolling backstage ahead of me and blindly taking a right.

"It's a left," I call, and she chuckles as she does a one-eighty.

We meet my band at the cozy little couch in the area below the stage. "Liv!" Waylon calls, throwing his arms around his cousin. "Why didn't you tell me you were coming?"

"It was a surprise." Liv laughs, clawing free of Waylon's embrace. "I missed you, too."

Nash and Ethan take turns greeting her, and then she spots the buffet spread out behind us.

"Is all of this for you guys?"

"Yep," I answer. "Take whatever you want."

"This is *awesome*," she exclaims, taking a paper plate and loading it so high that it strains under the weight of all the food crammed onto it. "I should've been a musician."

"It's just mini-subs and chips," I scoff. "You're easy to impress."

"Hey, between vet school and college, I'm on year seven of ramen noodles and PB&Js. This is the height of luxury for me."

"Jesus, Liv, let me Venmo you some money so you can get a real meal every now and then." I crinkle my brow. I didn't know she was so strapped for cash.

"Yeah, you owe me after paying eight hundred dollars for a front-row ticket tonight."

My pulse spikes, and I turn to Nash. "You made her *pay*?"

Olivia laughs as Nash throws his hands up. "No, man, I got her a free ticket."

"I'm just playing with you, Riley. Nash is right. He gave me a free ticket. I would never *pay* to see you. Although, it's encouraging that so many people do, huh? And that eight hundred dollars wasn't a lie. I checked this morning, and front-row tickets were up to twelve hundred a pop for tonight."

Ethan whistles. "That's insane."

"No kidding," Liv answers. "It's never been a better time to be Riley Coleman's sister." I chuckle, and she adds, "No, I'm serious. I mean, not that I advertise it or anything. That would be weird. But the other day, my lab partner saw my last name was Coleman and jokingly asked if I was related to Riley Coleman. When I said, 'Yes, he's my brother,' his eyes just about popped out of his head. It was pretty funny...but now he spends every lab, for the entire lab, asking about you. It's getting weird. I genuinely think he might have a secret altar to you or something."

Waylon chuckles. "That's Riley, our little heartthrob."

I roll my eyes.

"Seriously, that part is a little weird, though. Riley, once a thirst trap of you came up on my feed. It was absolutely disgusting," Liv says.

"You watched it?" Ethan laughs.

"Well, I was curious what the people see in him," she jests. "But then I reported the video as a scam, so luckily, the algorithm has adjusted to not show me any more similar videos."

"A scam?" I laugh. "Liv, these abs aren't a scam. They're perfectly real."

"Ew," she whines. "Stop it, you're disturbing me."

"Liv, if you think *that's* disturbing, Riley is totally boning Willow Jordan," Waylon adds.

"I am not!" I interject at the same time Olivia excitedly exclaims, "No way!"

"He totally is," Ethan adds.

I look to Nash, who bashfully shrugs.

"Don't believe them. We're just friends."

"Since when are you *friends* with *Willow Fucking Jordan?*" Liv asks.

"It didn't look like you were just friends when you were all over each other on that dance floor back home," Waylon says dubiously.

"I was just teaching the girl how to dance," I defend.

"*Willow Jordan* was the girl you brought home? Mom told me you brought someone, but for some reason, she didn't feel the need to specify that it was *Willow Jordan.*"

"Guys, can we please stop yelling, 'Willow Jordan.' Someone's going to overhear."

"Overhear that you're fucking Willow Jordan?" Ethan suggests loudly.

"No."

"Then why are you nervous someone will overhear?"

"Because...ugh. You guys are so annoying."

"And you weren't just 'teaching her how to dance,'" Waylon scoffs, completely ignoring my pleas for them to stop. "Liv, they were *all over* each other. She was wearing his hat, for Christ's sake."

"She was wearing your hat?" Liv squeals. "Riley, that's pretty damning."

"She didn't know what she was doing," I insist.

"Oh, yes she did." Waylon laughs. "That girl knew what she was doing. Or what about when you roundhouse-punched that guy to defend her honor? You should've seen it, Liv. It was straight out of a movie or something."

"Woah, woah, woah, you *punched someone* to defend *Willow Jordan*? Who the fuck are you?" Liv asks with a smile big enough to take up half her face. "Oh my God, she would make such an awesome sister-in-law. I bet she'd hook me up with the coolest clothes. Although, if she's interested in you, I'm beginning to question her taste."

"Alright, alright, that's enough. I was serious about that meet and greet. I need to go. Y'all have fun here. I'll be back in an hour or so. Try not to make Willow's ears ring too badly while I'm gone," I call over my shoulder as I walk out.

This is going to be a long night.

* * *

I was right—we were up so late that we saw the sunrise in Jacksonville. But I had a full night's sleep last night and I'm feeling plenty energized as I walk out onto the stage in Charleston, greeted by roaring cheers.

I do my typical little "I'm so glad to be here, thanks for coming out, etc." speech before jumping into my first song. After that song ends, I begin talking into the mic again. "So, I was here a few weeks ago. Well, I was in Kiawah. I was picking up a *friend*," I emphasize, looking sideways at Waylon, who smirks back at me. "Who was staying there, and I met the greatest guy. He told me he was a huge fan and that he would be at this show. Tim, if you're here, can you yell out?" I ask, taking off my earplugs.

I hear a shout from the left side of the crowd. "Sorry, could we try that again, but with the lights down so that I can see?" I ask. "And y'all, can we all point to Tim so I can find him?"

The lights go down, and I hear another yell, the crowd pointing to Tim.

"Tim!" I call.

"Hi, Riley!" he calls back, cupping his hands around his mouth to amplify his voice.

"I remember you told me you had all my songs memorized. What do you say you come up here and help me play one?" I offer, grinning.

Tim cheers, lifting both his arms in the air triumphantly.

"Alright, so I'm going to take that as a yes." I laugh. "Can we create a path so Tim can come up here? Thanks, guys, y'all are the best."

Tim makes his way up to the front of the crowd and climbs onstage with the help of a boost from a few security guards and my outstretched hand hauling him up. The crowd cheers as he straightens up next to me. Tim is grinning from ear to ear.

"Thanks for helping me out, man," I greet him with a masculine handshake.

"No problem, I know you needed the help," Tim jokes, and the crowd laughs.

"See, guys, I told you he was great. So, what do you want to play?"

"Anything?"

"Anything. Well, preferably something from my album, but hell, if you want to play some Skynyrd or something, we could do that too."

Tim chuckles. "Can we do 'Don't Tell Me'?" he asks, naming one of my punchiest songs.

"Fuck yeah, man," I say as a sound tech brings out another mic and a guitar for Tim.

The crowd goes wild.

Chapter 32

Willow

The good news is that Mom's surgery went well. The bad news is that she couldn't really talk for the first day or so...but I guess that's to be expected after lung surgery. Visiting hours ended shortly after Mom woke up that first night, so the rest of us—even Aspen, who has her own place in LA—went home to my parents' rented penthouse in the city. A few days after the surgery, Mom was able to come home. We spent the next couple of weeks taking turns fussing over her until it was time for chemotherapy.

"I'm canceling the photo shoot," I tell Mom, sitting on the couch next to where she reclines, her feet resting on me.

"Willow Elizabeth Jordan, if you cancel your *tropical Sports Illustrated shoot* to sit in a musty hospital with me, I will be absolutely livid. I'll tell the nurses that you're not even allowed to come into the room to sit with me. You'll be cooped up like you have been for the past two weeks. Please, Willow. Go."

"But I–"

"Willow. Are you seriously going to disobey your sick mother? You've done enough damage by arguing this with me and raising my blood pressure. Get in your room and start packing right this second. You need to leave tonight," she demands. My mom rarely gets serious, but I can tell she means business right now. She wants me gone.

"Mom, I want to be here with you, I want to help."

"I know," she says, softening her tone. "But there's nothing you can do to help. And I'll be damned if my little bump in the road gets in the way of you living your life. You've been here two weeks, Willow, and it means the world to me. But please, *please* don't put your life on hold for me. If you really wanted to make me feel better, you'd go. I can't stand the thought of holding all of you up."

"You're not holding us up. We want to be here," I say, holding her hand.

"Send me pictures of the water," she says, squeezing my hand. "It'll motivate me because your father promised me that when this whole thing is over, we'll take a big family vacation anywhere I want to go to celebrate."

"Okay," I say, trying to push back the tears threatening to spill over my eyes. "But even if I resume modeling, I'll be back to check in on you every week or so."

"Willow, honey, that's a lot on you. You don't have to. I'll be fine, I *promise you*."

"I know you will be." I nod. "I'll see you in a week, okay?"

"I can't wait to hear all about it." She smiles. "Little Willow on the cover of *Sports Illustrated*," she says merrily.

* * *

Forty-eight hours later, I'm on the beach of Turks and Caicos in a tiny white string bikini. I arrived yesterday, and the crew spent all day preening over me—massaging, exfoliating, tanning, manicuring...the list goes on and on. Then, before dawn this morning, they plucked my brows, expertly applied a

Strike a Pose

full face of "natural" makeup (including some fake freckles to make me seem more beachy), and then I had a fitting and lighting check.

"Let's try both hands in your hair, really mess it up a bit," the shoot director calls. "You're doing great, Willow."

I smile tightly and run my hands through my hair, tousling it. "More teeth, give us a real smile," the director calls. I do as he asks, cycling through a few different poses, all with my hands in my hair.

"Alright, let's get some seated ones. Well, actually let's start with you on your knees, legs spread a little. And give us more of a serious look. Perfect," he says as I follow directions.

After about thirty more minutes of that, I switch bikinis behind a flimsy little tent and we resume the shoot for a few more hours.

"Alright." The director smiles. "I think we have everything we need. Great job, Willow, you were an absolute vision."

"Thanks."

There are a few other models who were shooting simultaneously with me (although I have the cover spread), and we all go out to dinner together. I'm wrapped in a towel, sitting on a picnic bench eating fish tacos, when my phone lights up with a call from Riley. With my mom being sick, we haven't had much time to talk over the past couple of weeks, so I excuse myself from the table and pick up.

"Hey," I answer as I walk down the narrow beach access.

"Hey. How are you?" he asks.

"I'm alright. How's being back on tour?"

"It's great." I can hear the smile in his voice. "We're on the bus again, driving to Nashville. Last night, we played Atlanta, which was a blast. Oh, and a few nights before that, we played Jacksonville, and my sister surprised me. It was great."

"Aw, I'm so glad." My mood instantly lifts tenfold. "How is she?"

"She's great. I'm so glad she was able to catch a show. Your turn to watch one next."

"I will, I promise."

And I mean it. As soon as I get back to LA and check in with my family, I plan on figuring out when I'm free to see one of his shows. Even though his tour is sold out, I'm sure Riley could get me a ticket, or I could buy a scalped one if need be.

"How's your mom? Still doing well? And how's the Caribbean?"

"She's doing well, yeah. I called her earlier this morning, and she seemed happy. She started chemo yesterday, and she said it went well. But I know she feels like shit and is just putting on a brave face. I'll go back and check in with her in a few days. *Sports Illustrated* gave us all a few extra days to spend lounging around the resort, and my mom said, and I quote, 'The thought of you leaving free beach days on the table makes me sicker than any cancer.' So, since she made it very clear that I can't show my face back to LA until my free beach days are over, Heena is flying out to stay with me here for a few days tomorrow morning."

"That's tough. But I guess there are worse places to be banished to," he offers.

"Very true. Did you get any time on the beach while you were in Florida?" I ask, plopping down in the sand, close enough to the water that the waves lap at my feet.

"Yeah, I did. Finally got some color back. Although, unfortunately, nobody paid *me* to spend the day at the beach."

"Maybe you should explore your options. Find a rich Floridian sugar momma who'll pay you to lounge next to her all day."

Riley laughs. "If my next album flops, that's the plan."

"I'm sure it won't. I heard that song you posted on your Instagram the other day. If that's on the album, I'm sure it'll go triple platinum."

"Eh. I just had a good muse."

"Claire?" I ask reluctantly.

"What?" his brows bunch together, as if he's both offended and amused. "No, Willow, it's about you."

"Oh."

"Oh?"

"So you think I'm a masterpiece?" I tease, twirling my hair around my finger even though he can't see me.

"Doesn't everyone?"

I laugh. "You're great for my ego. I'm keeping you."

"Your ego needs a boost?"

"Every now and then, sure. I'm flattered, really. I'm going to add that to my resume: Superstar Riley Coleman's muse."

Riley laughs in my ear, making me grin as I run my fingers through the wet sand, disrupting it and then smoothing it back over. "Remind me to never write you another song," he says.

"I can remind you all I want, but something tells me you'll write another just to spite me."

"Probably."

Wow, I didn't expect him to agree with me. Suddenly, my stomach is full of butterflies. Addicted to the feeling of Riley's admiration, I get an idea to keep it going.

"On another note, I already got some proofs back from the shoot today. Want to help me narrow down the general idea of which one should be the cover shot?"

"You get to choose your own cover photo?"

"Sort of. It's a team effort. The photo gets approval from both the magazine and from me and my team. Want to see?"

"Sure."

I send a few photos over. One of me standing in a red one-piece with enough cut-outs to be skimpier than most bikinis, one of me kneeling in the surf in the tiny white string bikini, and one of me laying on my side in the same tiny string bikini, but in black.

"Did you get them?" I ask after a few seconds of silence on Riley's end.

"Yeah," he answers, his voice a full octave deeper than usual.

Mission accomplished.

"I sort of like the white one," I goad. The white one is definitely the most seductive in style, pose, and facial expression.

"That one's good," he responds, his voice still gravelly. "I like the water in that one."

The water, I kick my feet, practically giggling out loud.

"That's the differentiator? Because I have shots of the other two suits in the water, too."

"I like everything about that one," he corrects. "But I also like the other two...I mean *Jesus,* Willow."

"What?" I ask innocently.

"How do you *look* like that? You're like...from another planet, I swear."

"In a good way?" I fish. I'm almost ashamed of myself, but my inner-Heena is telling me to embrace the narcissism.

"In a great way. If I were you, I don't think I'd ever leave the house. I'd be glued to the mirror all day admiring myself."

A deep laugh escapes me. "Be so for real, Riley."

"I swear to God, Willow, I would. I'd also never touch a piece of clothing ever again."

"I think I'd probably get arrested."

"No way. Everyone would be too awestruck to arrest you."

"Maybe I'll have to try it sometime."

"Give me a call when you do. I'll come watch and see what happens. Purely for science."

"Of course. So, you don't think my tits look better in the red suit?"

Wow, I really must be possessed by Heena today.

"Willow," he groans. "I'm begging you, don't *ask* me to look at your tits."

"Why not? It's really important. It's for the cover."

"Do you want the honest answer?"

"Always."

"Because I'm hard as a rock, and I'm genuinely worried I'll come in my pants if I look at your tits again."

"Riley!" I laugh. "*Again?*"

"Willow. I'm a man. How could I *not* look? It's genuinely mortifying how turned on I am from a photo."

"Well, technically, it was three photos. Maybe one of the guys could help you out with your little...issue."

I laugh wickedly.

"Hey, watch what you call little, Willow Jordan."

"Or what, you'll come? I didn't peg you for a degradation guy, but hey, I'm not one to kink shame."

"Okay, I'm hanging up with you now." I can just tell he's shaking his head at me through the phone.

"To go jerk off?"

"I mean, yeah," he says. "Bye, Willow."

I laugh, hanging up. "Have fun."

On the way back to my room, I can't stop giggling to myself, thinking back over our conversation. And when I get there, I lock the door, grab my vibrator, and pull up some of my favorite thirst traps of Riley...it's only fair.

Chapter 33

Willow

The next morning, I'm lying on the beach listening to Riley's music while I wait for Heena's flight to land. I've listened to it a few times before, but after my trip with him and getting to know him better, the lyrics are particularly painful. For example, the opening track is just Riley and a guitar, and his voice is full of emotion as he sings:

You hate my questions,
    My lack of connections
    And you hate my backwoods roots
    You hate my accent and wish that I'd drop it,
    Along with my cowboy boots
    You never liked my friends,
    So baby you tell me how this ends
    When you tell me you love me do you even mean it
    Or are you just playing pretend

. . .

I mean, seriously, it's enough to make my chest physically hurt for him. That girl, Claire, is a monster. Soon enough, I'm struck by another song called "I Believe You."

And you tell me in private
    When I kiss you and you like it
    That you'd rather love than fight
    That he's just a friend and nothing happened
    When you brought him home last weekend
    You say I'm being crazy, that's why you didn't bring me
    And I believed you

I pull out my phone and text Riley.
    Me: did you write your whole album yourself?
He responds in seconds.
    Riley: Yep.
    Riley: Listening to it?
    Me: ...no
    Riley: Mhm. I can't wait to be the top artist on your Spotify Wrapped
    Riley: Thanks for the support, I love my fans <3

I chuckle, feeling a little less sorry for him now. Not knowing how to respond to that, I toss my phone aside in favor of the romance book I brought. I flip it open and get lost in it, uninterrupted for a couple of hours until a figure plops down next to me in the sand.

"Whatcha reading?" Heena asks.

"Just some trashy romance," I say, closing the book. "How was your flight?"

"It was good. I texted you when I landed, but I guess you were occupied by...*Hockey House*," she says, reading the title of my book. "So, I tracked your location."

"At least my stalker's pretty," I laugh. "How's my mom?"

"She's doing well. She told me to tell you to stop worrying about her, though. She knew it would be the first thing you asked." Heena smiles. "She also instructed me not to let you leave this island, under any circumstances, until your free stay is up. And she made me promise to take you out clubbing."

"That's all?" I joke, hearing my mom's laundry list of demands.

"Well, she also told me to send her tons of photos," Heena adds. "And she's tough to argue with, so I guess we're going clubbing later. I ran into a few other models on the way out here, and they seemed more than eager to have us come out with them tonight."

I hold back a smile. While the other models have been nice and gracious to me over the past couple of days, I can tell they're all incredibly nervous around me. I've walked with most of them on runways before, but they still struggle to make small talk with me, as though they're afraid I'll bite. But I get it—I'm a lot more famous than most of them, I'm known as a 'mean girl,' and my mom has cancer. Any one of those things would be enough to make someone nervous, let alone all three. Nonetheless, I'm excited that they invited Heena and I to hang out with them tonight.

* * *

Later that night, Heena and I strut past the flimsy saloon-style swinging doors and into the bar, where the other girls told us to meet them. Immediately, all eyes turn to us, and a couple of the models break off from the group to greet us.

"Hi guys, we're so glad you could make it," Shu-Fen, a Taiwanese model a few years older than us, says, air-kissing us both on the cheeks.

"Of course. Thank you for inviting us," I respond as we approach the gathered group of girls.

"No problem, we're happy you're here. You looked fantastic yesterday. I saw some of the proofs, and *wow*, they're going to look great in print. And you look great now, too, of course. You too, Heena," Shu-Fen adds.

"Thanks, Shu-Fen." I grin down at my skintight floral minidress. "You also look great tonight," I say, genuinely appreciating her bright orange dress. "And I meant to tell you, you looked great walking the Stella runway in London. Seriously *amazing*."

"Thank you," she says, her cheeks tinting slightly. "I didn't know you knew my name, to be honest."

Heena laughs. "Willow knows everyone. That girl's like an elephant, she never forgets a face. What are we drinking?"

Another model in the group grins deviously, holding up a pitcher and saying, "Long Island iced teas."

"Oh, God." Heena pretends to gag. "Seriously?"

"Sounds like a fun night." I laugh. "I'm down. Heena, you want one?"

"If I *have* to."

I have a love-hate relationship with Long Island iced teas: they get you plastered, but they usually taste like gasoline. An hour into sipping on our pitchers, Heena and I are spinning, literally and mentally. The club is full of rotating colored lights, complete with a disco ball, which only adds to the disorientation.

"You're so pretty," Heena tells me, throwing her head back

and laughing as we grip each other and spin on the dance floor. "Let me take your photo and post you. I need people to see how pretty my best friend is."

"Fine. But only if I can post one of you too."

We take turns snapping pictures of each other, but for some reason, we can't stop giggling, so it takes *way* longer than it should to take a few decent photos—not to mention we can't figure out where our camera apps are. The majority of the photos we take are extremely blurry.

"If you want, I could take a photo of the both of you," Shu-Fen offers, appearing out of nowhere.

"Ohmigod, that would be perfect!" I hear myself cheer. "Wait, Shu-Fen, get in here with us. Hold on one sec," I say before running up to the bartender and asking him to take our photo.

"Everyone, get in! Group photo!" Heena motions the other girls into the photo.

The bartender snaps a few before handing me the phone back. I manage to send the photos to everyone before Heena and I begin cackling to each other about God-knows-what on the dance floor again.

A couple of hours later, I feel my phone incessantly vibrating. I pull it out of my pocket and am disappointed to see the screen lit up with a photo of my dad. I don't know why, but I thought it might have been Riley calling me.

"Hey, Dad," I say, picking up. Then I realize I can't hear anything on his end over the pounding music. I leave through a side door, dragging Heena out with me. "Dad?" I ask again.

"Will? Hey, can you hear me?"

"Yep, what's up." I try not to slur. "How's Mom?" I ask, suddenly realizing it's probably not a good sign that he's calling me after midnight. "Is she okay?"

"Your mom's fine," he assures me, but something in his tone is off. His voice sounds...tight.

"What's wrong, then?"

"It's Aspen," he says. My heart drops into my stomach.

"Put it on speaker," Heena whispers, seeing my stunned expression.

I do as she says, and we both cling to every word my dad says next. "She—she had a bit of a...I don't know how to put this."

"Dad! Is she okay?"

"She had a breakdown, Will." The way my world rocks has nothing to do with the pitcher of Long Island Iced Tea I drank.

"A bad one," Dad continues. "She and Maple were helping your mom today while I was on set, and apparently, it wasn't a good day for Mom. She was really sick. And then, mid-afternoon, Maple called me. She was frantic, saying that Aspen couldn't stop crying and hyperventilating and could hardly form coherent sentences. I booked it to the house and drove Aspen to the hospital.

"The ER docs said she was having a bad panic attack. They contacted her therapist and a psychiatrist and gave her a choice between doing intensive outpatient treatment, meaning an hour of therapy every day until they deem her stable enough to cut it back, or a short stint in the hospital's in-patient center. Aspen chose the in-patient center."

Heena and I look at each other over the phone. I open and close my mouth several times, seemingly having lost the ability to speak.

"How long will she be there for?" Heena asks my dad, stepping up for me.

"A week," he answers. "It could be longer, but probably a

week. They're going to get her on medication and give her group and individual counseling."

"Can she see visitors?" Heena asks.

"Not for the first twenty-four hours. She should be good to see people by seven p.m. tomorrow. She only gets one hour for visitors."

"Send the jet to us," I manage to get out, my voice hoarse. "We're leaving for LA first thing in the morning."

"No, you girls should stay there, at least until early afternoon. There's no point in coming home before then, anyway," I hear my mom weakly interject on the other side.

The poor woman has been sick all day, and now this...it sends a strong stab of guilt through my chest.

"No, we're coming back. I never should have left."

"Willow, this isn't your fault," my mom soothes.

"Either way, I'll be there tomorrow morning," I say, with tears I didn't realize I was crying dripping onto my wrist. "I'm coming back."

"Okay," my mom whispers, as though she's given up fighting me. "We look forward to seeing you tomorrow, then."

I sniffle. "I love you."

"Oh, Willow. We love you too."

"So much," my dad adds.

"And you too, Heena," my mom says.

"And Heena," Dad echoes. "We'll see you girls tomorrow, alright? Chug some water and have some ibuprofen before you go to sleep, yeah?"

"Okay. Goodnight," I say, not even wanting to know how drunk I must sound if he added that last part.

"Come on, let's get back to your room," Heena says, letting me lean on her for the short walk back.

POP CULTURE PULSE PODCAST

Caroline: So we have some breaking news to talk about today.

Jenna: Yeah, and it's so sad so brace yourselves.

Caroline: According to multiple sources, Aspen Jordan was checked into an in-patient psychiatric ward last night.

Jenna: Apparently, the poor girl had a full-on mental breakdown. You know, I truly feel so much sympathy for her. She's only twenty, her TV show is ending, and her mom has cancer. I mean, when I was twenty, I was having breakdowns every other day, and all I had to worry about was passing my classes and whether whatever frat boy I was hooking up with at the time was seeing other girls. It's a really difficult time for anyone, let alone if your career and mom are both dying.

Caroline: I know. It's awful. On the other hand, Willow Jordan is completely unbothered, having the time of her life on some tropical island. She really must be a callous bitch.

Jenna: Oooh, what do you mean? I haven't heard about that.

Caroline: Well, yesterday she posted some photos from some *Sports Illustrated* swimsuit shoot on a tropical island. And then last night, as poor Aspen was having a breakdown, Willow went clubbing with her model friends.

Jenna: That's just awful. Doesn't she have any concern for her family? Why would she even do that shoot in the first place? She should be with her mom right now. I can't even imagine Aspen's stress from being ditched by Willow, left to take care of their sick mother all alone. Maybe Willow's leaving contributed to Aspen's breakdown.

Caroline: Yeah, it's pretty pathetic to see where her priorities lie. She'd rather slut it up on an island than put on some real clothes and tend to her sick mother. It's really fucked up.

Jenna: Well, what did we expect? It's Willow Jordan. She's always acted like that. She's one of the most selfish, narcissistic people in the industry.

Caroline: Still, it's a new low. Even for her.

Jenna: Well, let's all send supportive energy Aspen's way. The poor girl needs it. Hopefully we'll have some updates to bring you on her condition soon.

Caroline: Let's move back to Riley Coleman. I know a few weeks ago, we asked you guys to figure out who he's seeing right now, and so far, *no one* has been able to figure it out. Whoever it is, they're keeping it very tight-lipped...

Chapter 34

Willow

At precisely 7 p.m. the next day, I hug Aspen tighter than a drowning man clinging to a life preserver, and I don't let go. She grips me back just as desperately, and a muffled sob escapes my lips.

"I thought you were doing better," I choke out.

She sighs, still clinging to me. "I was."

"What happened? Why didn't you call me? I would have dropped everything and come back the second you even hinted that you were feeling overwhelmed, Aspen, I swear it. I only left because Mom insisted, and I thought I'd disappoint her if I didn't go, and I wasn't thinking enough about you or Maple or what you'd—"

"Willow," Aspen says, gently prying herself free from my grasp. "This isn't your fault."

"If I wouldn't have left, you wouldn't have been under so much pressure."

"Nothing you could have done would have made a difference. Really, Willow, please believe that," she reassures me earnestly, her blue eyes searching mine.

"You're actually feeling better?" I ask, looking her up and down as if her injuries were physical.

She's wearing flimsy blue scrubs and grippy socks, hair loose down her back. I can't tell if she looks especially thin or if my eyes are just playing tricks on me.

"I am." She gives me a small smile. "Stop worrying, Willow, it'll give you wrinkles."

"I'll gladly be wrinkled for you."

Aspen good-naturedly rolls her eyes before moving to hug Heena, who was respectfully standing back to give us a moment together. My parents were able to talk to Aspen on the phone earlier this afternoon, and despite their protests, she insisted that they stay home tonight and not come to see her since Mom still isn't feeling very well. Maple wanted to come but had tutoring scheduled for tonight, so she'll just come with us when we visit again tomorrow.

Maple hasn't been back to school in person in New York since Mom got sick, and even though her school has been accommodating these past few weeks, there's only so much that they can do from afar to help her keep up—so her tutoring sessions are pretty imperative. So, it's just Heena and me tonight.

"I'm so glad to hear that you're feeling better." Heena breathes a sigh of relief into Aspen's shoulder. "We were so worried."

"I promise, I'm feeling a lot better. In a weird way, it helps to finally have a game plan for how to deal with this. For the longest time, I just tried to shove my feelings down and pretend they weren't there. I guess if this is what it took for me to finally seek serious help, then it was a good thing in the long run."

"What is the plan?" I ask. "For when you come home?"

"Well, I was officially diagnosed with generalized anxiety

and panic disorder. But the doctors told me both are definitely manageable with medication and therapy. Today, I started on a medication that should help, but it won't start working for a few weeks because it needs to build up in my system. Until it's fully effective, they're going to have me do daily therapy, then cut back as they see fit once the medicine helps take a little of the weight off. And I think being here for a week will help me too. I like the group therapy sessions. It's nice to see other people struggling too—as fucked up as that sounds."

"I don't think that's fucked up at all," Heena says. "And I know it probably doesn't mean much, but I really admire that you sought help, Aspen. It's a hard thing to do."

"Coming from the bravest person I know, it means a lot, Heena." Aspen reaches for Heena's hand. "Thank you, truly. But enough about me and this stuffy place, I want to hear about the *Sports Illustrated* shoot."

And so we catch up, the hour flying by in what seems like minutes. Eventually, a nurse comes out and informs us that visiting hours are over. But then we all flash our trademark "we're famous and pretty, please do us a favor" smiles, and she grants us an extra ten minutes.

* * *

Six days later, Aspen is home, and Mom is feeling a lot better. So, obviously, a girls' day is in order, beginning with mani-pedis. Normally we call someone to the house for in-home services. But today, both Mom and Aspen are anxious to get out. So instead, we rent out a nearby salon for the morning—it would be a security nightmare if the five of us just walked in somewhere open to the public.

"I'm torn between white and this bright blue color," I say, holding two shades up to Maple.

"White," she answers definitively.

"Mmm, I think I want the blue," I say. "But thanks for helping me realize that."

"Why did you even ask if you're just going to make the decision yourself?" she huffs.

"Because I needed you to say something so that I could see what my reaction was. And my reaction was 'No, I want blue.'"

"Well, which of these should I get?" she asks, holding up two identical shades of black.

"The one on the left."

"Too bad, I'm doing the one on the right." She smirks, putting the left back. But then she hesitates to let it go.

"You liar, you want the left."

Maple narrows her eyes at me and slyly switches the shades so that the left one is now in her right hand. "Nope, I'm going with the right one."

"Maple, I saw you switch those."

"Whatever." She grins. "You get the point. It's annoying."

"I don't think I got the point at all, seeing as you chose the one I picked."

Maple just rolls her eyes and walks away, plopping down in the chair next to Mom.

"Teenagers," Aspen snarks, sidling up next to me. "I like the blue. That'll be pretty."

"Thanks. What are you doing?"

"I think I'm going with 'Ballet Slipper.' Classy, you know?"

"Ugh." Heena gags. "I've walked a hundred too many runways where they have my nails painted and repainted in various shades of light pink. Maple's got the right idea. I'm doing black."

We take our seats, and the staff begins to work on our nails.

"So, you guys will never guess what happened to me last week in New York," Heena says to all of us.

"What happened?"

"I was having dinner with some guy from the Jets—"

"Where?" my mom asks. She knows that Heena only goes out to the nicest places with the most desired men.

Heena's approach to dating is pretty much the exact opposite of mine. While I tend to keep a low profile, keeping my dates few, far between, and private, Heena doesn't mind her love life being in the public eye. But it actually works in her favor because since she goes on so many dates with so many men, the press doesn't even bother keeping up with her anymore. Meanwhile, the second I'm spotted in the mere *vicinity* of a man, the press is on me like flies on honey.

"We were at Zero Bond." Heena shrugs as though that isn't one of the most exclusive spots in the city. "But guess what he told me."

"What?" my mom asks, perched on the edge of her seat. She lives for Heena's dating drama since the rest of us don't have much to offer.

"He asked me what I gave up for Lent, and I told him that I wasn't religious, so I didn't give up anything. And then he kept harping on the issue, practically begging me to ask him what he gave up. So finally, I bite, and ask what he gave up. And he says he gave up *masturbation*."

We all burst out laughing. Even our nail ladies pause their filing for a split second to giggle. One of the qualities I admire the most about Heena is that she's so authentically herself. Because when Heena says something, she means it. She doesn't care who knows. She doesn't wait to say things in private. She'll unabashedly say them in public. And although we ensured that no other customers would be here, we're still very much in public, as the salon is buzzing with nail technicians.

"And that's not even the best part," Heena continues. "He then proceeded to tell me, in the middle of the very crowded restaurant, that *it doesn't count if someone does it for him.*"

"Was he gunning for an under-the-table handy?" Maple asks, eyes wide.

"Maple!" my mom scolds halfheartedly.

Heena laughs. "He totally was."

"What did you say?" I ask, knowing damn well Heena would never do that.

"I suggested that maybe one of his teammates could help him out," she responds with a smirk. "And then I ordered another drink and three desserts only to take a single bite of each. It's the penance God would have wanted for him."

"You didn't go home with him afterward, did you?" Aspen asks.

"No way. He didn't get so much as a kiss on the cheek." Heena laughs. "He didn't deserve anything. So, instead, I called up a guy I know on the Giants and went over to his place."

Aspen's jaw goes slack.

"What! A girl has needs. And I was already all dolled up and prepared for a fun night. And going for a Giants player after denying a Jets player was just too funny an idea to pass up. And, by the way, the Giants player thought the whole 'giving up masturbation for Lent' story was *hilarious.*"

"You told him?" Maple asks.

"Oh, of course. Come on, that guy forfeited his right to privacy when he told me something so heinous."

Maple raises her eyebrows appreciatively. "I like your style, Heena."

"Thank you."

"Heena, you need to help me set up Willow. She never dates," my mom says, grabbing a tabloid off a side table and flipping through it.

"I don't think so," I interject.

"Why not?"

"Because I don't like public dates. Everyone stares, and it makes my skin crawl."

"Then you could go on a private date. What about this guy? He's very handsome." She points to a photo of Grey Aldridge on the set of James Bond.

I roll my eyes. "I like that you set your sights so high."

"Oh, come on, Willow. You're the most famous model in the world. You could bag anyone, including him."

"I could *bag*? Mom, who taught you that?"

"That was me," Maple answers sheepishly. "We've been spending a lot of time together, okay? Mom made me teach her Gen Z slang one night."

As Mom laughs in her chair, Heena slyly points to her phone. I check mine.

Heena: Do you not want to go out with anyone because of Riley?

I told her all about our weekend together while in Turks and Caicos, including our kiss and my maybe-feelings.

Me: ...maybe

"Isabelle, I don't think Grey is her type. I could set her up myself in New York if you want."

"If he's not her type, then I'm disappointed by her taste." Mom raises her eyebrows. "But, Heena, that would be incredible. When are you girls going back?"

"I need to be back in a week and a half for a Vanity Fair panel I'm going to be on." Heena answers. "I could set her up, then. I know you have to be in New York to shoot that perfume ad anyway, Will."

. . .

"I don't think so." I shake my head. "I was going to cancel that shoot. The last time I agreed to leave, I was called back because you had another emergency. I'm not going to leave you guys again when you need me."

"Just a couple of days," Heena urges, pleading with me through her eyes. *Trust me*, her look says.

"Willow, I think you should go," Mom says. "You'll have the entire week to be cooped up in LA with us. And as much as we love having you here, I promise we'll manage just fine without you. In fact, I have a live-in nurse starting tomorrow to help take some of the load off of everyone."

"Seriously, Willy, a couple of days is nothing. You should go. I'll be fine too," Aspen agrees. "I'm going back to set next week anyway. My doctors said I should resume the normal pace of life. You should, too."

"We'll be fine," Maple adds on.

"Please go," Mom insists. "Really, it would only make me feel worse if you put your life on hold for me, Willow. I know I keep saying it and that you probably don't believe me, but it's *true*. And you can always come back and visit as often as you want."

"Fine," I reluctantly agree. "But I'm only leaving for a couple of days at a time. At least for now. And the *second* there's any trouble at home, I want you to send the plane and call me immediately," I warn, narrowing my eyes. "You promise?"

Mom nods. "I promise."

"Me too," Aspen agrees.

My gaze shifts to Maple. "I promise, too," she concurs.

"Yay! One hot date for Willow, coming right up." Heena grins deviously.

Chapter 35
Riley

Unknown Number: Hey it's Heena Badahl
Me: Proof?
A photo of an all-business Heena holding today's newspaper comes through. Damn, she's intimidating.

"Hey, Ethan, look at this." I tilt the phone toward him. Currently, the guys and I are getting drunk on a boat in the waterways surrounding Virginia Beach, where we're playing a show tomorrow night.

"No fucking way," Ethan says over my shoulder, jaw practically on the floor.

Heena: I see Willow taught you a thing or two.
Me: Haha. Yes. What's up?
Heena: I noticed you're playing in New York next week. What are the odds you could get me two tickets?
Me: Wow, Heena, I didn't know you were such a fan. Want an autograph, too? Don't worry, I won't tell anybody that you're a secret fangirl.

"Dude, she's not going to like that," Ethan warns.
Heena: 😑

Heena: I was going to surprise Willow with them, jackass. But nevermind, I think I'll surprise her with tickets to a Knicks game. I know Lance Davies has a huge crush on her, he'll hook me up with floor seats.

"See, I told you." Ethan laughs. "Fuck, Lance Davies? Good luck competing with him, dude. That guy drops panties like nobody's business."

"It's true," Nash adds from behind the boat's comically large wheel. "He's slept with Seraphine De Luca *and* Isolde Vega. That's the type of power that guy has."

"And he's like seven feet tall, isn't he?" Waylon adds, cracking open another beer.

"Y'all shut up, or I'll push you overboard," I growl, sending Heena two VIP tickets for my Brooklyn show next week as fast as humanly possible.

Luckily, there's some wiggle room in ticket numbers for each show so that the guys and I are able to squeeze in a few guests of our own if need be.

Me: So you don't want an autograph, then?

Heena: Nope. Thanks for the tickets, though. I'll text you when we get to the venue.

Ethan claps me on the back before fishing another beer out of the cooler for me. "At least she said thank you."

"Are we seriously going to ignore the fact that Willow's best friend thinks that taking her to see *you* is a good surprise for her?" Waylon asks.

"I wasn't going to think on it too hard. We're friends, and we haven't seen each other in a month. It makes sense. To be honest, I'm just relieved. I really wanted her to be there, but I didn't ask because I didn't want to pressure her to leave her family since both her mom and sister need her. In fact, I really haven't even talked to her since she had to rush home for Aspen."

"Well, it seems Heena pressured her on your behalf," Ethan says. "Maybe Heena deserves a surprise of her own for that, right?"

"Are you the surprise in question?" I narrow my brows.

"You certainly aren't," he scoffs. "Yes, me."

Waylon smirks. "You know, I think I could be into her."

"Don't you dare, Waylon," Ethan warns, his tone dangerous.

"I don't know." Waylon's eyes glitter with mischief. "She looked amazing in that bikini she posted the other day."

"Last warning, dude," Ethan threatens.

Nash brings the boat to an idle, seemingly sensing what will happen next.

"I'm just saying, her tits looked *great*. Do you think those are real or—" Waylon grunts as Ethan body checks him hard enough that the two of them fly off the boat into the water.

"Ethan!" Waylon gasps. "I can't—" He flails his arms as his head dips below the surface. "I can't swim!"

"Really?" Ethan asks, shaking his wet hair out of his eyes as he treads water.

"Does it look like I'm joking?" Waylon cries, ineffectually splashing frantically.

"Fuck, man, why wouldn't you *mention* that before you got on a boat?" Ethan rants as he swims over to Waylon and hooks his arm around his chest.

"That would make me a real idiot, wouldn't it?" Waylon grins, turning swiftly in Ethan's arm, pushing his head under the water.

"Guys," Nash calls from the boat. "Stop that."

I knew Waylon could swim—hell, we did swim team together as kids—but I was enjoying the show too much to warn Ethan. Even now, I'm not trying to stop it. I know neither of them would ever actually hurt the other.

"You dick! I was trying to save you," Ethan shouts, popping back up and wasting no time in trying to push Waylon under.

My phone buzzes, dragging my gaze away from the two fools in the water.

Willow: hi

Me: What's up?

Willow: sorry i haven't had much time to talk recently. i've been busy with family stuff

Me: Don't worry about it, you don't have to explain yourself. How is everything, if you don't mind me asking.

Willow: everyone's doing much better than they were a week ago, lol

Willow: also, just to clarify, my mom begged me to go to that shoot. i didn't want to leave them

Me: I never thought otherwise. Again, you don't have to explain yourself to me, Willow. I know you :)

Willow: well, i've seen what the tabloids are saying and just wanted to make sure you know it wasn't like that

Me: I know

Willow: but guess what

Me: What?

Willow: my mom is getting a nurse and my entire family practically begged me to get out of their hair and back to modeling. soooo i'm going to be in new york next week

Not wanting to give away the surprise, I don't mention my show there at the same time.

Me: Oh, no way! That'll be so fun. What are you modeling for?

**Willow: a perfume ad. but that's not the point lol. i

Strike a Pose

saw you have a show in brooklyn at the same time i'll be in the city

Me: Does it align? Maybe we'll have to meet up

I feel like an asshole typing that, but I really don't want to give the surprise away. I text Heena, asking what I should do.

Me: Willow just texted me asking about my show in NYC next week, saying she'll be there at the same time

Me: Should I spoil the surprise or be the ultimate dick and tell her it's completely sold out?

Heena: Tell her it's sold out. Her face will be worth it, I promise.

Heena: Tell her you could do dinner instead or something to soften the blow?

Me: 👍

I swipe back to my chat with Willow.

Willow: yes it lines up perfectly! do you have any extra tickets?

Me: Ugh I wish. It's sold out.

Technically, that's not a lie. The show is sold out to the public. I just have access to a few extra tickets.

Me: You know if I did, they'd be all yours.

That's also not necessarily a lie. The tickets I have *are* hers, she just doesn't know it yet.

Me: I'll be in the city the night before my show, too. Maybe we could get dinner or something?

Me: Also, I have another two-week break two weeks after the Brooklyn show. Maybe we could pencil in the "luxurious, fame-soaked weekend" you promised me?

Fuck, I'm over-texting now. Damn guilt.

Willow: it's okay

Willow: dinner sounds good. i can order it to my family's place and you can just meet me there. any requests?

Willow: and yes, i am down to show you a bougie weekend. first weekend of may?

Me: Perfect, I'll be there. And I eat anything lol you should know this by now.

Willow: joe's pizza it is!

Me: I look forward to it :)

Chapter 36

Willow

A little over a week later, Heena and I are walking through the door of my family's Manhattan penthouse, three bodyguards in tow. Normally, I'd yearn to be free of the guards, but I'm grateful for them today since they're extra hands to hold all the stuff I bought for dinner and sprucing up the place.

"You can just set it all on the counter," I say, placing my own bags on the huge marble island.

"Are you sure you don't want us to stay?" Justin asks.

He's worked for me sparingly throughout the last year or so, only working when I was doing something high-profile enough that Tito alone wasn't enough (like fashion month). Now, he's a new permanent fixture in my life as my second full-time guard.

Heena's guard, Cole, met us at the penthouse. While she shared my guards with me today, she's going out tonight and needed someone to accompany her. Cole must be relatively new, because I think I'd remember a face that attractive. Even among Heena's Rolodex of notoriously hot bodyguards, he stands out above the others.

"No," I reply to Justin's concern. "Don't be ridiculous. Riley's above suspicion."

Justin shrugs. "Hey, your dad would kill us if we didn't at least offer."

"Well, lucky for you, I'm not my dad. I let you go home and enjoy your night." I reach for the giant bouquet I bought today to make the penthouse feel more alive and pluck out two vibrant white roses. "For Anna." I give one to Justin "And Lucía." I hand the other to Tito.

"Thank you, Willow," Tito says, grinning broader than the small gesture warrants.

"You're welcome. Now get out of my sight," I joke, pushing the two giants toward the door.

"Hey, where's my rose?" Cole asks Heena when I return to the kitchen.

"You didn't walk all over the city today carrying our shit," Heena responds.

"So, no rose then?"

"Here." Heena plucks a rose and hands it to him. "If you want to hold on to that all night, feel free."

Cole tucks it into his shirt pocket, smirking. "Thanks."

"Mhm. Let's get out of here. We're meeting Zac Schwartz at Jean-Georges in—" She glances at her thin Cartier watch, "—five minutes."

"Good luck with that," Cole scoffs.

"I know we're going to be late, but let's not be later than we have to be. Bye, Willow, have a nice date," she whispers in my ear as she hugs me goodbye.

"It's not a date," I insist as she backs away.

Cole chuckles as he holds the door for Heena. "Sure it's not."

Interesting dynamic those two seem to have. Unlike

everyone else in the world, he doesn't seem afraid of Heena—he acts amused by her. But I don't have time to unpack all that. Riley's going to be here in ten minutes, and I have a long list of things to do before then.

I quickly change and touch up my makeup and spend the remaining two minutes trying to make the vacant penthouse seem more homely. I hide the three small gaps in the flowers, light a scented candle, turn on some low music, and get out some plates and glasses. Right when I finish, there's a call to our in-home system.

"Willow, Riley Coleman is here to see you," the doorman says through the small pad on the wall.

"Send him up," I answer.

The minute I wait for him to arrive seems to drag on for hours. I run my hands through my hair, stooping low enough (physically and metaphorically) to check my reflection in the oven. I run my palms down the strappy yellow dress I chose to wear tonight, flipping between thinking it's too formal and too casual. I walk to the door and walk back to the kitchen, debating whether it's polite or overzealous to meet him at the door.

What the fuck is my problem? I need to stop freaking out. It's only Riley.

As I'm scrolling through the music—finding the current classical song too *fluley*—I hear the elevator to the penthouse ding.

I walk as casually as I can to meet him in the foyer, trying to figure out why the hell I'm so nervous.

"Hi." Riley flashes his trademark boyish grin at me and I'm suddenly reminded why the hell I'm so nervous—because he's quite possibly the most attractive man I've ever seen in my life.

"Hi," I answer, drinking in his khakis and blue button-up.

His sleeves are rolled up, and his shirt is left slightly more open than is business-appropriate. It's like he read a manual on what women want or something.

"You look incredible," he says huskily, looking at me as greedily as I imagine I'm looking at him.

"Thanks, you look great too."

After a second or two more of staring at each other, he clears his throat and diverts his gaze from me. "So, this is where you grew up?" he asks, looking beyond me towards the large first floor.

Except for a select few rooms, the first floor has an open floor plan: the kitchen and foyer blend into the living room and dining room. The floor is flanked by huge windows on all sides, displaying an incredible view of Central Park and Manhattan.

"Yep, this is it." I awkwardly spread my arms before silently cursing myself for being so weird and dropping them back at my sides. "Can I get you something to drink? We have pretty much everything. My mom's a big wine fan, and my dad's into whiskey, so our drink cellar is pretty evenly divided between those two. But we also have beer, seltzer, whatever."

Riley smiles, dimples on full display. "Beer's good with me."

"You got it," I say, opening the drink fridge. "Budweiser or Coors or this IPA thing, or...you know what, just come pick one." I chuckle. "Who knew we had so much beer?"

Riley comes up behind me, close enough that I can feel his body heat, and reaches over me to grab a Corona. "This place would have been epic for high school parties," he says, leaning back against the counter and admiring the place again.

I pour myself a glass of wine and meet him at the counter. "Probably. But I left high school at sixteen, so I never got the chance."

"Ah. Probably for the best. Wouldn't want this place getting messed up. It's too nice."

"It's really nice, yeah. It feels a little sterile with everyone in LA right now, but I love it here nonetheless. I missed being home."

"I know the feeling," he says, and I meet his gaze.

Holy shit, his eyes are so many shades of green. I could stare at them all day, I swear. I need to stop lusting after him. This is getting pathetic.

"So, have you ever had Joe's pizza before?" I cut the sexual tension, opening the top pizza box.

"Nope, but I'm assuming it's your favorite?"

"Oh, mine and half the city's. This pizza is more famous than I am," I joke. "I got a few different ones because I didn't know what kind you like, so there's a veggie, a cheese, and a pepperoni."

"You didn't have to go to all that trouble. I'll eat anything. Seriously, thank you so much, Willow, this looks amazing."

"No problem. Any excuse to get pizza. And you're going to Venmo me for all this, right?"

Riley laughs. "Totally, I know how much you need the money. It must be so hard to be a struggling artist. I don't know how you do it."

"Well, Riley, not all of us can have sold-out tours. And do you get paid for those photos of your abs you post, too? Or do you just give that away for free?"

He raises his brows. "What photos of my abs?"

"Don't play coy. The ones from the tour, where you purposefully lift your shirt up. You're not fooling anyone. That's the oldest trick in the book."

"Oh, *those*! Yeah, those photos are actually only on my OnlyFans, babe, but nice to know you subscribe."

"Shut up. If you were on OnlyFans, I would've heard about it. In fact, it would probably break the internet."

"I don't know about that. But I'm glad to know I'd at least have one subscriber, Willow Jordan. I'll have to tell my manager about this lucrative new business idea."

"Yeah, you'd have thousands of subscribers between me and all those girls online who freak out anytime you do *anything*."

He quirks one side of his mouth into a smirk. "Careful, someone might think you're jealous."

"I'm not jealous. Just making an observation."

"Mhm. Don't worry. I kind of like when you get jealous. It's flattering," he teases.

"Like you don't scroll through my comments, either."

"Yours are turned off," he responds without thinking, eyes widening slightly.

"Aha! Caught red-handed, Riley!"

"Whatever." He raises his hands defensively. "Fine, I internet stalk you. At least I'm honest about it."

"I stalk you too," I admit. "I once went down a rabbit hole of some girl who had this elaborate theory about who you wrote 'Masterpiece' about."

"Who'd she think it was about?"

"*Lottie Lawson*," I scoff.

Riley's shoulders shake from laughing so hard. "You're totally jealous."

"I'm not jealous. I just know there's no way that song is about her. You've never mentioned Lottie before. I mean, have you ever even *met* her? This girl was making the most far-fetched connections possible. It was ridiculous. Horrible investigative journalism."

"I guess I'll have to name my next song Willow, just to prevent the confusion. Although, the song doesn't actually mention your name, so it might be a little weird to title it that...but whatever you want, it's up to you."

"You've already written it?"

"Yep. And a third is in the works."

"You're ridiculous."

"Want to hear it?"

"Why don't you play it for me at your show tomorrow?" I ask.

Riley pauses, narrowing his eyes. "But you're not going to that show, right? It's sold out," he emphasizes weirdly.

"I bought some scalped tickets." I shrug. "And they were *crazy* expensive, so you'd better play that song for me."

"Willow."

"What! You can't seriously expect me to be in the same city as one of your shows and not go, Riley. That's absurd."

"Willow, *I got you tickets to the show*. I gave two tickets to Heena, they were supposed to be a surprise for you."

"Oh my God. *You* were my hot date?"

"What?"

"Forget it. Ugh, you dick." I groan. "I paid six thousand dollars for two tickets!"

He roars with laughter. "That's such a rip-off."

I lightly shove him.

He rubs his arm playfully. "I'm very familiar with that set, and it's *definitely* not worth three thousand dollars a ticket," he keeps laughing. "Who would pay that much?"

"Apparently, me."

"Oh, God, I'm literally crying. That's so funny," he says, hunched over and wiping his eyes. "What are we going to do? Can you return them?"

"*Return them?*" I laugh. "No way, they're scalped."

"Fuck, I'll have to give you a free T-shirt or something for that."

"A free *T-shirt*? You better give me more than that."

"Like what? A free autographed T-shirt?"

"Famous Riley is unbearable," I reply, my stomach hurting from laughing so hard. "But fine, I guess I won't say no to an autographed T-shirt."

Chapter 37

Willow

After we finish eating, Riley and I get a second round of drinks and settle into the deep leather couches in the living room, not ready to leave each other's company just yet. Neither of us wants the pressure of picking the movie, so we just put on whatever was suggested by Netflix.

"I have to say, I'm disappointed in you, Willow," Riley says before the opening credits even finish rolling.

"Why?"

"Because I thought we were making great progress on the whole turning-Willow-normal thing. But normal people would never pay three thousand dollars for a single ticket to a concert. Well, maybe for Beyoncé or something, but certainly not for one of *my* concerts."

"I'd argue that a superfan would."

"So you're a superfan?"

"I guess I walked into that one."

We turn to each other. Two minutes into the movie and we've already abandoned the guise of watching it.

"Fine, so what if I am a superfan?" I ask. Riley's eyes search mine thoroughly enough that I squirm under his gaze. "What? Do I have pizza on my face or something?"

"No." His lips curl up into a smile small enough to go unnoticed by those unfamiliar with his expressions. Lucky for me, I've seemingly memorized them all. "Can I ask you something?"

"The way you're asking to ask a question makes me nervous," I answer. "But yes."

"Is it me?"

My brows furrow. "What do you mean?"

"I mean." He pauses, eyes searching the ceiling as though the words he's trying to form are written there. "The second I saw you in that dress tonight, it felt like my heart fell out of my body. Hell, I felt that way the entire walk here. I changed my shirt three times before I left my hotel. I wake up thinking about you, Willow. You make me nervous in the best way, and suddenly, I find faults with every other woman who makes a move on me."

He runs a hand through his hair, and a stray lock falls over his forehead in a way that makes my heart pound.

"What I'm trying to say—" Riley continues, his expression painfully earnest "—is that I'm falling for you. And I can't stop myself, no matter how hard I try. For some reason, I can't help but cling to the thread of hope that maybe you're falling with me because you haven't actually told me that you don't feel the same. You've given me other reasons why we can't be together, sure, but you haven't actually told me it's *me*. So please, I need you to shatter my hope so that I can try to get over it. Stop being nice, Willow, and please just tell me that it's me."

"I can't," my voice comes out in a whisper. "It's not you, Riley."

His eyes widen slightly, then soften. He beams like he's just won the lottery. His shoulders sag in relief and he starts to reach for my hand but stops himself, pulling back. "Then what is it? Because, Willow, I'll do anything I can to make this work. I'm fine with the distance. I'll come to you when I can. And I don't care that your family life is complicated right now. I want to be there to help you through it."

"And what about the press? Riley, you've seen what they say about me. They'll tear you to shreds if they know we're together."

"*That's* what this is about?" he asks incredulously. "Willow, I don't give a shit what they say about me. I want to be with you. I couldn't care less what other people think about that. It's our lives, not theirs."

"They can be awful. And they love you. I don't want to ruin that."

"I know they've hurt you, Willow. Believe me, I know how painful it is to hear people say such awful things about you. And although being with Claire was awful, she was only one person, let alone the millions that berate you. But my experience with Claire taught me something. Eventually, I realized that her hateful comments were coming from a place of insecurity in herself. The faults she found with me were just projections—they didn't mean anything, and they certainly didn't define who I was. The only opinions that matter to me now are those of the people I love. None of the rest. I can handle some bad press. It might even be good for my ego," he adds with a cocky grin.

"Really? You're not just saying that?"

"I promise you, Willow. If that's truly what's holding you back, then there's absolutely no reason why we shouldn't be together."

At this point, I can't hold back any longer. I put one hand on his shoulder, the other on the side of his face, and kiss him. He doesn't waste any time kissing me back, moving one hand to my waist as he wraps the other in my hair, pulling me closer until I'm straddling him. Unlike our first kiss in North Carolina, we don't waste any time being gentle with this one. His arm wraps fully around my waist, and he pulls me flush against him, my back arching as I feel his hard length pressing against my core. I can't help myself as I rock against him, grateful that I wore a dress so there's one less layer between us right now. Riley groans into my mouth as I move my hips against his.

Needing to hear it one more time, I break the kiss and try to keep my gaze off his slightly swollen lips, but instead, they land on his heavy-lidded eyes, making me somehow more aroused. "And you're sure you don't mind the distance, or my family drama, or the press?" I pry.

"I don't mind the distance," he growls, placing his hand on the side of my neck and drawing me back in for another deep kiss. "Or the family drama," he says a few seconds later after he reluctantly removes his lips from mine to speak. Then they're on my jaw, kissing the spot right below my ear, making a breathy sound escape my lips. I feel his smile on my neck. "Or the press," he assures me, moving to my collarbone. "I want you, Willow, no matter how many strings are attached."

"Then," I breathe, "as much as I love the third shirt you put on tonight, it's coming off." I unbutton it, and he leans away from me just far enough so I can slip the shirt off his body.

"And as much as I love this," he says as he fingers the strap of my dress, "it's coming off too."

He somehow takes the dress off as he lifts me and sets me down on the blanketed edge of the couch, kneeling before me. Unsurprisingly, he ripped the dress with that maneuver—though it was still impressive.

"Riley," I scold gently. "That was custom Schiaparelli!"

"I'll buy you a new one," he says against one of my now bare breasts, his hand working the other. "Fuck, Willow, how are you so perfect?"

"I must be God's favorite," I respond in a heavy voice as I lean my head back in appreciation of his work. "Do I want to know how you got so good at this?"

He looks up at me and smirks in a way that makes me eager for his head to be between my legs. "Probably not," he answers. "Let's just say I was sort of a slut before I met you."

"Thank God for those women, then," I say as he reads my mind and kisses his way down my stomach, fixating on the area just above where I'm desperate for him to be.

"Enough talking," he murmurs, his hand running up my thigh, again teasing me by stopping inches away from where I want him.

"Make me stop then," I answer, and he huffs at the challenge.

He slips my underwear down my body, and then, finally, his tongue is on me, making a slow swipe up from my core to my clit.

"Fuck, Willow. You taste even better than I imagined."

He focuses his tongue back on my clit, moving it in slow circles against me. I arch my back to try to get more pressure from him, and he laughs against me, the vibrations sending a jolt down my body. He slowly slides a finger inside me, making me whimper at how good it feels, yet still craving more. Riley's tongue keeps working its circles on my clit as he slowly pumps a finger in and out of me, drawing me closer and closer to the edge.

"Riley," I breathe. "I'm close."

He grunts in response against me, now sucking my clit. And just to torture me, he works another finger in, two fingers now hitting the spot inside me that makes me see stars. And then I come, hands gripping the leather of the couch, on the blanket, and at some point landing in his hair, searching for anything to grab onto. Riley continues to work his mouth and fingers on me as I come, dragging my pleasure out for as long as he can before, eventually, I'm a panting mess collapsed against the couch.

He slowly rises from between my legs, and his mouth is on mine again. There's something so erotic about tasting myself on him, and it makes me clench my thighs together, anxious for all of him.

"You have no idea how often I dreamt of that," he says against my lips.

"I hope it lived up to expectations." I smile against him.

"Oh God, I almost came in my pants," he responds, and I laugh at him.

"My turn?" I ask, reaching between us to stroke his hard length through his pants. As if he couldn't get any hotter, his dick is huge. Because, of course it is.

"No." He draws back. "I was serious about the almost coming in my pants part. And I don't want to do that until I'm inside of you."

I unzip his pants, eager for him to make good on that promise. Despite feeling how big he was, I still gape at the sheer size of him when he slides his pants off.

He laughs when he meets my wide-eyed gaze. "You sure know how to make a guy feel good about himself."

"As if everyone doesn't look at you that way," I retort.

"I like it so much more when you do it, though," he says, ripping a condom open with his teeth before expertly unrolling it on his cock. "Are you sure about this?" he asks as he positions himself between my legs.

"Positive," I say, pulling him on top of me. I gasp as he slowly rocks his hips forward me, stretching me inch by inch.

"Fuck, you're tight." He groans, eyes rolling back when he's finally fully inside me and his hips are pressing flush against mine. "You okay?" he asks, recovering himself enough to gaze down at me.

His expression displays an unbelievably hot mix of lust and concern as he looks down at me, brushing a piece of stray hair off my face.

"Amazing," I say, pulling him into a kiss and rocking my hips slightly, silently telling him to start moving.

He takes the hint, slowly pulling out and thrusting back in. A few minutes later, his strokes become faster and more desperate, both our breathing becoming labored. He lifts my right leg and angles himself deeper, eliciting a moan from both of us.

"I love the sounds you make." He smirks as he repeatedly hits my G-spot, making more breathy sounds escape me.

"Riley," I moan.

He groans in response. "You close?"

"Mhm," I whimper as blackness fills my vision and pleasure courses through my body, my nails sinking into his back as I arch my body against him.

"Fuuuuck," he drags the word out slightly.

He finishes seconds after I do, dissolving into messy strokes as he comes. As if that wasn't already the best sex I've ever had, the groan Riley makes as he comes is incontestably the hottest sound I've ever heard. Honestly, that sound alone could drench me.

"Willow," he whispers my name into my neck, still inside of me.

"Yeah?" I ask, catching my breath.

"I'm going to write a whole album for you."

"That's what you have to say right now?" I laugh as he

slides out of me and disposes of the condom before stretching out next to me on the sectional part of the couch.

"Yep." He smiles that stupid boyish grin I love so much as he turns on his side to face me. "In fact, I think every song I write from this point on will be about you."

"Stop sweet-talking me."

"I'm serious. I could write a whole album on your eyes alone. They're so blue. Like a deep, twilight blue on the outside before changing to a sea green in the center. They're mesmerizing."

"Maybe workshop that a little before putting it in a song," I tease, entangling my fingers with his as he laughs.

"I'm going to sing the song for you tomorrow."

"I'd love that." I move my head to rest on his broad chest. "But can we go a little slow with revealing our relationship to the public? Just so you're absolutely sure it's what you want."

"I know what I want, but okay," he answers, rubbing my back. "We can go slow. I won't tell the crowd it's about you, as much as I want to. We can stay private for as long as you want."

"Thank you." I kiss his shoulder. "Should we take this party up to my bedroom for the night? We wouldn't want Heena to walk in on us naked."

"You want me to spend the night?"

"You don't want to?"

"Oh, I want to," he answers, swooping me up into his arms as he stands.

"You're ridiculous. I can walk."

"Hopefully, by tomorrow morning, you won't be able to."

He walks me up to my bedroom and drops me on the bed, smiling wickedly at me, his cock rock hard and clearly wanting a round two.

Chapter 38

Riley

"Riley, do you want to tell me why I saw your clothes strewn all over the living room last night?" Heena asks as the security team escorts her and Willow into the backstage area where my band and I are killing time before tonight's show.

Willow is wearing a white baby tee with two red cowboy boots embroidered on it, paired with a red-fringed leather jacket, low-rise flare jeans, and the golden boots I gave her. Beside her, Heena's in a lacy black slip dress with black tights, black cowgirl boots, and an oversized black leather jacket.

Ethan freezes at the sight of Heena Badahl in the flesh. "Holy shit."

"No reason. I was just feeling a little warm and wanted to cool off," I respond.

I can feel Waylon and Nash's stunned gazes on me (Ethan is still staring at Heena, seconds away from literally drooling).

"Congrats, dude!" Waylon beams, hitting me on the back as he looks between Willow and me. "So, are you two finally together?"

"Yep," Willow answers, crossing the room to sit next to me

on the couch, the guys moving to the armchairs to give us space.

"It's about time." Nash smiles like a proud dad. "I'm so happy for you two."

Heena sits next to Willow, narrowing her eyes at Ethan and his 'Enjoy a Nice Cold Girl!' T-shirt. "What's his problem?" Heena asks me pointedly.

"He has a little crush. Just ignore him."

"Oh, I think I remember Willow mentioning something about that," Heena says before directing her attention back to Ethan. "Not. Gonna. Happen, okay?" she says, drawing out each syllable like she's talking to a baby.

"Okay," he answers glibly, obviously not taking Heena's words to heart.

I hear a low chuckle coming from the doorway and see two giant, attractive men facing us with their arms crossed. They're each at least 6'5 and built like boulders. One appears to be in his mid-twenties with dark hair and dark eyes that contrast his pale skin, which is decorated with black tattoos. The other seems like he's in his forties, also with dark hair and dark eyes, but with uninked, tanned skin.

Willow follows my gaze. "Oh, I forgot to tell you, but we decided to use the two extra tickets I had for Cole and Tito."

I feel my eyebrows raise all the way to my hairline.

"They're our bodyguards. Relax." She knocks my leg teasingly with hers. "'You're cute when you're jealous,'" she teases me, using my words from last night.

"I'm not jealous," I defend. "I was just wondering who they were."

"Nice to meet you." The older one grins warmly at me, instantly melting any unease I felt. "Willow told us you were a great singer. We're excited to see your show."

"Mhm," the younger one grunts, face still stony as he... glares at...Ethan? Interesting.

"I know we'll be right by the venue's security in the VIP section anyway, but I figured, why waste the tickets? A little extra protection never hurt anyone."

"That and the fact that Cole practically begged to come," Heena teases. "It's all he talked about last night."

"I wouldn't go that far." The younger one rolls his eyes, a hint of a smile grazing his lips as his eyes meet Heena's.

"All night?" Ethan asks. Cole's shadow of a smile instantly drops.

Okay, this is definitely weird.

"Well, on the way to and from my date with Zac Schwartz."

"Zac Schwartz?" Waylon whistles. "Good luck competing with that, Ethan."

"Hey, I could take Zac Schwartz any day," Ethan responds. "He's short."

"He's five-seven," Heena clarifies. "And more than makes up for that in other areas."

Willow turns to her friend, holding in a laugh. "Wait, you're five inches taller than him?"

"Eight in the heels I was wearing last night." Heena flips up her hand to stare at her nails. "But that didn't matter when we were horizontal."

"Cole, were you there for that part, too?" Willow asks innocently.

Cole doesn't answer.

"Nah, I sent him home. Zac's not into sharing," Heena answers for him.

"Well, just for the record, *I'm* six-three," Ethan says loudly into the void.

"And I'm six-six," Cole responds coolly. The two men glare at each other.

"What's up with that?" I whisper in Willow's ear.

"I don't know. I don't remember meeting him until last night. I think it's just Heena being Heena, though," she adds. "She has that effect on men."

"So, did you guys have work this week in New York?" Nash asks the girls. "Or did you come just for the show?"

"I had a Dior shoot," Willow starts.

"And I had a Vanity Fair panel thing," Heena finishes.

"What's it like doing a photoshoot?" Waylon asks.

"Usually not as fun as it sounds," Heena says. "They take hours to do hair and makeup, and then you have fittings and outfit changes and lighting changes and directors telling you what to do."

"But it *can* be fun with the right photographer," Willow adds. "Usually, they at least play music for you."

Willow's phone buzzes, and she leisurely brings it out and checks the screen before jolting up and bolting out the door, Tito hot on her heels.

"It's probably nothing, but she's had a few family emergencies recently," I hear Heena explain as I follow them. "So she gets worried about calls."

I catch the iron back door just before it closes, propping it open so we don't get locked out before I emerge into the alley.

"Are you okay?" I hear Willow ask the caller. "Is Mom okay?" she asks a few seconds later. Tito and I tense and then relax as we listen to the rest of Willow's end of the conversation. "You—what? Aspen, holy shit! Oh my God, that's incredible. I'm so excited for you! Yeah, I'm with Riley right now. Heena had tickets the whole time but didn't tell me because she wanted it to be a surprise. I know, right? Can I tell you about it tomorrow? It's a lot. Yep, by afternoon. Heena, too. Okay, see you then. Tell everyone hi for me. Bye, I love you."

She ends the call and turns to look at me, tears glistening in her eyes.

"Everything okay?" I ask.

She takes a running leap into my arms, wraps her legs around my waist, and laughs into my neck. "She got offered the lead in an upcoming Jack Mack film. He wrote the screenplay and is producing *and* directing it. And he personally called her and begged her to take the role."

"Holy shit," I exclaim. Jack Mack is one of the greatest screenwriters of the past decade, winning Academy Awards after Golden Globes for his films. His movies are *huge*. "That's incredible."

"God, I'm so happy for her. She's been so stressed. She really needed this. And she sounded so happy. I haven't heard her that excited about anything in literal years."

"I know." I squeeze Willow as I gently set her down. "That's great news."

"I can see the headline now. 'Aspen Jordan, starring in the highest-grossing film of the year.' And *I* plan on taking the hottest date." She quirks one corner of her lips, leaning up to give me a kiss.

"Just to be clear, you're talking about me, right?" I smile against her lips.

"Would you rather I take someone else?" she asks, running her hand through my hair in a way that sends a jolt through my body.

"Nope." I lift her up by the back of her legs and press her against the wall of the alley, kissing her plump lips.

Tito clears his throat.

"That's your cue to set me down," Willow says, giving me one last peck.

"Fine, but only because the show starts soon." I set her down and start towards the open door.

"Hold on." She giggles, pulling me back gently by the biceps. "Wow, somebody works out," she jokes, giving my arm another squeeze for good measure. Then she pulls out her phone and takes a photo of me.

"What are you doing?" I furrow my brows.

"Taking a picture so I can remember how cute you look with your hair all messed up and with my lipstick all over your face."

She turns the phone around, and I see my lips smeared with red.

"Willow." I swipe it off with the collar of my white T-shirt. "Did I get it?"

"Almost," she says, wiping the edge of my lip with her thumb. "But now your collar is red."

"Eh, I don't care."

"People will wonder whose lipstick that is."

I smirk. "Make sure to reapply then, so they'll know."

Willow playfully scowls at me before walking through the open doorway. I can't help but smack her ass as she passes me, prompting a laugh from her.

Chapter 39

Willow

We all hang out backstage for another thirty minutes or so before the stage crew pops in to lead Heena and me to our seats. Although Riley isn't supposed to come out for another ten minutes or so, the screaming is so loud by the time Heena and I take our seats that I look toward the empty stage anyway. Then I notice *our* faces on the jumbotron. They're cheering for *us*.

Heena, ever the professional, gives a sultry smile and wave, somehow making the crowd cheer even louder. I smile and wave beside her. I don't even care that I hear a few boos mixed in with the cheers. Riley's words last night really resonated with me—I need to stop caring what strangers think of me. I should only care about the opinions of my friends and family. And speaking of my friends and family, they all seem to be doing well. Mom is doing okay, Aspen was cast in a prestigious film, and Riley's about to perform for thousands of screaming fans, including me. I'm in a great mood.

"Give the people a wave, guys," Heena teases our guards, who can be seen behind us on screen. Tito's jovial smile is gone, replaced with an impassive expression that means he's purely in work mode right now.

"Come on, Tito, I know you're as excited for this show as I am. At least give us a smile," I prod him, poking his arm.

Heena giggles beside me. "As excited as you are? I highly doubt he is, Will."

His mouth twitches into a minuscule smile before disappearing back into a stony stare.

"Alright, I guess I'll count that," I tell Tito. "And I don't know what you mean," I direct at Heena, hardly able to suppress *my* smile.

"Oh please, as if he didn't keep you up all night with his—"

"Heena!" I cut her off. "Lip readers are going to be all over that. We're still on the screen."

"They're too obsessed with us for their own good." She chuckles before covering her mouth to obscure her words from the screen. "With his *monster cock*."

Cole and Tito's eyes widen slightly, betraying their eavesdropping.

Luckily, I'm saved from having to reply by the dimming of the lights. The crowd quiets as the opening act comes out, a guy who looks to be in his early twenties. Then their cameras start flashing, at least half of them pointed at Heena and me instead of at the stage. I feel bad for stealing the poor kid's thunder, but what can we do? It's not like we're doing anything to catch their attention. We're literally just standing here. Besides, I have a feeling everyone will be focused on the stage again once Riley comes out.

The opener is actually really good, but I'm glad his set was only a few songs. The crowd's anticipation to see Riley is palpable as the opener clears off the stage and the stagehands come in to rearrange a few things. The crowd begins cheering

Riley's name over and over, and I'll be damned if I don't join in too.

It's a weird feeling to be standing with a crowd of thousands of people all waiting to see your boyfriend—it sounds weird to say that, too. I feel incredibly proud of him and his success, but I also feel a twinge of jealousy that all these people want to see him as much as I do. Like...calm down a little, guys.

The lights dim for a few seconds, and the cheers become deafening. Then, the stage is flooded in blue-white light, with Riley standing front and center.

"Hi guys," he says into the mic. "Wow, I think you're the loudest city to date."

The thunderous roar of the crowd swells with pride.

"Alright, alright, I hear you. I'll shut up now and give y'all what you really want," he grins. "This one's called 'Vicious.'"

The crowd goes wild, singing each word in time with Riley. I look to my side and see that even Heena's singing along, jumping up and down with a huge grin on her face. Cole's mouthing the words, and even Tito has cracked a smile.

Riley sings two more songs with brief asides to the crowd between each. After the third song, he takes the mic off the stand.

"So, New York is a very special place to me." The crowd erupts. "I played my first big show here on New Year's Eve. Truly, that night changed my life in more ways than one. I'm getting sidetracked. Because I love this city—and because y'all are such an amazing crowd—I thought you deserved something special."

The crowd 'ooohs' in response.

"How about a brand-new, never-heard-before song?"

The crowd roars.

"I don't know, though. Do you really want to hear it?" Riley revs up the crowd.

They scream loud enough that I can feel my ears ringing.

Riley raises his brows. "Alright, I'm convinced. This one's called, 'Put It on the Radio.' Let's hit it, guys," he says to his band.

You had windburnt cheeks and a bottle of champagne
    On the first night on that rooftop on Main
    I had a country attitude and a cigarette
    And had just seen a face I'd never forget

Now on the road, I wake up with a smile
    Because all I dream about is you
    My band teases me each mile
    Say they're sick and tired
    Of all my songs being about you

But you make me sing of honey,
    Away from all my bitter tunes,
    You've turned my melodic minors,
    Into blissful "I love you's"
    So put it on the radio
    That I never want to let you go
    Now that I've got you ...

Riley doesn't sing the last word in the chorus. He mouths, "Willow."

I don't think anyone else in the crowd caught it, except Heena and me, but that totally was my name.

As the crowd screams, Heena looks at me, shocked. "Holy shit," she says into my ear.

"Holy shit," I echo.

"He mouthed 'Willow,' right?"

"Yep," I respond, too stunned to speak.

"Holy shit," she says again, dumbfounded.

After Riley plays the encore and exits the stage for good, I race backstage with Heena and the guards hot on my heels.

"You were incredible," I squeal, throwing myself into his arms.

"Thanks," he chuckles, wrapping an arm around my waist before loosening it and taking a step back. "You probably don't want to be touching me right now. I'm all sweaty. I know that was your fear with my cowboy hat in North Carolina."

"I don't care," I scoff at him. "I was just teasing you. And anyway, I've seen worse. You should see how sweaty Heena is after hot yoga."

"That's a lie, I don't sweat," Heena defends.

"Fine, you should see how much Heena 'glistens' after hot yoga."

"I, for one, would love to see that," Ethan offers.

Heena rolls her eyes at him. "Keep dreaming, buddy."

"I will," he smirks in response.

"Great show," a middle-aged woman says, entering the room.

"Thanks. Tracy, meet Willow and Heena," Riley introduces us. "And Willow and Heena, meet Tracy, my manager."

Tracy looks me up and down and frowns slightly, seemingly seeing right through the public guise of our 'friendship.'

"I hope you two know what you're doing," she says.

"We do," Riley answers bluntly.

"You know you two are going to be plastered all over the internet tomorrow, right?"

I raise my eyebrows. "For what? I just like his music."

"You were making sex-eyes at him all night. And Riley, you only looked at one particular spot in the crowd all night, even serenading it with a brand new love song. I think people are going to see through that."

"We'll cross that bridge when we come to it," Riley answers.

"You'll be there by morning, I guarantee it."

"We'll manage," I respond to the woman. I'm sure she's just doing her job and looking out for Riley, but I sense a little disapproval in her tone—disapproval of his choice in women.

Nobody's opinion matters except those of the people I love, I tell myself, finding Riley's words calming.

"Well, as nice as it was to meet you, Tracy," I say. "Heena and I should get going. We run on a tight schedule, you know, being supermodels and all." *Why did I just say that?* I never rub my status as a supermodel in people's faces. I find it tacky. "Riley, you'll meet us at my penthouse, right?" *Jesus, I did it again. What has gotten into me?*

Waylon snickers behind Riley, no doubt at my blatant humble-bragging in front of Tracy.

"Nowhere I'd rather be, babe." Riley grins, also amused by my uncharacteristic outburst.

"Tito, can you have the car pulled around?" Heena says, straightening her posture and narrowing her eyes down at Tracy. "I'm so glad we decided to bring your custom Rolls-Royce, Willow. I don't tell you enough how much I love it. The backlit Swarovski crystals outlining the night sky on the day you were born were *such* a nice touch. But my favorite part is the built-in champagne fridge under the seats, of course. You put in that bottle of the Krug Clos d'Ambonnay that Oliver

Rousteing gave you as a gift for walking in Balmain's Paris show, right?" Heena says, straightening her posture and narrowing her eyes down at Tracy.

Even though my cheeks heat at Heena's obvious flaunting of my wealth and connections, I'm eternally grateful for her backing me up in the face of Tracy's disapproval.

Heena's message is very clear underneath her thinly veiled words: *Willow is worlds above you, bitch. Your complaints are so far below her that she can't even hear them.*

"The car's already outside." Tito's eyes glitter mischievously, and I can tell that he enjoyed Heena's defense of me as much as I did.

POP CULTURE PULSE PODCAST

Jenna: So, I think we've finally solved the mystery of who Riley Coleman is dating. Well, the internet and tabloids have.

Caroline: What, really? Who is it?

Jenna: You haven't heard? I'm shocked. It's plastered all over the internet. I swear, I was scrolling this morning on TikTok and every. Single. Video. Was about these two. Now, it's still just conjecture—unconfirmed by the couple—but I have to admit, the evidence is pretty compelling.

Caroline: Ugh, I know what conjecture is! Just spit it out, the anticipation is killing me.

Jenna: Alright, alright. It's Willow Jordan.

Caroline: *Willow Jordan?* The self-proclaimed Eminem super-fan? The girl who starred in a 50 Cent music video? She's with country singer Riley Coleman? Nah, no way. That's impossible. How would they even know each other? And what the hell do *those two* have in common? She was born in the industry, and he just released his first album six months ago. Not to mention, isn't she an absolute selfish bitch? And Riley seems so sweet. No way, I don't believe it.

Jenna: Well, let me explain the theory, and you might

change your mind. I'm going to go back to the beginning, so just bear with me. The first little breadcrumb comes from the second week of February, so a little more than two months ago, when Riley began following Willow on Instagram.

Caroline: And does she follow him back?

Jenna: No, but she only follows five people. Anyway, he likes every single one of her posts, and Willow liked one of his photos in March, which was probably an oversight on her part because she doesn't like *anyone's* photos, except for her family's.

Caroline: And Heena Badahl's. And I'm still not buying this theory. I need stronger evidence than this.

Jenna: Well, Heena's a given. Okay, I'll jump to the strong stuff. So the first week of March, the Jordan family went on a beach vacation, remember? They didn't publicize where they went, but some sleuths on the internet were able to identify the Ocean Course Clubhouse as the backdrop in some photos posted by Aspen. Which is on Kiawah Island, South Carolina.

Caroline: Okay?

Jenna: And then, at Riley's show in Charleston a few weeks later, he brought up a fan onstage, who he said he *met at Kiawah while he was picking up a friend*. So obviously, people are assuming the friend is Willow Jordan, since she was in Kiawah.

Caroline: I hope there's more.

Jenna: There is. So, in between Riley talking about Kiawah and Willow being there, Willow posted a photo of herself riding a horse. When has Willow Jordan ever ridden a horse? People scoured the internet, and there are literally no photos of her with horses other than random ads. But you know who rides horses? *Riley Coleman.* So people think that Riley picked her up from Kiawah and brought her home with him to North Carolina. And the timeline matches up, because he was on break from tour during that week.

Caroline: Okay...

Jenna: Also in March, Willow was spotted entering one of Riley's Instagram livestreams, and she even *commented*. And she said, "Did you ever find the right rash cream?" Like, that's a weird thing to ask a stranger, right? They're definitely at least friends.

Caroline: Did Riley acknowledge her on the livestream?

Jenna: He pretended not to know who Willow Jordan was —which is fishy in and of itself. I mean, she's Willow fucking Jordan—but he was smiling like a kid on Christmas. He totally knows her. And there's more. Remember when Willow did that *Sports Illustrated* shoot while her mom and sister were sick?

Caroline snorts.

Caroline: How could I forget? That'll probably go down as one of the worst celebrity moments of the year.

Jenna: Well, she posted some photos of herself and the other models from that trip and captioned it "fuck Claire." And guess who's named Claire?

Caroline: Who?

Jenna: Riley Coleman's ex-girlfriend. The one that half of his songs are about. The one who clearly treated him like shit and broke his heart.

Caroline: Holy shit.

Jenna: Yeah. And there's one more thing, the thing that made people finally connect all these dots. Riley played a show in Brooklyn last night and guess who was in the audience?

Caroline: Willow?

Jenna: Willow *and* Heena. Shit must be getting serious because even Heena Badahl looked thrilled to see him perform. And Riley surprised the audience by playing a brand new song nobody's heard before. The song is titled "Put It on the Radio," and it's one of the most romantic songs I've ever heard. So, do you finally believe it?

Caroline: Unfortunately, I don't think there's much room to deny that. It seems pretty damning. And there's no way it's fake because it seems like they've worked pretty hard to keep it from the public.

Jenna: Agreed. I hate to say it, but this relationship is definitely real.

Caroline: Fuck. Well, it's only a matter of time before he dumps her, anyway. I mean, what would Riley Coleman want to do with a bitchy supermodel? Once the thrill of sex with her wears off, he'll kick her to the curb. I'm sure of it.

Chapter 40

Willow

"Hey, Heena, you might want to put on noise-canceling headphones or something," I tell her as we walk through the doors of the penthouse.

"Oh God, Willow, you can't seriously be thinking of having sex with Riley tonight. My poor, innocent ears!"

"Don't be so dramatic. You won't be exposed for long. We'll be done within thirty minutes...well, on second thought, maybe give us an hour, just in case we decide to go for round two. But I'm exhausted, and I'm sure he is too, so probably just one round. As you know, we were up most of *last* night..." I trail off, smiling deviously at Heena.

"Yes, and I'm actively trying to block that out," Heena interrupts me. "Because, in case you forgot, I was also staying here."

"Oh please, you didn't hear a thing. We were really quiet. But if you're tired now and want to go to sleep, you could just crash in my parents' room or in one of the guest bedrooms," I suggest.

My room, along with Aspen's and Maple's, are all on the second floor, while my parents' bedroom and a few spares are on the third. Heena also has her own room here, but it shares a wall with mine on the second floor, so I'm guessing that's out of the question for her tonight.

"I know. I slept in a guest room last night. You two aren't as quiet as you think you are."

I blush. "Sorry."

"Don't be sorry. I'm just giving you a hard time. You deserve a good orgasm as much as anyone. He's delivering, right?"

"Like a UPS driver the week before Christmas."

Heena gives me a funny look. "It's a good thing you're pretty, Will. I'll be in one of the guest bedrooms if you need me," she says, heading towards the stairs. "The one on the opposite end of the penthouse from your room," she adds over her shoulder.

"Goodnight, Heena," I call after her.

I decide to use the few minutes head start I have on Riley to change into something a bit...sexier than my concert clothes. After a couple of hours of jumping around in an arena, they feel gross and a little sweaty. I decide on a lacy golden lingerie set, sheer enough that I'm practically naked. The gold matches my boots, and those are staying on until we get to the bedroom. I have a feeling Riley would be into that.

I hear the intercom buzz as I'm admiring myself in the mirror and tell the doorman to let Riley through. Then I head downstairs, meeting him just as the doors open.

"Hey, sor—holy shit," he interrupts himself mid-sentence, taking in my outfit (or lack thereof). One thing about being a supermodel is that you get incredibly comfortable with your naked body since it's practically plastered everywhere. High fashion doesn't really do modesty.

"You like it?" I ask, giving him a little spin. When I turn back around to face him, his face is pinker than it was three seconds ago and I notice he's already *very* happy to see me. "Pathetic," I scold, making a point of looking down at the tent in his pants. "You're too easy, Coleman."

"Well, when you look like *that*."

"Like what?"

"Like you," he says, wrapping me in a kiss and sneaking an ass grab. "So, should I pretend to ask you how you liked the show, or should we just get straight to it?"

"Ask me how I liked the show." I wrap my arms around his neck, my tits on full display if only he looked down a few inches. But he clears his throat, moves his hand from my ass to my waist, and, like the gentleman he is, makes a valiant attempt at keeping his eyes on mine.

"How did you like the show?" he tries, his voice thick with lust.

"I thought it was really good. You were amazing. I especially liked that new song... 'Put It on the Radio,' was it?"

"That's the one." His jaw is clenched, and his hands are statue-still on my waist.

"And I thought Waylon, Ethan, and Nash did wonderfully, too. Who knew your friends were so talented? You must audition all your acquaintances and only actually befriend the ones with musical talent."

"I do," he answers, but the look in his eye tells me that he's not thinking of his bandmates right now. No, with that look, he must be imagining fucking me in a thousand different positions, each raunchier than the last.

"Fine, Riley." I look up at him through lusty eyes as I attach my lips to the spot where his shoulder meets his neck. "I'll stop torturing you." I run my tongue over his skin, drawing a throaty groan out of him.

"Thank God," he grabs me forcefully, and I squeal in surprise as he grabs my ass and presses my hips into his, allowing me to feel how rock-hard he is. "I don't know how much longer I would've lasted," he rumbles into my ear.

I kiss him in response, running my tongue over his bottom lip. He eagerly parts his lips for me before drawing back just long enough to murmur, "Where's your shower?"

"Shower?"

"Shower."

"Upstairs, in my en suite," I answer before yelping in surprise as he bends and throws me over his shoulder in one smooth movement. He carries me as though I weigh nothing.

"Riley!" I laugh as he begins walking toward the stairs. "Put me down!"

"I don't think so." He climbs the stairs, and I can feel every muscle in his back and shoulders rippling. God, this man is hot.

When we reach my bathroom, he turns the shower handle, and water starts spraying from the three showerheads—one long one on top, simulating rain, and two on either side.

"Holy shit, this is fancy," he chuckles, and I feel his laugh reverberate since my upper body is still pressed to his back.

"Care to set me down now?"

"Can these get wet?" he asks, skimming a finger under the thin waistband of the lace thong.

"Yes."

"Good," he says, gingerly bending to set me down in the shower.

The warm water rains down on me. If I wasn't soaked before, I am now. I watch slack-jawed as Riley strips. He's not giving me much of a show—he's quick and efficient—but it makes my blood rush all the same. A few seconds later, he joins me in the shower, closing the glass door behind him.

"Hi," I say, resting my hands on his chest.

"Hi." He grins, ducking his head to kiss me deeply. I've

only tried shower sex once before, and kissing was akin to waterboarding. But despite the direct water flow, Riley angled his head just right to keep our faces free of water.

His hands wander as his tongue wrestles with mine, toying with the fabric of my underwear before tugging them down my thighs. He wraps a hand around one leg, and I lift it obligingly, allowing him to slip one side of the thong off, repeating with the other leg. He ventures a hand between my legs, and my hips buck into his hand, vying for any friction.

"Jesus, Willow, you're so wet."

"As if you haven't been hard as a rock since the second you walked in," I retort, wrapping my hand around his cock and lifting my leg around his hip so our bodies can more easily connect. One of his hands slips under my knee, helping me keep my leg up.

"You sure you're good to go?"

In response, I grab the back of his neck and push his lips back onto mine as I stroke his cock. He growls in response. Without disconnecting our lips, he lifts me entirely and presses me into the wall of the shower before setting me back down on one leg, still holding my right leg around his waist. Then he reaches behind him and angles one of the side showerheads so it's spraying right on my clit. I arch my back at the sensation and whimper into his mouth. I feel him run his cock up and down my core teasingly before slowly sliding in. We moan in unison, finally breaking our lips. I fix one hand around his shoulders and the other fisting a clump of his hair as his lips fix on my neck.

"Riley," I breathe. "I'm not going to last long like this."

On their own, either the water spraying my clit or his cock filling me would be enough to make me come. Together, it'll be a miracle if I last sixty seconds.

"Good." I feel him smirk against my neck before he kisses

his way down, sucking one of my nipples into his mouth while rubbing the other between his thumb and forefinger.

His thrusts aren't especially fast, but they're so deep, thanks to this angle, that I feel him in my stomach. A pressure builds between my legs, and before I know it, my vision is crowding with black.

"Riley," I moan, trying to stave off the orgasm a little longer.

"You're okay, baby. Come for me," he whispers into my ear.

And suddenly, my vision fades almost completely, crowning with stars. I'm floating so high out of my body right now that I can't even imagine what noises are escaping me. I'm overflowing with that familiar ecstasy, my skin feeling like it's brimming with fire. Finally, I slowly return to my body, my head heavy with pleasure as Riley comes back into focus, his huge arms now on either side of my head, my legs wrapped completely around his waist, my arms around his shoulders as he pins me to the wall with his hips.

His lips meet mine as he continues thrusting, faster than before but just as deep. The water's still targeting exactly where I need it to, and I squirm under its focus. I tear my lips from Riley's to chance a glance down at where our bodies meet, and the sight of him thrusting into me is enough for my stomach to drop out of my body. *That was a mistake*, I think, leaning my head on the wall and staring up at the ceiling, trying to imagine my grandmother to abate the pleasure already rebuilding within me. I'm trying desperately to hold out so that we can come together, but I'm struggling to contain myself.

"Fuck, Willow," he breathes.

I move one of my hands to rest on the side of his face, moving it so I'm staring directly into his green eyes, just inches from mine. His heavy-lidded eyes, combined with the feel of his five o'clock shadow against my hand and everything else, make my breath catch, twisting my insides into a ball of pleasure.

"I can't hold out much longer," he groans, managing to keep his eyes on mine instead of rolling back in pleasure.

In response, the pleasure between my legs overflows for the second time, this time even stronger than the first. I try to keep my eyes on Riley's and am vaguely aware of Riley falling off the cliff seconds after I do, his green eyes shutting in bliss.

Chapter 41

Willow

Thirty minutes later, Riley and I are cuddled up in bed. He's on his back, wearing only a pair of briefs, and I'm on my side in a pink negligee, with my head and arm resting on his bare chest.

"So, do normal girls typically have sex with country singers?" I ask him.

"The lucky ones," he responds. I can hear the smile in his voice, even though my eyes are fixed on the New York City skyline sprawled out just beyond my window.

"Speaking from experience?" I prod masochistically.

"As a girl who's fucked a country singer? No, I can't say I have any experience with that." He chuckles, toying with a lock of my hair.

"Fair enough."

"Or as a country singer fucking normal girls," he adds. "Don't have much experience with that either."

"What do you mean?"

"Well, since my record came out, I've only had sex with two girls—one was a gorgeous, compassionate, smart, witty, leggy, blonde angel on earth—" I hide my smile, though I'm sure he can feel it on his chest. " —and the other was Willow Jordan."

"Dick." I smack him lightly on the stomach.

"Ow," he moans, as though his rock-hard abs didn't hurt me more than I hurt them. "At the risk of being hit again," he says after recovering himself, "I honestly don't remember the other girl's name. I'm ashamed to say it, but it's the truth. I met her at some bar in Nashville in December. Claire had been texting me nonstop that week—unrelated to my success, I'm sure," he adds sarcastically. "I didn't respond to a thing she said and changed my number, but she still got in my head. I guess I just wanted to get her out of my system, and I thought that sleeping with someone else would do the trick. But all it really did was make me feel gross. At heart, I'm not the hookup type of guy. Even though I slept around a good bit when I was a teenager, it never felt right. I only did it to fit in, or seem cool or something. Not that there's anything wrong with liking hookups, it's just never been me."

"So wait, you're telling me you haven't slept with anyone since December? Since literally last year?"

"Nope."

"Why not? It wouldn't have had to be a hookup. I'm sure millions of girls would happily volunteer to be at *least* friends with benefits."

"Because you ruined me, Willow." He huffs a laugh. "After I met you, no one else could measure up."

I sit up and turn to face him, finding his eyes cast in the dim glow of the city. "You're seriously telling me you haven't slept with anyone since we met?"

"Nope," he answers simply, holding my gaze.

"I haven't either," I admit. "Not since December, too, actually. It was with an ex. Just a one-time thing. I'm not the hookup type either."

"He's out of the picture?"

"It was Arm$trong. What do you think?"

Riley erupts in laughter.

"Yeah, yeah, keep laughing. What does it say about my taste in men, though? Think about how that reflects on you."

He stops laughing.

"That's what I thought," I lay my head back on his chest. "No wonder we've been all over each other the past twenty-four hours. We've been so repressed."

"I have a feeling it'll always be like this between us," he says. "I don't think I'll ever be sated around you."

"You're sure you're going to be okay?" I ask, changing the subject. "I have a feeling your manager was right. Tomorrow's going to be a media storm—if it's not already. I don't even want to look at my phone."

"It's that bad to be seen with me?" he jokes.

"They're going to rip us to shreds. Both of us. They hate seeing people happy. I just want to make sure you're absolutely *positive* that this is what you want."

"Willow." His voice is somber now. "I want *you*. I don't give a shit about anything else. I can handle it, I promise. Don't worry about me."

"I'll try not to."

"A year of bad press is worth a minute with you," he assures me, his large hand rubbing slow circles on my back.

"It's worth maybe like fifty-one-and-a-half weeks with you," I reply.

"Still a good deal."

I smile. "Marginally."

"So, do famous people have sex with supermodels?" Riley asks, turning my earlier question back on me.

"Definitely."

"I guess we'll have to incorporate that into our fame-soaked New York weekend, then."

"For authenticity's sake, of course. One more week to go, then I'll make sure you have the true famous-person experience, supermodel sex and all."

"Why wait? I only have two more shows before the break. Come with me."

"I wish I could, but I have to go back to LA to check in with my family."

He sighs. "Okay, fair enough. It's hard to argue with that."

"It's hard to argue with me in general," I tease. "I'm just so cute."

"And humble, too."

"But the silver lining is that now we can go out in public together. Since the news has already broken about us."

"Where would you want to go?"

"The finest restaurant in the city, at a table right in the middle of everything. And a long nighttime walk through Central Park, preferably with Magnolia Bakery's banana pudding in hand."

"I think we can manage that."

POP CULTURE PULSE PODCAST

Jenna: Sorry in advance to our listeners who don't give a shit about Riley Coleman and Willow Jordan's supposed relationship because we just can't seem to shut the fuck up about it.

Caroline: Can you really blame us though? It's all anyone's talking about.

Jenna: True. Anyway, according to the guy online who tracks celebrity flights, Willow's back in LA now. And Riley's in Boston, gearing up for his show there tomorrow night.

Caroline: Any hope that they've gone their separate ways because they had a massive fight and broke up?

Jenna: Unfortunately, probably not. You know how those celebrities are, always jet-setting. I don't think it means they're broken up.

Caroline: I agree, but let me still hold on to some fool's hope.

Jenna: Stay delusional, girl. I support it.

Chapter 42

Willow

I open the door to the family's apartment in LA, where Aspen is currently staying too, despite owning her own house twenty minutes away. Tito follows behind me, carrying a huge box of Aspen's favorite New York treat, Levain cookies.

"Willow!" Aspen calls, bounding down the hallway. "Congratulations on making things official with Riley!"

"No, I should be the one congratulating *you* for landing the lead in a Jack Mack film," I reply, pulling her into a tight hug. "I brought you a little something from New York to celebrate."

Tito steps out from behind me, and Aspen sees the huge blue box. "Holy shit! Levain? Willow, you shouldn't have," she squeals giddily, in a way, reassuring me that I very much *should* have.

She thanks Tito and grabs the box, tearing into it. "Ooo," she says at the sight of the twenty-four cookies in front of her. She grabs a dark chocolate peanut butter one and takes a huge bite, her eyes practically rolling back in her head. "Willow, these are *amazing*," she moans.

"I'm glad you like them." I smile. "I know I should've gotten you something bigger for such a huge accomplishment, but this was the best I could do on a time crunch."

"No, don't be silly. These are perfect. Actually, I also bought you something to celebrate your new beau."

"Please don't ever say the word 'beau' again," I tease. "And seriously, you didn't have to get me anything."

"Yes, I did. You never date anyone. This is a momentous occasion. Look on the kitchen counter," she says around a mouthful of cookie.

I do as she says and see a huge bouquet of multicolored flowers. It's large enough to take up half the kitchen island... and that's a feat, considering this isn't a small kitchen by any stretch of the imagination.

"Aspen, these are beautiful."

"Almost as beautiful as you."

"As if you don't look just like me."

"Exactly, that's why I said it."

Maple rounds a corner, followed by my parents.

"Hey, Willow. Congratulations on going public." Maple wraps me in a hug and snags a chocolate chip cookie from the box.

"Seriously, honey, we're so proud of you. It's a big step, but you won't regret it. Just keep off the news sites for about a week or so," my mom says.

"I know, Mom," I say, giving her a hug. She sees me eyeing her wavy ravenette locks.

"I thought I'd try something new." She shrugs. "There's a small upside to losing your hair to chemo, and it's getting to try out all different sorts of hair colors and styles. The wig supplier for your dad's films was kind enough to lend me a month's worth of wigs at a time. A new style every day." She beams.

"Yesterday, she was wearing a lime green bob." Maple shudders. "You're lucky you came today."

"You know, I really liked that one. Maybe that'll be my new signature style."

Maple groans. "Please, no, Mom."

She winks at her youngest child. "I'll do it just to annoy you."

"How was New York?" Dad asks, giving me a hug.

"It was good. Still standing."

"I miss it." Mom sighs wistfully. "The second I'm done with this chemo, we're going back there, Bobby."

"Fine by me," Dad affirms. "My film is almost wrapped, and I could fly back to LA for the production process a few days at a time."

"And by this time next year, you'll have another Oscar?" I goad.

"Well, it'll be this time in *two* years. The release date is next March."

"Hey, maybe you and Aspen will win Oscars together, then," Maple suggests. "Isn't your Jack Mack film set to release sometime next year, too?"

"Probably a bit later than Dad's since we don't start filming for a couple more months. But hypothetically, yeah, it'll be released next year."

"Just think, my two favorite movie stars winning Oscars together." My mom smiles. "Thank me in your acceptance speech?"

"You've already been thanked in three Oscars acceptance speeches." Dad rolls his eyes playfully. "And you were nominated for one."

"But I never won one. And you know it doesn't count unless you've been thanked in at least five Oscars speeches. I'm counting on you two."

Strike a Pose

"Is that the rule?" Dad smiles bemusedly.

"It is now. Get that fourth Oscar so we can at least beat Mercer, that cocky fuck."

"Is this about the bet you made with him when you were drunk in East Hampton?"

"No," Mom lies.

"What bet?" Maple asks.

"Four years ago, your mother made a bet with James Mercer over who would win a fourth Oscar first—him or me. So far, it's still a tied game."

"What did you bet?" Aspen asks.

"I wanted Princess Leia's golden bikini, and he wanted Trykie." Mom shrugs, referencing the partial triceratops fossil my dad has tucked away in the den of our Hamptons home.

"I still think that was a bad bet," Dad grumbles. "I mean, how much can a bikini be worth?"

"And how much can a dead animal be worth?"

"More than a bikini," Dad answers.

"Well, that's all the more reason for you to win that fourth Oscar first, Bobby," Mom cajoles.

"So, how are you doing, Mom?" I ask, capitalizing on the brief pause in conversation.

"Since three days ago, when you last saw me? Nothing's changed. I'm still doing well. The doctors say the chemo is working...I just wish it would work faster and with fewer side effects."

"Still feeling super nauseous all the time?" I ask. My mom has always been naturally thin, but right now, she looks thinner than I've ever seen her.

"Yeah. It's been a diet of 'whatever I can stomach at the time,' so not the healthiest balance. Mostly cereal and banana bread."

"She's a fighter, though," Dad says. "With the progress she's making, the doctors say she'll be in remission in no time."

"It's easy to be a fighter when there's no choice," Mom adds.

"Don't diminish your accomplishments, Iz. Getting up every morning is fight enough, you know that."

"I know. See, Will? You need someone who will cheer for you like your dad cheers for me. Does Riley cheer for you?"

I chuckle. "Yes, Mom."

"Good."

"When are we going to meet this guy, anyway?" Dad asks.

"I'm afraid you'll scare him half to death," I tease. "He still gets nervous when he remembers who I am. I can't imagine throwing him to my entire pack of wolves."

"We'll play nice," Aspen says with a mischievous smile.

"Yeah, we won't bite," Maple adds, with a look that screams that she will, in fact, bite.

"Maybe in a few months. He's still getting used to his own fame, let alone ours. Your interrogation will have to wait, Dad."

"I wouldn't *interrogate* him..."

"Yes, you would." My mom laughs. "I remember laying in the hospital bed holding Willow, and you said that you'd tear any boy to shreds who tried to hurt your sweet girl."

"I was emotional." Dad chuckles. "I'll play nice if you bring him, Willow—scout's honor."

"We'll see. Maybe in a month or so. Aspen's already met and pre-vetted him."

"I met him very briefly. I'd like to vet again."

"I want to meet him," Maple interjects.

"Maple, you'd be the worst out of any of us. You'd scare him senseless."

"But I'm not even famous."

"First of all, you're Maple Jordan. You'll always be famous," Dad tells her. "Second of all, yes, you'd make that poor guy piss his pants."

"Dad!" Maple laughs. "I would not."

"I don't believe you," I say. "But I'll pre-warn him that you failed an exam, so you're in a bad mood."

"Hey! Do *not* say I failed an exam. Any other excuse, but not that one."

"That you were recently diagnosed with rabies?" Aspen offers.

"Better than failing an exam."

"See why I'm hesitant to bring him?" I ask.

Aspen smiles. "Come on, you know you have the greatest family in the world."

"I do," I confirm. "I love you guys."

"We love you, too," Mom says, bringing us all in for a group hug. "Now, who wants my homemade tater-tot casserole for dinner?" she asks, referencing her signature dish. It's a remnant of her childhood in Indiana and a family favorite. "I may not be able to stomach it, but I sure can cook it."

She winks at me as she nudges her way into the kitchen, letting our chef know that she can take off for the night.

Chapter 43

Willow

"Are you sure you're ready for this?" I ask Riley as my Rolls-Royce comes to a stop along the curb of 20th Street in front of Gramercy Tavern. Tonight is the first night of our weekend together in New York and we had decided that we'd have our first public date tonight. So, rather than dine at one of the exclusive clubs my family has membership to—like 10 Cubed, Casa Cipriani, or the Century Club—we're here, dining like anyone else in the city. "Really, I wouldn't blame you if you got cold feet," I say as paparazzi begin to climb out of their cars or throw their bikes to the side, cameras already flashing as they try in vain to capture us on the other side of the tinted windows.

We should've taken the more nondescript Cadillac Escalade, I curse internally. *Then they wouldn't have found us so easily.*

"I'm sure. I want to do this, Willow." Riley squeezes my hand reassuringly. "Do you?"

"Of course."

"Then let's do it," he says, reaching over me to open my car door.

I exit the car to shouts of, "Willow, are you really dating Riley Coleman," "Willow, who are you wearing," and "Willow, come on, give us a smile." They quiet for a fleeting moment as Riley climbs out of the car behind me before starting up even louder this time. "Riley!" "What's it like dating Willow Jordan?" "Are you in love?" "Don't be shy, give her a kiss for us!"

I don't realize I'm frozen in place until Riley appears at my side, wrapping his arm around my stiffened waist. I instantly relax at his side, his presence doing more to calm my nerves than any drug ever could.

"Have I told you how much I love this dress?" he whispers in my ear, soft enough that only I can hear it.

I love the dress too. I specifically requested it custom-made from Di Pesta after fawning over something similar I saw at a Milan afterparty. The sheer, baby-pink fabric is intricately draped and sewn to create the illusion of being soaking wet. The skintight, floor-length gown is more heavily layered —and thus opaque—over the more private areas while leaving the rest of the body on display through the fabric. It's dazzling, and I couldn't imagine a better time to wear it than on my first public date with Riley.

"Thank you." I smile at him as Justin cuts a path through the paparazzi for us, Tito following.

Justin opens the door for us, and we're met with warm lighting and soft jazz playing below the indiscernible chatter from the tens of tables. Then, slowly, everyone in the restaurant goes silent, staring at us with wide-eyed gapes.

"Hi there," Riley drawls to the stunned hostess. "We have a table under Coleman."

"Yes—I—" she stumbles, looking from me to Riley, then back to me again. "You're Willow Jordan," she states, then her eyes widen as though surprised by her own statement.

"I am," I answer, trying to calm her nerves with an easy smile. Unfortunately, it only seems to make her more flustered.

"Right, this way, guys. I mean, just follow me." She walks us to a cozy two-top in the center of the dining space. She places the menus on the table and scurries away with a quick, "Enjoy your meal."

Riley is holding back a laugh as he settles into his chair.

"What?"

"She was so into you."

"No, she was just starstruck."

"Nope. She hardly looked at me, only at you. I'm pretty sure she had literal heart-eyes."

"As if you don't have the same face when you look at me," I tease.

"Exactly. That's how I knew she was into you," he answers smugly.

"But you're not jealous?"

"Nope. Because you look at me that way. That's how your dress got wet. All that drool."

"Really, *that's* how you think it got wet?" I laugh. "When we left the apartment, it was dry, Riley. Then you put your hand on my thigh in the car, and now it's..." I look down at the dress dramatically.

Riley chuckles. "Glad to know I have that effect on you."

"As if you didn't know already. Weren't we supposed to be here thirty minutes ago?" I raise an eyebrow.

"They didn't seem to mind that we were late."

By now, the other patrons are turning back to their own conversations, growing tired of gawking and taking photos—photos I'm sure have already been uploaded to different social media platforms.

"You okay?" Riley asks, noting my silence.

"Yeah, sorry. I'm just thinking about how, by this time tomorrow, the entire world will have seen the photos of us from tonight."

"Is that worrying you?"

"No. They deserve to see this dress."

Riley laughs. "Yeah, I'm sure the dress is what they'll be talking about."

"For sure."

A waiter approaches and takes our order, momentarily interrupting us. Once he leaves, I ask the question I've been dreading. "So, what's the plan after this weekend? We haven't really discussed it."

"What do you mean?"

"How often will we get to see each other? I mean, obviously, we would be doing long-distance. You're based in Nashville, and right now, I'm mainly between New York and LA."

"My label has offices in New York and LA, too. I'm sure they wouldn't mind if I asked to work on my next album in one of those cities."

"You aren't tied to a specific Nashville producer?"

"No. I work with a few different producers. And anyway, these days, they can do pretty much everything remotely. No need to physically record the song in the same city that someone else is producing it in."

"Really?" I ask, excitement creeping into my voice.

He smiles bemusedly. "Really."

"So, you could come to New York?" I ask, needing to hear the words stated plainly to believe them.

"I could come to New York."

"Oh my God, Riley! This is such a relief. I thought we'd only see each other every month or two."

"Come on, Willow. As if you don't have me wrapped

around your finger tight enough that I'd crawl to the ends of the Earth for you."

I practically swoon in my seat. "I think that's the most romantic thing anyone's ever said to me."

He smiles, candlelight dancing across his face. "There's a lot more where that came from."

Chapter 44

Riley

"My family wants to meet you," Willow murmurs as we stroll through a shadowy Central Park, our own protective shadows following us. She looks over at me. "I knew you'd make that face."

"What face?" I ask.

"That one. You'd think I said that I wanted to take you to the gallows." She shakes her head with a small chuckle, taking a bite of her banana pudding.

"That's not true," I insist. "This is my 'wow I'm so excited I was asked to meet my girlfriend's family' face." We pass a streetlight, and her blue eyes and blonde hair momentarily shine underneath it before dimming, once again blurred by the moonless night.

"Mhm," she tuts disbelievingly.

"I'm serious. I would love to meet them. Say the word, and I'm there."

"They wouldn't scare you?"

"Oh, they'd scare the shit out of me." I chuckle. "But that doesn't mean I don't want to meet them. They're your family. I want to meet them."

"You're handling all of this surprisingly well," she muses.

"What do you mean? You and me?"

"Yeah. I would have thought you'd have run away screaming by now."

"I've told you, Willow, I'm not going anywhere. Remember when you said that it was every woman's dream to have a 'hot, tall, broad, muscular, sexy, musically talented, hilarious, magnetic, strong, confident, charming cowboy' stand up for her?"

"I don't know if those were my exact words." She giggles. "But yes, I remember that."

"Well, isn't it every man's dream to be photographed with the world's most kind, caring, funny, beautiful, radiant, gorgeous, dazzling, alluring, show-stopping woman on his arm?"

"I suppose that's me?"

"You're damn right it is."

She smirks at the compliment, then says, "But nobody likes having their privacy invaded."

"Willow, baby, my privacy has been invaded for the past eight months, ever since 'Moonlight and You' blew up. And I'd rather have my privacy invaded with you than have my privacy invaded alone, wishing I was with you."

"Has anyone ever told you how romantic you are? You'd make a great songwriter."

"Once or twice."

She exhales a sigh of relief. "I'm glad to hear that you haven't changed your mind. I knew you were okay with the idea of the paparazzi following us everywhere, but to have it happen in real life is a completely different thing. I was worried they would scare you off."

"Change my mind? Scare me off? When I have a prize as great as you, I don't think anything could change my mind or scare me off. As you once said to me, I'm keeping you, Willow Jordan." I pause pensively. "Well, actually, I think one thing could scare me off. Your dad. Would it be weird to ask him to sign a *Bloodied Waters* hat for me?"

"Yes, that would be weird. You could try it, though. At the very least, it would throw him off his rhythm, maybe disarm him a bit."

"This is after you ask him to be nice to me, right?" I tease.

"I'll tell him. But I'm sure he'll attempt to be all macho with you anyway. But don't mind him. He's all bark and no bite."

"Has he ever met one of your boyfriends before?"

"Nope. To be honest, I've never seriously dated anyone before," she confesses, avoiding eye contact by staring at the path ahead of us.

"What about Arm$trong?"

"What do you think?" She chuckles. "It was never more than a fun time between him and I. No real feelings involved... at least, not on my end."

"Willow Jordan, you heartbreaker," I tease. "That poor guy."

"What can I say? I can't help it if every man falls at my feet."

"I guess I'm no better than the rest of them."

"No, but the difference is I *want* you to fall at my feet. I'm already at yours."

"Does this mean you have a foot fetish?"

"Don't ruin a perfectly sweet moment, Riley."

"Fine. To make it up to you, I'll turn that into a song on my next album. You know, the one titled *Willow*?"

"So you're going to make it up to me by plagiarizing me?"

"Exactly. Isn't naming the album after you credit enough?"

"No, I want royalties, too. In the form of more of this banana pudding."

"Fine, but you'll have to do a little more to earn that banana pudding money. Will you sing a duet with me?"

"No way. I sound like a dying whale. It would tank your sales."

"I'm sure that's not true."

"It is."

"Prove it?"

"I don't think so. I finally got the guy, I'm not going to scare him off now by singing."

"You've heard me sing. A whole concert, in fact. And I serenaded you," I point out. "You owe me."

"I'll sing to you when we're married. That way, you can't run."

"Well, I could still divorce you if it's that bad," I joke. Willow gives my arm a playful shove.

"Nope. I'll have it written into the prenup that you can't divorce me on the grounds of my terrible singing voice."

"But I can divorce you for any other reason?"

"Why? Have you already started thinking of a few?"

"Oh, shut up, Willow." I laugh, wrapping my arm around her shoulder. She's the perfect height for me. "I won't divorce you."

"But you'd marry me?" she asks, throwing her empty pudding cup and spoon in a trash can, then wrapping one arm around my waist to steady herself against me, intertwining her other hand with the hand I have resting on her shoulder.

"Are you proposing?" I answer her question with another question.

"You wish," she says, squeezing my side. "How is every part of you rock hard? I'm going to break my hand just trying to hold on to you."

"Every part, huh?"

"Shut up."

"Never. And to answer your question, I think I would marry you, Willow Jordan. But I want to be the one doing the proposing. I think I'm going to need a huge rock to entice you, anyway."

"I don't think you would."

"No?"

"No. But a huge rock would certainly be nice."

"I knew it."

"I'm not superficial. I'm just... a little-ficial," she jokes.

I kiss the top of her head. "One of the many reasons I find you so alluring."

We spend the next hour or so weaving our way down the dark park paths, drunk off wine, the ephemeral late-spring breeze, and a feeling neither of us is brave enough to name.

Epilogue

WILLOW

The First Week of October the Following Year

Yesterday morning, the morning after this year's September fashion month, I stepped onto my private jet, thinking I was going home to New York to spend the week with Riley in our new little—okay, maybe not so little—apartment. He's been busy the past few months between the release of his new album, *Willow*, paying off his parents' mortgage and his sister's student loans, buying his bandmates each a new car, and signing the lease to the new apartment with me.

I've been busy, too, planning the launch of Heena's and my new fashion line. My family also finally went on our two-week-long grand vacation to celebrate my mom being cancer-free (Something she achieved months ago. It just took forever for all of our schedules to align). After that, I organized and threw a huge party to celebrate Maple heading off to college.

I was excited for some long-awaited alone time with Riley. But instead of boarding a jet full of other models headed for New York, I was met with my handsome boyfriend holding a bouquet of flowers, declaring the jet was headed to Palermo, instead.

"Change of plans," Riley said with a smirk. "I rented a seaside Italian villa for us for the week."

I was absolutely thrilled. When we arrived to the quaint, bucolic town that afternoon, I thought I was in heaven. Then we rounded the corner, and I was met with a beautiful, sunset orange villa with ivy climbing the exterior and a spotted cat lazing on the porch, and I *really* thought I was in heaven. We spent last night there, taking an evening stroll around the city before having a huge meal of pasta and wine at a local restaurant.

As I open my eyes this morning, I'm greeted by the bright Italian sun and cool sea breeze. I briefly wonder where I am before I remember yesterday's surprise and smile. I turn the other way and see the god of a man I'm dating sleeping shirtless beside me. I kiss his cheek before rising and accidentally wake him.

"Sorry to wake you," I whisper after his eyelids flutter open and his green eyes land on mine.

"Don't ever apologize for kissing me, Willow Jordan," he says in his gravelly morning voice, wrapping his arms around me and pulling me against him. We fall back asleep holding each other for a few hours longer before waking up for good.

"Want to go to the beach?" he asks, brushing his teeth.

"Sure," I happily oblige, rifling through my bags for a bikini.

After we're dressed and fed, we grab our towels and make our way down the rocky path to the beach. The air smells gloriously salty, and despite it being October, the temperature has risen to a comfortable level while the sun further warms our skin.

When we finally make it down far enough that our feet sink into the sand, there are a few other sunbathers already lounging around.

"Want to see if the other side of the beach, around this cliff, is a bit more private?" Riley asks.

"Sure, lead the way," I reply.

He holds my hand and leads us around the large rock formation. But my eyes are drawn away from the beach on this side and toward a white dinghy perched on the edge of the surf. Behind it is a large white yacht, inscribed with pink letters reading, *The Seashell Princess*.

"Riley James Coleman. You did not," I say, sliding my sunglasses off the bridge of my nose to get a better look.

"Oh, but Willow Elizabeth Jordan. I did," he says, smiling as wide as I must be.

"It's ours?" I ask, still in a state of disbelief.

"It's yours."

"No, I mean, it's ours all week?"

"Yes, ma'am." He chuckles, amused by my shock.

"How did you *do* this?" I squeal as he walks us towards the dinghy waiting to take us to the main ship.

"I know the owner." Riley smiles. "And I asked her parents if we could arrange to have the boat this week."

"Wow." I beam as he helps me into the small boat. "I think you've outdone yourself, Riley. This is incredible."

Riley joins me in the dinghy, still smiling broadly. "I'm glad you like it. We're set to take a leisurely trip to the Aeolian Islands and back this week...does that sound good?"

"That sounds *great*," I exclaim as the dinghy's captain begins to motor us toward the yacht.

Riley just smiles, clearly very pleased with himself that he was able to pull this off.

"This must be the last surprise, right?" I ask curiously. I thought his showing up in Europe to begin with was the grand surprise.

"Yes."

"You're lying."

"I am not."

"Yes, you are." I laugh. "You keep blinking. You're definitely lying."

He smiles. "I guess you'll just have to wait and see if I am."

We climb the ladder and board the ship, which is just as large and beautiful as I remember it. I stand by the railing and close my eyes, letting my head fall back. I bask in the sun and drink in the briny sea breeze.

I feel a familiar hand snake around my waist. "I'm so happy you like it," Riley whispers in my ear, kissing my neck gently.

"Like it?" I ask, turning to face him. "Riley, this is by far the most thoughtful, romantic thing anyone has ever done for me. I can't believe you remembered this ship. The only time I ever mentioned it was that first weekend at your house, right?"

"I have a good memory when it comes to you."

"Good luck topping this, Riley."

"Topping it?"

"Yeah. You have to keep raising the bar to keep the romance alive, you know," I tease, expecting him to grumble that this is the best he's got.

"Happily," he says instead, the loving look in his eyes telling me he truly means it. He will continue to surprise and romance me for as long as he can.

I hear the engines crank beneath us, and slowly, the ship turns and sets off into the Mediterranean.

"Want to lay in the sun?" I ask him.

"Sure," he responds, following me to the chaise lounges spread out on the bow deck.

We lay there for hours, reading, talking, napping, and reveling in each other's company before a deckhand comes and apologizes for disturbing us. He announces that a small sunset dinner is ready to be served if we'd like to follow him. We do as he asks and make our way to the stern deck of the boat, where a little above-deck dining area resides.

I gasp when we round the corner, not at all expecting the elaborate display before me. Hundreds of red and pink roses are arranged around the space, the sight enough to make my heart skip a beat. The table is draped in a long white tablecloth, and a bottle of champagne sits in a crystal bottle chiller in the center. I turn to face Riley, tears welling up in my eyes, but before I can say anything, my eyes fall to his right hand, which is holding a small black velvet box.

Holy shit.

Riley moves to hold my hand with his free hand.

"Willow," he begins as the first tear falls down my face. "I hope that's not because you don't want what's coming," he jokes.

I shake my head, laughing, giving his hand an encouraging squeeze.

"I've been yours since the very first time I laid eyes on you on New Year's. And every day since then...every conversation, every glance, every laugh...I've fallen deeper and deeper. I knew I was in love with you the moment you stepped through those hotel doors in South Carolina and ran into my arms. But the feeling I had then...it doesn't even *compare* to what I feel now. I've fallen deeper in love with you than I ever thought possible, and I don't see an end in sight. There's no limit to how deep I've fallen, or for how deep I know I will continue to fall for you."

He drops to one knee and opens the ring box to reveal the most beautiful ring I've ever seen. A huge, sparkling marquise-shaped diamond sits atop a twisted golden band, accented with several smaller, similarly shaped diamonds on either side, creating a whimsical design reminiscent of leaves on a vine.

"All this to say...you're the love of my life, and I can't imagine a future without you by my side. Willow Elizabeth Jordan, will you marry me?"

"Yes," I squeak out, nodding emphatically. "Yes, yes, yes," I repeat, bending down to kiss him deeply.

"Thank God," he murmurs into my mouth. "My heart's been resting at one hundred and sixty beats per minute ever since you met me on that plane yesterday."

"Aw, you were nervous?" I tease.

In response, he slides the ring onto my finger. "I was."

I gasp, admiring the way the ring sparkles, turning my hand to see it from all angles. "Riley, it's gorgeous."

"You really like it? I can get you another one if you don't. Heena and Aspen helped me pick it out, but still, you're hard to buy for."

"I love it, Riley. And I love it even more because you chose it for me."

His face melts in relief, and he pulls me in for another kiss. "Good," he says.

I grab the bottle of champagne off the table and lift it up. "So, are we celebrating or what? Surely *that* was the last surprise, right?"

"That was the last one," he chuckles. "For now."

I pop the cork and squeal as the foam bubbles pour out over the top of the bottle, dripping onto my bare feet. Riley holds out two glasses, and I fill them before setting the bottle back in its chiller.

"To the rest of our lives," I say, taking a glass from him and clinking it against his.

"With the greatest woman on Earth, who said yes," he cheers.

"And the greatest man on Earth, who finally asked," I answer.

Author's Note

Thank you for reading STRIKE A POSE! If you enjoyed this book, please leave me a review on Amazon and Goodreads! This is my debut novel, so every review and share helps! My newsletter, Instagram, and other links are accessible through the below QR code or here: https://linktr.ee/lilahmorrisauthor

Acknowledgments

First and foremost, I want to thank my friends Elizabeth, Grace, and Sarah. Your encouragement, beta reading, and invaluable advice have been instrumental in this journey. You've been my greatest advocates and supporters. I also want to thank Lee, Molly, Fernanda, Lizzie, Manon, Aubree, and my grandparents (I hope I haven't missed anyone) for their support and belief in me. Your encouragement means the world.

Also, I'd like to give a special thanks to my ARC readers for the initial reviews and feedback, which were crucial in polishing this book. Thank you also to Summer for the stunning cover design and to Sherri for her meticulous edits. Your contributions have been essential in bringing this book to life. Finally, thank *you*, the reader, for giving my writing a chance. I hope that by making it this far you enjoyed the book. I look forward to sharing more with you in my next novel. <3

Made in the USA
Columbia, SC
18 November 2024